~Cecile~

Also by Janine Boissard

A Matter of Feeling
A New Woman
Christmas Lessons
A Time to Choose

Cecile

A NOVEL

by Janine Boissard

Translated by Mary Feeney

LITTLE, BROWN AND COMPANY
BOSTON   TORONTO

FIRST ENGLISH-LANGUAGE EDITION

Originally published in French, under the titles
Cécile la poison and *Cécile et son amour,*
by Librairie Arthème Fayard, Paris, 1984.

Library of Congress Cataloging-in-Publication Data

Boissard, Janine.
  Cecile.

  "Originally published in French, under the titles
Cécile la poison and Cécile et son amour . . . 1984" —
T.p. verso.
  I. Feeney, Mary.   II. Boissard, Janine.   Cécile et
son amour.   English.   1988.   III. Title.
PQ2662.054C413   1988   843'.914   87-22666
ISBN 0-316-10103-6

10 9 8 7 6 5 4 3 2 1

FG

*Published simultaneously in Canada
by Little, Brown & Company (Canada) Limited*

PRINTED IN THE UNITED STATES OF AMERICA

To Claude Désiré
who believed in the Moreaus
and opened the doors of La Marette to everyone

and

to Maurice Biraud
who brought a sensitive and moving Dr. Moreau to life onscreen

The Family Tree

The Parents   Dr. Moreau: Daddy or Charles to his daughters; Grandpa to his grandchildren.

Mathilde Moreau: Mom to her daughters; Mattie to Charles and the grandchildren.

The Four Daughters   Claire, the Princess.

Bernadette, the Horsewoman.

Pauline, never had a nickname.

Cecile, the Pest.

The Husbands   Antoine Delaunay: surgeon, husband to Claire.

Stephan de Saint-Aimond: law clerk, husband to Bernadette.

Paul Démogée: writer, husband to Pauline.

The Children   Gabriel: Claire and Antoine's son, six and a half.

The twins: Melanie and Sophie, Stephan and Bernadette's daughters, five.

Benjamin, Pauline and Paul's son, four.

The Burgundians   Grandmother: won't tell her age.

Great-Uncle Alexis: one year older than Grandmother.

Aunt Nicole: one year older than Mom.

The Normans   Count and Countess of Saint-Aimond: Bernadette's in-laws, with a castle in Normandy.

Friends of the Family   Tavernier: lives across the way, known as Roughly Speaking; Poppy to the younger generation.

Beatrice de Kervolec, called Bea. Pauline's best friend.

Melodie, Cecile's best friend.

Cecile

1

Spaghetti Alla Carbonara

GERMAIN DIED YESTERDAY. The horse that belonged to my sister Bernadette, pushing thirty. Germain, not my sister! Toward the end he wasn't much more than an old nag; his main pastime was to munch on the lower branches of my father's carefully pruned poplar tree and then turn to look at you with an expression that was enough to break your heart. I liked to touch my lips to his cheek where it was smooth and quivering. Now I'd never feel it again, so soft, or smell his smell, so warm and still fresh in my mind.

In a way it was good because a death always seems to reunite the living. My three sisters came to La Marette, with their husbands, Antoine, Stephan, and Paul. The smell of bacon floated through the funeral proceedings since Mom was making a ton of spaghetti alla carbonara for dinner. Carbonara — *charred:* Bernadette had wanted to have her horse cremated so she could keep the ashes, but apparently there are no furnaces big enough, and anyway Stephan wasn't hot on the idea of keeping the urn on the mantel of their tiny apartment in Neuilly. So, as usual, we consulted with our next-door neighbor, Roughly Speaking, and he came up with the idea of a backhoe. In three scoops, a hole was dug at the back of the yard, by the banks of the Oise. All that was left to do now was deposit Germain's mortal remains.

Bernadette had brought him to us at the beginning of the week, once it was clear that he wouldn't last much longer. Of course there was no question of riding him. It was enough to have him alive and looking at us with trusting eyes. Daddy couldn't object when he found Germain living in the garage, because, after all, the horse was sick. What better place for him than a doctor's garden? "If he's in the way, you can just finish him off," our Horsewoman suggested. With Germain listening, rough waves breaking under his coat.

Two days later he was dead. Very big, very dead. It made me think of war. I'm not sure why. Maybe because war wears a blindfold or because during his lifetime Germain's eyes were so full of peace.

Bernadette, true to form, said, "Life sucks," but shed not a tear. She got right on the phone to Heartbreak, her old riding master, who was like Germain's father even though he once tried to send him to the glue factory because he was so old and they were short of stalls. And this morning, here was Heartbreak with the surcingles.

We put them around Germain's middle and hitched ourselves up so we could all drag him to the gravesite, leaving a deep furrow in our wake.

We might have called in a horse butcher instead. They keep the good parts, and you never know what happens to the rest. The advantage is how quickly they dispose of the corpse. Then you have only pleasant memories: galloping through the morning dew with the sun slowly pulsating at the edge of the field; the feeling of closeness, mutual admiration. But Bernadette wanted him here at La Marette, and she made us solemnly promise to scatter her ashes over him when the time came.

Germain's grave was very near the spot where I buried my collection of poisonous mushrooms when I was a little girl. I took a secret pleasure in noting one of life's little coincidences. I say "coincidences," but I don't really believe in them. A mysterious chain lies beneath things: there are links between people, events, and even places. At times the chain becomes apparent, like one I saw the sea uncover on the beach at Houlgate but was never able to follow to the end.

It took forever to cover Germain with soil, but now there was no way we would use a machine. Just our arms, our hearts. Pauline dug in with all her might to keep from crying; Claire worked by spoonfuls, careful of her nails; at one point Bernadette touched my arm and said, "Hey, Pest, remember the time you went on TV?" That was how I had saved the dear departed from the glue factory and how he had started to belong to me too in a way.

"This is one lucky horse," remarked Mr. Tavernier, our neighbor. "There's no finer resting place than our own backyard . . . roughly speaking."

That made everyone think of his bomb shelter, the only one in town, sleeps twenty. He'd reserved room for all of us and now stocked powered milk for the grandchildren.

Stephan stayed close to Bernadette, trying to find the right words of consolation. But Bernadette is not easily consoled. Claire and Pauline more easily, I suppose, but not me. Either it's something minor and I don't need help, or else it's something that goes so deep nobody else could help if they tried.

Eleven of us sat down afterward to pasta alla carbonara. The three young couples, our parents, the riding master, Roughly Speaking, and me. A sauce of cream, grated cheese, and bacon. I added a touch of catsup, over everyone's loud protests. Even if you make mistakes, it's best to try new things. You only live once! Mom had already fed the kids and put them to bed, but up in his room Gabriel was sobbing that he wanted to pet the dead horse one more time.

Someday I'll show him the pictures I took right after I found Germain. I was the one who found him. I noticed a slight increase in the silence when I woke up, so I ran out to the garage without even putting on my slippers, and there he was. I wasn't surprised. I felt something like a big blank form inside me. I don't know how to explain it. As if suddenly all of life wavered, and there was nothing I could do about it.

I didn't cry out. I went back in to get my camera and I shot a whole roll of film. His eyes are what show that he's no longer there. They're like the crystal on my watch after I forgot and went swimming with it on. The hands stopped dead and Mom couldn't fix it. She said it was "kaput," which was how they used to say "dead" during the war. I didn't have the heart to close Germain's eyes. And at any rate that was Daddy's domain.

The pasta was delicious, especially the bacon. The more you use, the better it is. The cream tastes smooth and the bacon is strong and crunchy. Eating it made me wonder what the difference was between pork, horse flesh, human flesh. All of it courses with some warm spark that eventually goes out. Why is it that we cry over people, mourn certain animals, but cut up and cook and season others? It's all in the way you look at it.

2

The Pest

MY FAMILY calls me the Pest. People give you a nickname just for fun and it sticks to you like glue for the rest of your life. Even when you're a toothless old grandmother someone's still around to call you Sissy or Kitten or Freckles or some other stupid thing.

So it seems from day one I have been a pest. Made life miserable. Wrecked things. But when you're the fourth and last daughter in the family, you have to raise your voice, show your claws, and sharpen your beak to survive the pecking order.

I also came in last in looks. Claire, "The Princess," is a beauty and makes the most of her assets. Bernadette is the tomboy type, strong and lithe with an iron will, a mouth to match, and a lot of admirers. Nobody can resist Pauline. All she has to do is look at you with those eyes that could wring tears from a rock. But Cecile, nothing special. Height, hair, face: average. Average legs. At eighteen, I don't think I'd ever inspired physical desire, unless you count Bobois down at the hardware store who took me into his storeroom last winter to show me where he was digging for buried treasure, but made me look at something else instead. Anyway, he was just a pervert who could even get turned on by a chair — a hormonal problem, Daddy said. He made me promise not to go to the hardware store alone anymore, as if my virtue was in danger — and besides, Bobois wasn't a rapist, just an exhibitionist who picked on defenseless young girls.

I came to understand the expression "pay for someone else's mistakes" last year when I finished high school and asked my parents for a year off to think. They cited the example of the Princess, whose year off stretched into thirty-six months, practically up to the time she married Antoine. All right, they knew I wasn't Claire, but they still didn't want me to start off on the wrong foot.

The careers that appealed to me were missionary work, medical relief, social work. Mom and I had some serious discussions and concluded that I seemed to want something having to do with young people who were disadvantaged, either kids who from the beginning had problems fitting in or teenagers who couldn't figure out what life meant and in the meantime were making trouble so someone would pay attention to them.

It didn't take much figuring to see why work like that would interest me. When I was thirteen there was Gabriel, a runaway from a juvenile detention center. I hadn't been able to save him. Now, after my normal period of adolescent rebellion, I was also feeling the natural desire to emulate my mother. I'd wanted her to stay home, but my mother had gone to work counseling prisoners, as a volunteer.

She tried to convince me that working with offenders was a difficult career, underpaid and without opportunities for advancement. No wonder there are so many repeat offenders! Among other things, she thought I might be romanticizing criminals, inventing excuses for their behavior and imagining the miracles I could work with my kind heart, my charm, and my new insights.

To make sure I was serious about my choice, my parents

had me enroll in a new school of social work in Pontoise. We studied communication skills, report writing, psychology, first aid. At the end of the school year there was fieldwork in a prison or at a summer camp for disadvantaged youths.

Speaking of pyschology, let me add that between my godson, Gabriel, who was going on seven and would have to be told sooner or later that the man he'd always called Daddy was not his biological father; Bernadette's five-year-old identical twin girls, who should be in store for a full-blown identity crisis; Pauline's four-year-old, Benjamin, who understands things before you even explain them; and then Mom and Daddy, who must be secretly struggling with their mid-life crises, menopause, and the prospect of retirement, I had plenty of case studies right in my own backyard.

At school I made a new friend, Melodie. She was about my age, but her reasons for wanting to work with delinquents were different. She needed order. Melodie couldn't stand for things or people to be out of place. She had to straighten them out. Her career choice didn't go over very well with her mother, who was hoping Melodie would come to work in the family business, an intimate apparel shop. But fitting bras was not Melodie's cup of tea, besides being a constant cruel reminder that she herself was a double A.

And so, that evening, that beautiful autumn evening when everything was russet, golden, crisp, and inviting, I took Melodie home, then went home myself. It was six o'clock, almost dark. Mom was in a meeting until seven. No one was there to greet me except Germain, who wasn't in much shape to listen. Fall is beautiful, but sad. Summer gets raked up along with the piles of leaves. We'd have at least ten wheelbarrow loads of them. That was how I'd spend my Sunday.

3

Soufflé for Two

I WAS IN THE KITCHEN looking for the bag we use to gather windfalls when the telephone rang. Pauline!

"Cecile?"

"Speaking."

"Are you doing anything tonight?" She spoke in a strange, cramped voice.

"Why? Do you need a baby-sitter?"

"I need to see you, you Pest."

I said yes even though I can't charge for social calls and I make a fortune baby-sitting. Plus, if you counted meals away from home, it saved my parents a tidy sum. Everyone said I was tightfisted. I wasn't, really, but all you ever heard around La Marette was about money and pinching pennies, and so I'd been doing my part for the past couple of years. Between Gabriel, Benjamin, and the twins, I've saved a lot of wear and tear on the sheets at La Marette.

"Paul's not there?"

"Don't even mention that bastard," Pauline said, and hung up, leaving me hanging with all my questions.

I went out to gather apples. The apple tree is on its last legs too, losing its sap and producing heart-shaped fruit. I picked the ones the birds go after: they eat them on the branches and know which ones are the ripest, sweetest. I picked up a few walnuts along the way, husking them first with the heel of my shoe so the stain wouldn't get on my hands. And I kept hearing Pauline say "Don't even mention that bastard."

That bastard is her husband, Paul. Thirty-six years old and already referred to in the press as Démogée, a good sign for a writer. And my sister was the one who had gone after him, before she decided he was a bastard. She wanted him in spite of everything and everyone, starting with Paul himself. She wouldn't listen to reason, Daddy said. And she got him five years ago in our village church, when he said "I will" and slipped the ring on her finger before God, family, and friends. For me, the church ceremony is what counts, not the civil one. What happens at the town hall can be dissolved in three months by mutual consent. What God joins can't, at least not yet. And now Paul and Pauline had Benjamin, a dark little boy with his father's eyes and an uncanny look in them for a four-year-old.

Walking slowly back to the house, I tried to think about marriage. It was hard. The first thing I saw was a bed. For my parents, it was the opposite. I couldn't imagine a bed. When I could picture a bed for my parents, I'd be an adult and would accept the fact that they had to have sex to have me.

Back in the kitchen, a nice surprise: Mom was home. Milk, flour, eggs, cheese, all the signs of a soufflé. My mother felt guilty about being at home less, and to make up for it she would cook wonderful dinners. No wonder we were all gaining weight.

"Have a good day, honey?"

"Sure."

I cracked my walnuts, careful to leave on the thin, bitter

skin that means they're fresh from the tree. I ground them up with honey, added a lump of salted butter. Now, what had she done with my raisins?

"In the buffet, on the right, next to the vinegar."

Mom stirred her white sauce. When I was little, she used to let me add the milk in a thin stream, and I felt all grown up. Now that I was grown, I still liked pouring it for her — just so I could feel small again. I told her that. She laughed and handed me the wooden spoon to stir the sauce with while she beat the egg whites with the electric mixer that breaks down egg fiber and ruins conversation. I announced that I was sorry I'd have to miss her soufflé, but I was going to see Pauline. She needed to talk to me right away. That was all I could say. Top secret. For a minute Mom forgot about her egg whites. I could see that she didn't want me to go, and I felt sad for her but glad to find out that she'd miss me.

4

Even Mommies Cry

N O," SAID PAULINE. "I just can't accept it. Never. Or at least he should have warned me. Just said, 'Being faithful means nothing to me.' "

"And you wouldn't have married him?"

She stopped to look at me, thoughtful, with a dark expression that spoke her pain.

"I probably would have anyway. But at least I would have known."

Now she knew. Had found out three days ago, from a gossip column. One of Paul's books was being made into a movie; he was on location as a consultant. The columnist mentioned that he was doing quite a bit of consulting with the star of the film, Nina Croisy, on and off the set. . . .

"The bastard. The bastard. I hate him!"

Which meant she loved him. When she had confronted him, he hadn't tried to deny it. He had taken my sister in his arms and told her it didn't mean a thing, didn't change anything between them — and headed right back to Saint-Tropez, where they were filming the tragic farewell scene, to continue consulting with Nina Croisy.

Pauline was curled up on the sofa, clutching a pillow as if her stomach ached. Jealousy! They say it eats away your

13

insides and gives you no rest. According to Mrs. Roughly Speaking, who ought to know, you can compare it to having a toothache on top of shoes a size too small. I went to sit at Pauline's feet; I leaned my head against her knees. I'm not very good at hugging — it's too physical.

"How were things between you? I mean sex-wise?"

She bashed my head with her knee and gave me a look as if to say she regretted having me as a sister. I wish someone would explain it to me. Sex is all you hear about from morning till night, with all the details, and then when you ask a question about it out of concern for someone's personal fulfillment it's as if you were holding a knife to her throat. When I asked our neighborhood baker how it was with her second husband, she blushed redder than her strawberry tarts and slammed the door in my face.

"That's not the question," Pauline said. "What Paul's looking for is outside stimulation. He says an artist thrives on change, and that means women, too."

She clutched my arm and dug her nails in: "Know what he told me, Pest? That I was free, too. That's what hurt the most."

She was on her feet again. She couldn't sit still. Since we're talking bodies here, I have to say she was losing hers. Not that she ever had much to begin with, top or bottom, but now she was really turning into a stick.

"I can't stand this place anymore. And besides, it smells. It smells like him." Paper, tobacco smoke, and some other scent, the same as Daddy's, which used to turn my stomach when I was working through my Oedipus complex (all over now). But Pauline was right about this place. His place. Paul had lived here for years. After five years of marriage, my sister was still a homesteader. Paul took her and put her in a little corner, asking her please not to make too much noise. Pauline added Benjamin in another corner. You get the picture.

"I'm going to get a tissue," she said.

That gave me time to check on my nephew. He slept in the library, a strange, round room with books up to the ceiling. His bed got wheeled out when it was in the way. Needless to say, it did a lot of traveling.

You might expect the under-five set to be asleep by nine, but not Benjamin. Remote control in hand, he was watching a shoot-out on the TV. No one seemed to care how much he watched; when I was a kid, we were limited to one hour a day and weekend cartoons.

"Cile!"

That's what he calls me, Cile. I like it. It floats. He turned off the set and shrank as he watched me do Dracula homing in for a meal. I got a taste of neck, a bit of ear and cheek, remembering to brush my lips over his eyes. But no reaction! Getting a smile out of him is a major accomplishment. A laugh, unheard-of. He always seems to be on the verge of tears.

"Hey, Ben, isn't it a little late for television? Everybody's asleep, even Daffy Duck and Speedy Gonzales."

"What about Daddy?"

"Not your dad. He's at work." And I was in no hurry to see *him* in bed.

"Daddy is at the seaside," he declared. "Monica told me."

Monica was the English au pair who watched him when he wasn't in nursery school.

"And Mommy cried, besides," he added.

His eyes asked for an explanation. I was in no hurry. I knew him. When you talked to him, he seemed to turn your words and phrases over and over in his mind, like cats-eye marbles, trying to decide on their color. And once he decided, he'd throw it back at you six months later.

His mommy cried because his daddy was a bastard. I

15

couldn't tell him that. A father gets cracks in his image soon enough.

"Even mommies cry," I told him. "And it seems funny to kids because it makes the mommies feel bad, and feel better, too."

He nodded gravely. "The mommies cried about Germain and they wouldn't let us watch when they put him in the hole."

And he added, "What's Germain doing now?"

I tapped his forehead so he'd understand: "He's galloping around. In there. We call it remembering."

Benjamin closed his eyes a minute, to see him. Sometimes, late in the afternoon, at the hour when you're not quite sure whether it's still daytime or already night, I got the feeling the whole yard was alive with Germain's hoofbeats. I seemed to see the branches of the acacia move at the touch of his lips; I even heard him whinny. I suppose that's why he was buried at La Marette.

"Can we read about him, too?"

Benjamin pulled a book out from under the covers, an English book full of animals that Monica had given him.

"Of course. First we'll write a story, then we'll read it. A book just about him that's called *Germain, A Family Horse.* But now you need to sleep."

I kissed him near the eyes I found so intimidating and slipped out with the remote control switch, leaving the door open because he's afraid of being abandoned.

Pauline was waiting in the living room. She was smoking. Something new.

"I have a favor to ask."

She said it just the way she used to at La Marette when she wanted me to go break some bad news to Mom and Dad.

"What?"

"I want you to take Benjamin home with you."

16

"Take him with me?"

"I'm going out of town. A feature assignment. Beatrice is doing the photography. I leave tonight."

She had it all figured out. She'd drop us at La Marette on her way to the train station. Mom could watch him in the morning, Mrs. Roughly Speaking could take him in the afternoon since she was stuck at home with her stroke-victim mother anyway, and I'd take over when I got home from school.

I looked her right in the eye.

"Why did you have Benjamin? Was it an accident?"

Her eyes opened wide. "Of course not! What on earth makes you say that?"

"Because you're always leaving him, and it doesn't seem to bother you."

"It does bother me. I had him because I loved Paul."

"And what about Benjamin? Do you love him?"

"Of course I do. But I just can't stand staying here by myself while that bastard . . ."

And back to the waterworks.

"Come to La Marette. You won't be alone."

"Home to Mother? That would be too easy." And almost in a whisper she added, "And too nice."

"Can't you at least call Mom and ask her what she thinks?"

"I know what she'd tell me: 'Just sit tight.' "

"Where are you going?"

She didn't answer. In case we might come after her, I guess.

"Then may I inquire as to when you'll be back?"

"When things are going better. I'll try to get a story for the magazine."

"So when Paul gets back, no more Pauline?"

"No more us, anyway," she murmured.

I stood up and walked to the window. "No more us." Paris hurts me: the sky, the roofs, the chimneys, and

17

beneath them all the people with no thought of me. There was something like a weight inside my chest: something dead. I could remember when Pauline had cried because she ached to form an "us" with Paul. But does such a thing even exist? I wished I could be ten years old again, all four of us girls at La Marette with Mom at home, and that would be the end of it. That's what I felt was dead. Those days.

And to top things off I was hungry. Pauline apparently hadn't thought about eating. She knows that misery makes me famished! Claire and I are the same. At funerals, we eat for ten, for everyone who doesn't dare. Grandmother understands everything; she says it's a question of metabolism. Metabolism or no, half the time we end up with indigestion.

"You must be hungry," Pauline said. So she did have a smidgen of heart left. She went to the kitchen, excusing me from further comment, which, considering that I was all choked up, was a good thing. "No more us." I went to find my sister. Her refrigerator wasn't exactly overflowing. Nothing but frozen dinners.

"If Paul thinks sex doesn't mean a thing, maybe you should've tried food. You know what they say about the way to a man's heart."

I wasn't sure how she'd take it, but I had to try something. It worked, and suddenly we were laughing. We put some frozen soufflés in the oven — one of life's little ironies — and while we were waiting for them to thaw Pauline composed her note to Paul. I made some toast to keep my stomach from rumbling.

In her note, no blame, no emotional blackmail. A brief explanation of the situation. "Leaving on assignment. Benjamin at La Marette. Not sure when I'll be back."

I got her to add "See you then." That left things open.

After our dinner, Pauline packed the bags: Benjamin's, her own. And it was already ten-thirty. Seeing her lift her little boy out of bed, his hair like black hay, seeing him bury his head in her chest as if struggling to crawl back into her, seeing her look as much like his sister as mine, my throat started aching again, this time so much that I'd even have had to turn down a spoonful of caviar if it was offered. I took along his little English book with the pictures of horses.

I sat with him in the backseat. Out toward La Défense, at the edge of the city, the sleepwalking skyscrapers stared at each other, saying, "Madness, madness." What a symphony of shattered glass they'll make when the bomb drops. Benjamin sat up and looked hard at all the lights without asking a question. I bent over him and whispered, "Just wait till you see how much fun we're going to have, Ben, my boy." I saved the *I love you*s. It seems you don't need to say it to children. They need love so badly, being alone and fragile, that when it's there for them they sense it, smell it like the scent of life.

5

More Wife than Mother

I TOLD BENJAMIN: "We're heading for that big boat. Grandma and Grandpa are in there, fast asleep." I slung his bag over my shoulder and held his hand tight, and we navigated through the darkness, guided by the storm beacon over the front door. The wind blew in long waves over the trees, the yard seemed deeper, full of traps the night might have dug.

Benjamin lifted his feet high because of the gravel in the drive; he still got some in his slippers. We stopped to empty them. We heard Pauline's car out on the road, already distant. He threw his head back and looked up at the sky as if he was going to start crying.

"This is no time to waver, Captain," I said. "We're the good guys, and we're going to get them!"

He straightened up and we made our way into the harbor.

We fortified ourselves with a glass of milk and my nut mixture, which he really liked, especially the raisins. Now all we had to do was get upstairs without rousing the enemy. To keep the stairs from creaking, you have to walk close to the railing: it was the mast and we were the pirates. A hard climb: when Daddy coughed, we thought we'd been

20

found out, but no! A stunning victory. I didn't have to show Ben to his room, he headed straight for it: his mother's old room, on the top floor, across from mine.

When my sisters got married, Mom and Daddy offered me my choice of bedrooms, since I had the worst one on account of being born last. But no way. I was used to it now. And then, too, La Marette had become a resort hotel for my sisters almost every weekend (the price is right). So they all kept their old rooms with rollaway beds for the kids.

I tucked Benjamin in right up to his chin and left his door open so he could call me if he felt homesick. He was looking at the seascape a painter friend had given Pauline to remember him by, as she told me in confidence. No one's allowed to touch it.

On Saturday, Mom and Dad never got up till nine. At eight, I was down in the kitchen getting everything ready to lessen the shock. The yard was shrouded in mist; you could barely make out the swing on the old apple tree. Kids don't need help to get on it, and the grass cushions their falls. That made me think of the Princess, who would never swing without a pillow under her.

When Mom came down in her bathrobe the party was ready to go: hot chocolate, coffee, warm milk, toast and butter. Benjamin, perched on two phone books, had already tested the jam. I'd made twice as much coffee as usual because an extra cup can help when the going gets rough.

The fumes had reached the master bedroom, so Mom was expecting to see me, but not her grandson. She kissed him, beaming: "Is Pauline letting us have him for the weekend?"

"A long weekend," I said with a meaningful look.

I felt Mom consider asking a question, and I added, soberly, "Little pitchers . . ." I was so worked up that I didn't even feel sad about the situation. Human nature really is miserable. Sharing trouble is more invigorating than sharing happiness. Problems, you sympathize with; happiness, only if you've lost it.

At this juncture Daddy came down, thrilled that it was Saturday, the day he would prune the rosebushes. In the doorway, he held up his hands: "Ladies, take a good look, tonight they won't even look human." He was thinking of the thorns that get through even the sturdiest gloves. But pruning, to him, meant the first preparation for spring.

When he saw Benjamin, he went wild. With no male offspring, he was crazy about his two grandsons. He thought that Mom must have known that Benjamin was coming, and he welcomed our young guest by ruffling his hair, stealing his piece of toast, and tossing it in the air — all the things grown-ups do to make kids laugh. When Benjamin was almost in tears, Mom said, "I think that's enough, Charles," and Daddy turned back into an adult.

I told them the whole story over the dishes. Benjamin was upstairs doing something important. Charles was doing the washing, unfortunately for us wipers: one teaspoon takes him an hour.

"Paul is having an affair with Nina Croisy. Pauline took an out-of-town assignment with Beatrice to save face."

Daddy dropped the knife he'd just washed every particle of and gave me the kind of black look emperors must have used when they mercilessly executed bearers of bad tidings. Mom just sat down. I sensed how hurt they were and felt less excited. I explained about Nina Croisy and outside stimulation.

"Where did she go?" Daddy asked, looking out toward the phone.

"Address unknown."

"She shouldn't have," he said, vehemently. "She really shouldn't have. It's the last thing she should do."

I was expecting that. In my parent's day, the wife stayed, while husbands cheated as long as they could. Since women didn't have the Pill, or careers, they waited, wasting the best years of their lives, until the husband came home to them as a last resort in old age.

"Women don't put up with that anymore," I permitted myself to point out. "Even if you don't like it, you have to get used to the idea."

"And I have to bear the consequences!"

It shocked me to hear Benjamin referred to as a consequence, even if it was just because Daddy was so worked up.

"Mom will take care of him in the morning, Mrs. Roughly Speaking in the afternoon, and I'll take the night shift," I retorted. "Unless you're worried about what it will cost to feed him, for you the consequences will be almost nil."

Daddy was so upset that he ran the soapy dish-brush through his hair, throwing Mom into a nervous fit of laughter he didn't really appreciate.

"Should we tell Claire and Bernadette or not? It's Saturday, they'll be over tonight. We ought to decide," I said.

"Do me a favor and use some discretion for once," Daddy thundered. "That's for Pauline to decide, not us."

Out the window, I saw that the mist was giving way to warming sun. Now you could make out the swing, its damp seat a shade darker. When the kids get here, they all rush out to get the first turn, and the fighting starts. In a little while, I'd give Benjamin a head start.

"What I see in all this," I said, "is that Pauline is more of a wife than a mother."

If you believe what you read, it's usually the other way around: women quickly become more mother than wife, and it's one of the major causes of infidelity, along with the inevitable and tragic loss of passion, the attraction of novelty, and the desire to prove you still can.

Mom and Daddy didn't seem terribly interested. Daddy finished the silver, then took Mom up to their room to continue the conversation without further interruptions, leaving me with the rest of the dishes.

He came down three minutes later to ask me if Paul knew that Pauline had left. Of course he didn't. Then Daddy bolted back up the stairs to tell Mom this additional piece of good news. That's the advantage of being married. You share everything.

6

Hopscotch
with Heaven and Hell

"BENJAMIN LOOKS LIKE a houseplant," Mr. Tavernier was saying (that's Roughly Speaking's real name). "He's white as a sheet. With parents like his, it's no surprise, but if you want my opinion, a bit of fresh air won't do him any harm."

"He won't be too much trouble, then?" Mom asked, smiling. "With your mother-in-law, I was afraid . . ."

In fact, Benjamin was looking at the old lady. He studied her, trying to digest what Mom had explained to him on the way over: that she couldn't move from the waist down and he shouldn't mention it or it might hurt her feelings. From time to time he'd pinch her legs through the blanket to make sure there was no reaction.

"Too much trouble?" Roughly Speaking protested. "You know you children are like a family to us, roughly speaking. . . ."

Mrs. Roughly Speaking couldn't have children. Blocked tubes: a sexually transmitted disease she had gotten from her husband, whose whole life would not be long enough to make up for it.

". . . And I didn't retire just to sit around," he said. "We'll do some gardening, right, son?"

"All right," said Benjamin, "but I'm my daddy's son."

Benjamin was obsessed with getting things straight when it came to his family, as if he had to defend his place in it. Fortunately, Roughly Speaking took it well. We arranged that Mom would drop him off Monday at two, before she left for work, and that I'd pick him up on my way home from school at six.

"Anyway, it will just be for a few days," Mom explained.

"What is this story Pauline is covering?" Mrs. Tavernier inquired.

Before she had time to answer, Mom noticed that it was four o'clock. My sisters would be there any minute, with their children, meaning seven extra for dinner, and we still hadn't picked the plums for the tart!

Mrs. Tavernier allowed as how her mother had trouble chewing plums. And we were off, with Benjamin taken care of.

Mom took him to the orchard. He helped her carry the basket, pulling as hard as he could; you could tell he felt important. One kind of happiness; feeling useful. I went for a swing. A pleasant sensation. I could see my father the doctor, my father the gardener at prayer in front of his roses, and when he stood up, took off his gloves, and lit his pipe, I sensed we were slated for a serious father-daughter conversation. He walked over without hurrying, his eye on his surroundings; he picked a hazelnut on the way and gave it to me.

"Maybe I was a little rough on you this morning, about Pauline. It wasn't easy to deal with first thing in the morning."

"Or last thing at night, either," I told him. "What worries me most is the part about outside stimulation."

That meant it wasn't accidental. And considering that Paul was only thirty-six, the pain would kill Pauline before he found enough of that stimulation. "I hope your sister's suffering will help him get back on the straight and narrow."

I smiled at his choice of words. "And where does Benjamin come in? I guess he has no say."

"Right or wrong, children usually don't have much say in these matters."

We looked over at the orchard. Benjamin tugged so hard on the plums that it looked as if he'd bring the tree down. He was so small next to Mom, who was showing him how.

"Have you and Mom ever cheated on each other?"

"Some questions don't deserve an answer," he said. "And you'll have to realize someday that people have their private gardens, which you shouldn't go tromping on with your heavy boots."

"Sorry to bother you," I said, "and you're welcome in my garden anytime, boots or no."

I pumped hard on the swing, jumped off, landed ten feet away, and walked out of the yard without looking back. It was five o'clock. With any luck, Jean-René would be in church. There was a six-o'clock Mass for the lazy.

He was sweeping the vestibule where autumn had come with its dead leaves. I regained my calm by the holy-water font. The smells came to me: the cool gray stone of the walls, the warm brown wood of the pews, the presence of someone who spoke to me of my childhood. When I opened my eyes again, Jean-René had spotted me. Standing next to me, he waited for my return to earth.

"Come over here, Cecile. I have something to show you."

In the aisle near the confessional was a hopscotch grid drawn in the shape of an airplane. Heaven at the top, hell at the bottom, with *Heaven* spelled like *seven*.

"I guess the sidewalk wasn't good enough for them," I said.

Jean-René laughed. "Don't you think God likes to have children play in His house?"

I borrowed his broom while he went to prepare the altar. The leaves crackled like sugar wafers. I didn't miss a one. I felt good again. In churches, things fall into place. My father was right about private gardens: I think it's fun to invade them, especially if something smells a bit off. I guess I'm just not a very nice person.

Jean-René was in his vestments, in front of the altar, his eyes on Jesus. I went to his side and looked with him. I felt something rise in me, a kind of tingling. I asked him, "What can I do to help?"

"First, go ring the bells for my Mass," he said, "and ring as loud as you can to make a lot of people think about Him. Then you can go to the theater for me. I need someone to sit in for me and applaud hard."

7

The Other

THE AUDITORIUM was grim, like everything in the high-rise housing project that had come to grow on our fields, replace our wheat and wildflowers, loom over our old steeples, swallow the little bistros where we'd go on Sunday to eat french fries and apple tarts different from the ones at home.

A modern hall with lighting bright enough for a police interrogation and walls filled with the kind of paintings that don't look like anything: deformed faces, wild colors. And art is supposed to be a reflection of life! If that's the mirror, no thanks!

The only nice thing was the soft, reclining seats, or it would have been if they hadn't been riddled with cigarette burns and crawling with gum.

There were about thirty of us, all ages. No one had sat in the front row yet, so I did. Theater means seeing the actors close up, touching their voices, feeling them vibrate, laugh, feel afraid, like us, like everyone. Otherwise you might as well be watching a screen. I'd barely taken my seat when several more people followed my lead.

It was a new acting company from the new town. The

kind of thing that ought to be encouraged, according to Jean-René. The play was called *The Other,* by an author called Tanguy. Judging from the program, he'd cast himself in the lead.

At the appointed time, the lights dimmed. Total darkness. Silence. Suddenly it was like being in your own bedroom and wondering if you were dreaming, and then: the spotlight, the stage, him.

He was very thin, almost painfully so, blond and with eyes of a particular blue, at once hard and transparent: sword-eyes. He looked at us one after another, each for a moment or two, without saying anything, and only then did he begin.

He said he was waiting for someone, another person, the Other. They were to meet here, tonight or never: the last chance for them both, in a way. One by one other characters entered, men and women. Each time he had hope. Could this be the one? No. Despite appearances and his sincere efforts to believe, it was never the one he was waiting for, and when the play was over, after an hour and a half of disappointments, Tanguy had seen the light. He was wasting his time. The whole world could walk across this stage and it wouldn't change anything. The Other doesn't exist.

The curtain fell. Applause. But not mine. When a play moves me, I can never clap afterward. I'd rather keep silent, stay with the feelings that will all too soon disappear. I feel sad to be only myself again.

The curtain rose again. Tanguy was alone on the stage. He didn't smile. He gazed at us as before, one by one, as if accusing us, too, of failing him. The house lights went on. People hurried out of the auditorium, looking relieved that it was over. They talked in low voices, clung together. "Heavy stuff, heavy stuff," one woman kept muttering. Evidently she hadn't come to hear that, live as we may in a country of many millions, we're basically alone in the world.

I was the last one out, and instead of heading for the exit I slipped backstage. After two or three tries, I found the right door: a sign with the playwright's name on it.

Tanguy was removing his makeup with tissues by the handful: he must go through a box a day. He looked at me: not a bit surprised to see me there.

"Yes?" he said.

"Jean-René sent me."

"Jean-René?"

"The parish priest in Mareuil."

I wish someone could explain to me what's so funny about the word *priest;* half the time it gets a smile. I pointed out, "Without him I never would have known."

"Known what?"

"That your play was so good."

He didn't react right away. He looked at his eyes in the mirror, then at mine.

"I don't think that was the majority opinion," he said.

I tried to make him see why I *had* liked it. How without even noticing I had found myself waiting for the Other with him. And — it had just come to me — his play also concerned Pauline and Paul: "Is it ever really possible to say 'us?'"

"That's the whole question," he answered. "But it might help if you told me who Pauline is."

I gave him a rough sketch: four sisters, two parents, a house on the Oise, nothing very artistic but you don't get to choose your family. I was afraid he'd sneer at all this, but instead he seemed interested: could our house be that big red one with all the chimneys, the one with a fire going most of the time?

"That's the one! The working fireplace is the one in the living room; the others aren't up to code."

"You sound sad about it."

Of course I was! Hadn't he ever fallen asleep watching a banked fire?

As we talked, a girl came in — the one who'd been handling the box office. Open seating. Her name was Maryse. She laid an envelope on the table. "Not so great. Let's hope we do better tomorrow." And she walked out without noticing that I was there.

Tanguy slipped the envelope into his pocket. I didn't move. He stood up. "Want to come have a drink with us?"

I would have loved to, but I couldn't. I explained that to keep my parents from getting ulcers I had agreed, even though I was of age in the eyes of the law, that I wouldn't ride my moped after dark. My father had dropped me off at the center; my brother-in-law would be picking me up. In fact, he was probably already waiting. I'd better go.

I said, "I have to go," but I stayed. I can't explain it. I had a feeling I wasn't finished with Tanguy. He put on his jacket.

"Tomorrow we're having a matinee, if you'd like to come back."

A kind of breeze went through me. I was flying: we'd see each other again. His matinee was at three o'clock. I told him I'd be there for sure. He didn't shake my hand; smiling inside, he stared at me. Why on earth had I worn these wool slacks that made me look like an elephant? Better back out to minimize the damage.

His car door opened into the darkness, Antoine was listening to Bach. He seemed relieved to see me.

"I was beginning to think you'd been spirited away."

Spirited away? In a way I had been. I sat as close as I could to him. Even though he always looks sad, Antoine makes me feel secure. He seems to know where he's going.

"How was the play?"

"Not bad."

I steered the conversation toward small talk, and while he told me about dinner, the exploits of La Marette's third generation, Dr. Moreau's hand-shadows, everyday life, I tried to think things over lucidly.

I wasn't in love. No, love at first sight was not my style. What attracted me to Tanguy, besides the fact that he was handsome, and an actor, was what I saw in his eyes: a sort of black flame. The same look as Jean-Marc, who had died of blood cancer before his child was born; the same as in Gabriel's eyes when he had left the world before even turning twenty. An absence of hope. I've always been able to read that in people's eyes. Sometimes I see it in the subway, or in the street: a way of looking at things, as if to say, *What's the use?* Maybe it's because we had so much hope at home, but it always stopped me dead, as if a hole had opened up in front of me. And earlier in the evening, when Tanguy was waiting for the Other who never showed up, I seemed to hear cries from deep within that hole. The reason I had gone to his dressing room was to make sure. I had resigned myself to hearing him say "You can get lost, it's not you either." But instead he had said, "Come back tomorrow. " I hadn't been around long enough to disappoint him.

Why is it always "love at first sight"? It can happen with friendship, too. When it does, it means there's a "before" and an "after" in your life. The "before" is already far behind you — for instance, me that afternoon on the swing, discussing marital fidelity with my father; Mom picking plums with Benjamin; the family arriving; all those rather small things that happen the same over and over — and the "after," like now, is a feeling of freshness, like a wind sweeping the countryside and giving it back to you brand-new. If only it could last!

Antoine let me go on meditating. From time to time he'd just throw a questioning look my way. I opened the car window. The night was no longer the same, as if tonight it was opening for me, somewhere. There was a heavenly smell of freshly mown hay. The smell of the Oise, too, the walks we used to take, the crayfish caught out of season, by flashlight, and swims hugging the banks to stay out of the way of barges. That's all over now: pollution! I'd forgotten about the Oise; and also how strong life is. Tears came to my eyes.

I felt like telling Antoine to slow down to make it last longer, but instead he drove faster than usual because they were holding some gnocchi in the oven for me and a double helping of plum tart à la mode (our Horsewoman's idea).

It was eleven when he pulled up to La Marette. We shut the car doors quietly: everyone was in bed. Since I didn't head for the house right away, Antoine asked me, "Everything going the way it should for you?"

"Fine."

But I couldn't help smiling. Now, just now, I had my own private garden.

8

Sunday

I LOOKED IN ON my sleeping orphan. He was breathing in little gulps, his head turned to the wall. He'd
stashed his English book with its pictures of animals under
his pajama top, as if he was afraid someone might come
in and steal it while he slept. My heart ached; I felt responsible for him. And all over the world, other children
slept, some with no precious object to cling to and perhaps
with no one to love them. That hurt; I wished I could help.

I knelt by Benjamin's bed and told him, "Hey, little guy,
I'll never let you go." He seemed to breathe more deeply,
as if to say, "Right, Cile." Children are supposed to hear
everything you tell them in their sleep. Maybe grown-ups,
too; anyway, it can't hurt to try.

On my pillow was a wrench and a note from Bernadette
asking me to tap the radiator with it three times as soon
as I got in, no matter how late. She had to talk to me.

First I got ready for bed. Ten seconds after I tapped,
Bernadette appeared, in Stephan's pajamas with the sleeves
and legs rolled up. I like to wear other people's clothes,
too, especially sweaters that hold a person's smell.

She got under the covers with me.

"What's up with Pauline?"

35

I was expecting it. I looked into the darkness, full of fascinating things, no matter what anyone says.

"Nothing special. Didn't Mom and Daddy fill you in? She left on a featured assignment with Beatrice."

"Yeah, but out of the blue?"

"That's journalism, Bern. You have to be ready when something comes up."

"OK, then what's the story?"

"Top secret."

"Enough of that," she said. "You're not fooling me."

She pinned me to the bed, and the torture started. Bernadette has studied the martial arts. Holding your torso with one knee, your arms with the other, and tickling you all over with both hands is child's play for her. Not for her victims, especially one wearing a nightgown! In three minutes, I gave up and told all.

She fell back, her hands behind her neck, and gathered her thoughts while I tried to recuperate.

"If I understand you right, Paul gave her no choice. That bastard! 'Take it or leave it.' "

"Exactly. And you didn't leave me much choice either. If Mom and Daddy find out I told you, they'll put me through the shredder."

"They won't find out. Trust me."

I was just working up to a good discussion of life's fascinating problems, mundane but never dull, when she sprang from my bed.

"Stephan is waiting! Sweet dreams, Pest."

Talk about feeling used! Just worm it out of me and say goodnight, not even a word of thanks!

I dreamed of Tanguy. I was trying to tell him something; he couldn't hear. It was as if I wasn't there, or he wasn't — I don't know, everything was fuzzy. And when I woke up, in a way I felt saved. Things were back in their place: my body beneath the sheets, the smell of bread toasting downstairs, the house so sturdily planted in front of the pond, with lots of sunshine out in the yard.

The whole family was around the table. Sunday breakfast lasts forever at our house. Then we have a huge lunch around two and all anyone needs for dinner is a cup of cocoa. Everyone commented on my personal best for sleeping in. So many cheeks to kiss! I sorted out the twins without even peeking at the labels Bernadette sews on their clothes to avoid mix-ups. Easy as pie! Melanie is left-handed, Sophie right-handed. It's our good fortune to have "mirror-image" twins, meaning they spend their lives copying each other, believing they're the same: great outlook for the future.

With their blue eyes and thatch of blond hair, they're the image of their father, to the continuing delight of the Saint-Aimonds, Bernadette's aristocratic in-laws.

On Antoine's lap, little Gabriel, who showed talent as a food mixer, filled up on a blend of cereal, honey, and orange sections. His shock of hair is on the reddish side. It looks more and more like his biological father's: Jeremy, from California. I'm always afraid Gabriel will find out someday. Then what will happen? Sometimes it seems it would be better to get things out in the open, to clear the air.

Benjamin's napkin was spread on his lap. Leaning back in his chair, he declared that his legs were dead, like the old lady's, but nobody had better mention it or he'd feel sad.

"What old lady, honey?" Bernadette asked.

"The old lady in that house where they're going to take care of me," he said. "Poppy's house. He's the one who's not my dad and he plants stuff."

Completely baffled, Bernadette turned to Mom, who stared at her husband, who took a sudden interest in the wallpaper.

"What house? And who is this Poppy?"

Benjamin pointed out the window at the Taverniers'. And there was Roughly Speaking, at work on his mixed border. From here I could smell the good smell of newly worked soil.

"That house," Benjamin explained. "And that Poppy. The lady's legs are in heaven, but the rest of her is still here."

"Her soul must have been kind of low," Bernadette cracked.

Daddy couldn't keep from laughing.

"What's all this about?" Claire broke in. "If it's not too much to ask, I'd like an explanation."

"Me, too," said Bernadette. "And if you can handle it, Stephan, would you mind helping the kids dress so we can discuss this in peace?"

Antoine took the hint, too. Our "liberated fathers" got right up, leaving the dice game they were starting in the living room (they play for money). I don't like it when Bernadette talks to her husband like that. It seems as though she loves him less. Mom says it's her life that she doesn't always like: no more riding, and two kids at one shot.

Speaking of her daughters, the twins jumped Benjamin with twenty tickling fingers to see if his legs were really in heaven. He miraculously regained his use of them and flew out. They galloped up to the bathroom in a pack. Bernadette shut the kitchen door and leaned against it, just like in the movies.

"Why should we come here for the weekend if all you do is hide things from us?"

"Hide things?" Mom asked.

"Benjamin's going to Roughly Speaking's. What does that mean?"

Daddy got up. To him, breakfast is sacred. Especially on a Sunday, when he doesn't have to eat on the run, his mind already on the patients he's going to see. He took a deep breath, eyes closed, to regain his composure.

"The Taverniers have very kindly agreed to watch your nephew for a couple of hours every afternoon until his parents are back."

"Didn't you forget to mention," Bernadette interrupted, "that the parents in question have gone their separate ways?"

"What do you mean, their separate ways?" inquired the Princess, always quick on the uptake.

"That's exactly what I'd like to know," said Bernadette. "Where, when, and why?"

That was the last straw for Daddy. I could tell by the way his neck swelled and turned red. He walked right up to our now steedless Horsewoman.

"What goes on between your sister and her husband is their business, and only theirs. They can answer your questions if they like, but don't expect us to do it for them."

Bernadette scowled. Daddy pocketed his pipe and tobacco pouch and headed for the door. Then he turned to address the group.

"And since I'm the only one who seems to care, if you don't mind, I'm going to keep the yard from being choked by dead leaves."

The door slammed. Bernadette turned to Mom, who was starting to clear the table. She wouldn't be any help, obviously. A racket coming from the direction of the bathroom grew loud enough to distract us; we headed upstairs.

The barely controlled flooding indicated that bathtime was over. The twins were sobbing. The dads were pretending to console them but were laughing their heads off. Gabriel, naked and proud, paraded himself. He was the one who had started it, it seemed. He had pointed out to his twin cousins, not without a touch of scorn, that they had nothing down there where *he* had something really neat, and they had gotten all upset. Facing each other, the little girls checked each other out and echoed their dismay. Benjamin, standoffish as usual, had taken refuge in a corner, pulling his sweater down over the parts in question.

Bernadette scooped one daughter up on each knee and told them the good news: maybe they had nothing there now, but just wait, and one of these days — no hurry, ladies — you'll be the ones with babies inside. Yes! Right in there. . . .

Now it was good old Gabriel's turn to wail because he'd like to have a baby there too. Sophie, the right-handed twin, stuck a doll inside her T-shirt and danced around him to show him all he'd have to miss out on. And that's how sex education ought to be! With no brothers and a father who locked the door before he took his tie off, the four of us had never had a chance.

But in the end no one is ever satisfied with his lot in life. Girls want to have what boys have because it means they get all the breaks, good jobs and high salaries. Boys get fed up with their thing because it creates responsibilities they're not always ready to shoulder. The best solution is the snail, both male and female, in its own house.

That gave me the idea that we might find some snails out in the yard. It had rained during the night. I suggested a hunt. My troops pulled on boots and grabbed pails, and off we went.

9

A Cat Named Missile

FOUR SQUARE WALLS on the third floor of a gray concrete cube the same as a dozen others that lined the very straight, very dead streets. In the four corners of the square, one by one: a mattress, a sink, a table with a hot plate, a heater. And in the center, something like a flea market. A jumble of clothes, knickknacks, books — tons of books.

Sitting on the mattress, Melodie and I. Cross-legged on the rug between the sink and the heater, the room's tenant, Tanguy, as well as two other actors, Manuel and Maryse, counting the day's take.

I'd paid Melodie's way. We didn't agree on who the Other was. To her, it meant her ideal man, the Prince Charming she dreamed of, and when he showed up you could bet she wouldn't let him get away. I thought the Other was God. Not the one you hear about in church; the one you feel inside, which leads you higher in spite of yourself, and I wasn't prepared to speculate on what that implied. The interesting thing would be to find out what the author's version was.

He'd just finished counting the receipts, and from his face and his friends', you could tell it was a bust.

41

"We'll have to close," said Maryse.

She looked about our age, a little younger than Tanguy. In the play, to make him believe she was the Other he was waiting for, she did some amazing acrobatics, splits, juggling, the kind of thing that takes a lot of training and practice, all to perform for ten old fogies who cramp up when they leave their seats and yawn as they watch you. Sad.

"No," said Tanguy. "We'll go on again Saturday night. That's still the plan."

"What will we rent the hall with?" asked Manuel.

"I'll find a way."

Tanguy lit a cigarette — another cigarette — and, leaning on the wall, stared at the ceiling as if he'd like to go through it. But above his ceiling was another one just like it, and so on up to the eighteenth story.

Missile, a black, skinny, half-bald cat, observed his world from the radiator. Now and then he cautiously inspected his dish near the table, licking it to make sure it was still empty. Without even realizing she was doing it, Melodie had started sorting the piles of junk into categories. I stood up. What was I doing here? Where was all I had felt the night before? My "before" and "after"? I must have thought I was still at the theater. I had put on my own little show for myself. Today the curtain had come down for good: there was only this sinister room, with a boy just a little more handsome than most, who was acting as if I didn't even exist, while this was the best year ever for mushrooms and I could be out there hunting them with nice people, people who got something out of life, which hardly seemed to be the case here.

I went out on the balcony to see if I could find the edge of the forest. Night was beginning to blur the landscape. The streetlights were already lit. These towers, cubes, parking lots, streets at right angles all looked like a set.

Not one roof, one blade of grass; a few trees that didn't look real. It was the first time I'd set foot in the "projects" we could see from La Marette, through the branches in the orchard. Now I was on the other side, and I was afraid.

Below, a man washed his car. His wife sat inside knitting. They had a dog, Rowdy; every time he tried to live up to his name, the man threatened him with "If you want the chain, just keep it up."

"How's it going out here?"

Tanguy was at my side.

"Not so great."

My answer seemed to surprise him. People usually say "Fine, thanks, and you?" without even thinking. Even if they plan to knock themselves off the next minute. Someone did that last winter. Had lunch with friends, laughed, drank, joked, helped make plans, then went out and put a bullet through his head.

"Want to talk about it?"

I turned to him. He had the look in his eyes I remembered, the one that strip-searched you.

"I feel strange here."

"Not the style you're accustomed to, I guess."

"I don't like big buildings, and I hate new ones. They scare me."

"Why?"

"I could have been born in one. I'm afraid I'll live in one someday."

I gestured toward the stone landscape: "It's so lonely."

He laughed. "You can be lonely anywhere."

Down below, the man emptied his bucket onto the tires. The soapy water flowed, eager for cracks. I asked — not without feeling a twinge — "Who *is* the Other in your play?"

"No one. It doesn't exist."

"But aren't you really expecting someone?"

43

"A dream. An illusion."

"And if it wasn't an illusion, who would it be? What would it be for you?"

"You ask him for me," he said.

His voice was icy. Like his eyes. He turned away from me and stared down at the guy polishing his chrome with a chamois cloth. His wife had just gotten out of the car; she measured her work against her husband's back. A good thick sweater for the winter. They looked satisfied with their Sunday.

"For them, everything's fine," I said. "They're not waiting for anyone."

"Fine?" He laughed. An ugly laugh that deformed his face. I wanted to leave and at the same time I had the feeling I wasn't finished with him, just like the night before.

"They have each other," I said, "and that's enough for them. They keep each other going. It's a life."

"You call that living?"

His scornful look swept over me. There. He'd made up his mind about me. Stupid little girl with middle-class values. I should have told him right away and not wasted my time. Especially since he was exactly the kind of guy I can't take for more than three seconds, showing off his tortured soul, thinking he's different from everyone else, but still willing to count the box-office receipts and play the romantic lead.

In his crummy little room, behind us, someone had put on music. Melodie was laughing at something. Missile, his three hairs on end, stuck his head through the rungs of the balcony to challenge Rowdy the dog.

I said, "I don't think there's much left to say. I'm going."

That was when it happened. Tanguy's boot moved forward, Missile's claws scraped on concrete, a black ball catapulted. Down below, all hell broke loose as a dog chased a cat. My heart beat wildly. Two stories! He could have killed it. Tanguy went back into the room. I followed. He ignored me. I got my coat, bolted down the stairs. Leaning over the railing, Melodie protested, "What's the matter with you?" She was having a good time. She'd found treasures in Tanguy's stuff: earrings, a watch that played music . . .

I couldn't answer. In my throat was a long mewling of terror, in my ears the sound of claws on the edge of the balcony. I think she yelled at me to wait. I was already on my moped. It's after me, Melodie! Something I had touched, that had stuck to my skin, made me feel dirty. I didn't know whether it was evil or only trouble.

A car passed me, the driver screaming out the window: it seems I had run a red light and I was going to end up in a ditch. Who cared? Just give me wind whipping my face, to clean it. Give me a village with patched roofs, meandering streets that tremble when trucks pass, private gardens edged in bramble and columbine, the bright flowers you pick for your mother. Give me a church with or without a hopscotch grid, the gate to a real house, a big pile of leaves with a fire eating the heart out of it, and a mountain of wild mushrooms on the kitchen table.

"I don't know what's wrong with them this year," Mom remarked. "They're full of pine needles."

Give me back my life's friendly smile.

10

Love, Pauline

PEST, IMAGINE A LAKE *like a clear gaze, in spots shaded and moving. All around the lake, imagine a band of green dotted with chalets and hotels, and above that the dark, tight crown of pines, some of them so high that when you lean back to find the top you fall into the sky.*

Imagine, on the shore of this lake, a hotel closed for the season. Blankets folded on the beds, chairs tipped onto the tables in the dining room. There are only three guests here: Beatrice, her friend Martin, and me. The owner, a dedicated cook, is Martin's uncle, which explains Bea's presence, with me in tandem.

I'm glad I left. Paris is for happy people. Paris is loaded with crowds, noise, beauty, the past, chances taken or wasted, every second, and when you're hurting, all that crushes you. Cities cannot console; I'm sure you understand. When animals are wounded, they go lick their wounds in a corner, they hunt for what nature has that can heal them, plants or herbs, sometimes just dirt. I'm finding my remedy here: pine trees, the overhang of a farmhouse roof, almost brushing the ground, ready for snow, the smell of the huge wheels of cheese they make next door, the smell of bare tree trunks resting inside their bark. I'm finding the old bellmaker, the big bells they hang around cows' necks with wide leather collars. He tells me about life here: the

46

year everything froze, the year high winds blew a path through the forest like a giant's stride, the year of the wolf, the year of the carp so big, so old that no one wanted to eat it, out of respect. There are my salves, my dressings.

And you can imagine what Bea said when I showed up. Not so much surprised about Paul as bewildered by my reaction. "So you think you were going to keep your famous author to yourself your whole life long? You're really out of it, Pauline. That's not where to look for fidelity anymore. The physical side is nothing to build a marriage on. What if he cheated in secret? Would you like that any better?" Just what I wanted to hear. . . .

But Beatrice doesn't know. She never had both a mother and a father. She never had a home. She can't know.

Our nights at La Marette, around the fire with Mom, our daily bread of warmth so natural that we took it for granted, never suspecting its importance . . . what it was to be simply home. In Paris I've never felt I was home, and it's when I think of La Marette that I cry, over a teenage girl who'd known nothing but good in her life and was dying to get away. And, damn it, I still haven't really left home.

Pest, I have a decision to make and I'm in a fog. To choose Paul again, the way he is and not my dream of Paul — to quote him — would mean accepting other women in his life. But how can I? The bastard. Or leave him! Face the hurt and get over it. You do get over it, they tell me. Or go back to him and wait for it to hurt less, without accepting it. But that seems most horrible to me, because hurting less would mean not loving him passionately, and that doesn't interest me. And if being grown up means accepting the fact that passion doesn't last — well, no thanks.

I see you . . . I hear you from where I am. "And Benjamin?" You think I've forgotten him. I'm not forgetting him, but Paul takes up all the room. How to explain it? He's the absolute priority, the devouring thought, like a curtain closing over everything else. And then, listen, even if it shocks you, all that talk about "flesh of my flesh," "my blood, my life," I never really believed it. I carried my child, gave birth to him, I feed and care for him, love him. But I have never really had, in either my brain or my body, the kind of savage feeling for him that some women would build their lives around, and that to my way of thinking would put our son before everything else. I don't feel like a mother. I don't. Was I too much a child when we married? Is it because Paul didn't really want to be a father?

"So why did you have him?" you asked me the other night. I just did. Without really thinking it over. You love each other, get married, have children. I wanted four, like us, remember? I saw myself writing books the way Mom made cookies, and Paul coming home at night, like Daddy after work. Paul can't stand schedules or limits. I could never stay home like Mom. I need new faces. And Benjamin is not an easy child.

Pest, I have to go now. Beatrice is calling me. She's doing a photo essay on the Jura Mountains. Bea says photography has to capture life, the brief moment when life truly happens. It all boils down to the same thing: I try to capture it in words, Bea in pictures.

The lake is called Saint Point, the town is Malbuisson, the hotel Les Terrasses. I'll give you the phone number in case you need it, but don't tell anyone, promise?

Ciao, because I can't see too well and teardrops would smear the ink. . . .

Love,
Pauline.

11

Words of One Syllable

IT WAS SEVEN O'CLOCK in the evening beneath the freezing drizzle the onions had predicted with their four layers of skin. I put the road atlas back in the garage that smelled of Germain, life, death. I'd found the way to Malbuisson, to Saint Point. If I'd had my license, I'd have already been on my way.

On my way back to the house, I heard someone ring at the gate and went over to open it. It was three neighbors: Ferré, the butcher, Cadillac, the baker, and Charpier, who runs the pharmacy.

"You should always find out who's there before you open the gate," Cadillac scolded.

They had the somber yet pleased look of bearers of bad tidings.

"Can we have a word with your father?"

At that moment he appeared on the front porch, book in hand. For a while now he'd been reading poetry, Victor Hugo and all that. He looked at our visitors, then at me, and frowned. It was easy to read his thoughts: What's the Pest been up to now?

Sorry, Doctor, for once, nothing!

The three of them filed into the living room and sat

down by the fire, and I served them drinks. Beer for our dealer in wonderful lamb roasts, a finger of port for the specialist in giant éclairs with a half-chocolate, half-coffee filling, and Scotch on the rocks for the owner of Pill, a testy dog that was rather hard to take. Plus a splash of red wine for the doctor, since that's all that agreed with his stomach.

From the kitchen, the scent of herbs, tomato, and olive oil: Mom was baking a fish for dinner. She was upstairs putting Benjamin to bed. "A song," he demanded enthusiastically. I sat on the stairs so I could listen, too, but when my own childhood rose like a lump in my throat, it was too much. I headed back to the living room, stopping by the dining room table so as not to be conspicuous. I expected to be asked to leave, but no. So I sat down discreetly.

For the moment, they were talking trees. It had been such a hard year for them. Heavy winds in the spring, now this freezing drizzle. We'd lost one of our walnut trees. Then Charpier came to the point: "I suppose you've heard what happened in town yesterday, Doctor. Poor old Mrs. Lamourette . . ."

"Yes, I did hear about it," my father said. "Have they found out who did it?"

"They'll never catch whoever did it," Cadillac said. "That's the only thing that's certain."

"Have you heard how she's doing?"

"Not so well. They're not sure she'll ever walk again. And who knows what she'll live on. They really cleaned her out. Found her life savings, too."

There was a silence. They all stared at the fire.

"No need to beat around the bush with you, Doctor," Charpier continued. "We've decided to form a neighborhood protection association. We'd like you to join."

"Protection association?" my father repeated.

"Because things can't go on like this," Ferré piped up. "I don't know about you, Doc, but I'm afraid. I don't rest easy at night anymore. Today they break into houses whether or not anyone's there. And they park their vans right in front so they won't have to walk too far."

"What kind of association are you talking about?" Daddy asked in his doctor voice.

Charpier took the floor. From the looks of things, this was his idea.

"A preventive association. Let's make that clear from the outset. We don't want to take the offensive. You know us, we're not aggressive people. We just want to let potential troublemakers know that from now on Mareuil is off-limits, that they'd better try somewhere else."

"And just how would you let them know?"

"We plan to get as many people together on this as possible. Then we'll all install alarm systems — nothing elaborate or expensive, as long as they make noise. Form a sort of chain, see. Then when one alarm goes off, we'll all head over. We could also use the phone if anything looks suspicious. So we'd all act together anytime there was trouble. All for one, one for all."

"The self-help principle," added Ferré, savoring the phrase.

"And you'd all be . . . armed?" Daddy asked.

They didn't answer right away. There are ways of asking a question so it sounds like a reproach. Cadillac and Ferré turned to Charpier.

"We won't need guns," he explained in calm voice. "At the very most we'd fire a warning shot."

"Don't you think it's asking for trouble to carry a loaded gun? Isn't that how innocent people get wounded or killed?" Daddy inquired.

"Not in our case, Doctor," Charpier protested. "When you're alone, you act out of fear. Accidents happen. But not when you're with twenty friends, shoulder to shoulder."

He leaned closer to my father and explained his own case. In the past two years, his pharmacy had been robbed six times, more than once by the same offenders. Last year he'd been beaten, almost lost an eye. The perpetrators were free now. Every one of the robbers had carried a gun. He needed one for his own protection.

Then it was Cadillac's turn. He pulled a sheet of paper out of his pocket and read a list of crimes committed in the district since the first of September. Two murders, two rapes, two assaults with a deadly weapon, six burglaries. That wasn't even counting the vehicle thefts that happened every day. Ferré explained that they had all worked hard to get where they were and to have what little they did. They were hardly what you'd call capitalist pigs; no, they just wanted to live in peace, that's all. And they were fed up with waiting to be massacred in their own homes, because that's what it was coming to, a massacre.

"Let's say you catch one of these perpetrators," my father asked. "What would you do with him?"

"We'd teach him a lesson that would make him think before he tried it again," Cadillac said. "That's all. We probably wouldn't even hand him over to the police. That costs the taxpayers money, and besides, sooner or later they'd let him go."

"Almost everyone in Mareuil has signed up," Charpier went on. "It's . . . exemplary. The whole country would be the better for it. Well, Dr. Moreau?"

Daddy didn't answer right away. I looked over at him. In fact, his eyes were on me, and I understood that he was answering for us both.

"Sorry, gentlemen, but I can't."

There was a silence. The air was thick with disappointment. Charpier's glass clinked on the table.

"May I ask why?"

"It goes against my thinking," Daddy said simply. "Protection is up to the police and the judicial system. If citizens' groups take things into their own hands, that's anarchy, and who knows where it will lead."

"But what if the police and the courts aren't doing their jobs?" Cadillac asked bitterly. "What if there is no protection for private citizens?"

"They still have the power to demand it," Daddy said, "and loudly. I'd be glad to help with something like that."

Ferré stood up. He went to the window. He pulled back the curtain and looked outside. I'd hardly ever seen him without his white butcher's apron, and it seemed strange to have him here in a checkered jacket and matching cap, the latter tucked under his arm for the time being. I remembered that Charpier wore white behind his counter, too, and Cadillac sometimes, and my father as well: that could have formed a kind of link between them.

"You see, Dr. Moreau," Ferré said, turning back to face my father, "if it had been your mother they'd found with the soles of her feet toasted with her own iron, like poor old Mrs. Lamourette . . . or if it was your daughter those bastards — " He broke off and looked over at me. "Then you might see things differently."

"Yes, I might," Daddy admitted.

Charpier and Cadillac had gotten to their feet, too. "As long as people like you refuse to help us," Charpier remarked sadly, "we'll be less successful in putting a stop to the harm being done."

That was when Mom came in. She smiled at each of them, and thoughts of violence were no longer possible.

Ferré had donned his cap. "At any rate, we're here to help you, Dr. Moreau. Just call and we'll all come running."

"Thank you," Daddy said.

He saw them to the door. And if my mother had been

the one to have her feet burned? I would have shot to kill.

When Daddy came back in, he didn't look as though he'd quite convinced himself.

"What did they want?" Mom said. "They looked so serious."

"They're starting a neighborhood crime-fighters group. They wanted us to join."

My mother stopped clearing away the glasses and looked at her husband emptying his pipe against the fireplace, which always annoyed her because it left yellow stains. He swept the spent tobacco into the flames.

"What did you tell them?"

"What do you expect I told them? How can I heal with one hand and fire a gun with the other?"

Mom sat down on the couch, next to her husband. She leaned her head on his shoulder, very briefly.

"Don't blame yourself. But don't blame them either. They're good people. They've just been pushed too far."

Daddy looked at her, astonished at the tone of her voice.

Mom added, more quietly, "What happened to poor Mrs. Lamourette last night is very upsetting."

"Have you seen her?"

"I stopped by the hospital on my way home," Mom said. "She still hasn't said a word. Talk about ripped off; that's what happened, literally. They almost strangled her to get the watch she wore around her neck."

"So you would have said yes to Charpier?" Daddy asked her.

"If I'd been with that poor old woman last night, I would have tried to defend her," Mom said. "And if I'd had a gun, I would have used it. But that doesn't mean I wouldn't have told those men the same thing you did. That's why we all feel so uneasy."

Daddy fell silent. Mom took the glasses to the kitchen. I heard her voice as she had sung to Benjamin earlier, the songs you sing to children to make them feel secure, the stories where there are good guys and bad guys and the good guys always win.

In my mind I saw Tanguy's foot shoving Missile. I heard the muffled cries of the old woman being ripped off. There were people in the world capable of plugging in an iron to burn an old woman's feet. Not everyone feels screams in the same way. For some, life is written in black, in stormy weather, in death. Why is that so?

An answer took shape in me: it fit in a single word, but I didn't feel like saying it. According to whether you'd had this word or not, whether it had been held out to you like a mirror with the world in the background, you were the kind of person who created or the kind who destroyed, the kind who enjoyed life or the kind who failed to and in so doing sowed death. A very simple word.

Gripping my shoulders, I felt the two hands of Dr. Moreau. I couldn't see them, but they weren't hard to recognize: the grip of a father who sometimes hurts you, trying to help.

"I thought tissues were for wiping tears," he said, "and not cloth napkins. And if my own daughter has a problem and won't share it with me, it makes me wonder what earthly good I am to anyone."

A word of one syllable I'd always been surrounded with and that gave me no right to judge others. Like *love*.

12

Which Side Is the Prison?

I FOUND HIM sitting on the low wall near the gate to La Marette. He was wearing a leather jacket, a silk aviator's scarf around his neck, boots. Not the long, pointy kind with metal tips, but solid rawhide boots, like a cowboy's.

He jumped down from his perch and smiled, and the emotion of that first night swept over me, like a wind from the depths of the earth, and I knew I'd been waiting to see him again, Missile or no Missile.

I was still holding the handlebars of my moped. He reached over and gently removed my helmet.

"It's her," he said. "Yes, the girl who lives in the house of a hundred chimneys."

"And you've come to take the tour, right?"

He laughed. My tone of voice scared him half to death! But I'd guessed it. He'd come to take a closer look at my chimneys and me.

We parked both our bikes in the yard and started the tour with the outside, where the roosting birds were already anouncing night; green was fading into blue, and a few lights twinkled in the distance.

I showed him the path to the shed, the old wasps' nest,

the place where a huge rat had once nipped the Princess on the ankle. In passing, I introduced Tanguy to our "old-timers": the twisted oak, the tall cedar, the three walnut trees. The fourth one, victim of last winter's heavy frost, was still on the ground waiting for my father and Antoine to cut it up on Sunday. No use counting on Stephan's help. When he was trying to win the family over, he used to do yard work like mad, but now that he was one of us that was all over.

Since my father couldn't do everything, the orchard hadn't been mown lately and was knee-high in grass. A tangle of green was starting to creep all over Germain's final resting place. We stopped there a moment and I told Tanguy about him.

"Do you think it's a good idea to plant a tree over someone's grave? A fruit tree, for instance?"

"Probably good for the fruit," Tanguy said. "But some people might not want to eat it."

That was just what I thought. But in spite of everything I wanted Germain to go on in some way, even if it was only two or three peaches a year. Maybe it wasn't one of my better ideas.

We went as far as the fence that separated our grounds from the Oise. It had been fixed recently so our third generation could explore freely and remember La Marette as a huge adventure.

The river transported the evening's last barges. It smelled of silt and diesel fuel. Two blackened cans and some greasy paper flowered on the banks. And yet somewhere inside me it was still the clear water we used to know, and I still tasted it, up to my neck in the river with Bernadette holding my chin as she taught me to swim.

I looked over at Tanguy. His head pressed to the fence, he was staring through the mist at the tall outline of his housing project.

"You look like a prisoner behind bars," I remarked.

He turned to face me. "Which side do you think is the prison? In here or over there?"

Saying "in here," he pointed to the house, and I could see that while for me the family was life, for him it may have been prison.

As we walked toward the house, I asked him how he'd decided to become an actor.

"When I was a junior in high school, we put on a show at the end of the year. A comedy. I had a big part. On the big day, when everyone was there, the parents, teachers, the principal, instead of saying my lines I told them what was really on my mind, that school was full of shit and so were they. At first they thought it was part of the play, and they laughed. Then they saw what I was doing, but they didn't stop me. It was fantastic. I held them with my voice. They had no power to stop me."

"Then what happened?"

"I got kicked out of school. But at least they knew what I thought of them."

"Was it really all that bad?"

He didn't answer.

We passed the swing. He sat down and stretched his legs straight out in front of him.

"Give me a push."

I put both hands flat on his back and started slowly, as you would for a child who's afraid. He was heavy compared to Benjamin, who takes right off. His eyes were closed.

"See, there's how the wind usually feels," he said. "Then the way it feels when you're going a little too fast on your motorcycle, and then when someone pushes you on a swing . . ."

"And sometimes that can get to you when you're all grown up," I said.

"Sometimes."

He jumped to his feet. The swing came zooming back to hit me in the stomach — nice guy! He was walking toward the house without waiting for me. I caught up with him. Claire has gotten all of us used to unfinished sentences. Just when you least expect it, she throws you a bit of rope, almost regretfully. Before you have time to catch on, she cuts you off. But sometimes you're left with something that helps you understand her better.

I took the key from the hiding place under the third step, opened the door to the house, and preceded my guest into the living room.

"And here we have the one working fireplace, the chimney you see smoking."

I tossed in a match. Every morning before he left for work, Charles laid a fire. You're never all alone with a fire.

"You alone here a lot?"

"Some."

He paced the room without a word, checking everything out carefully. Since the swing ride, it was as if something had closed in him. Suddenly I wished Mom was home, but she'd taken Benjamin out to buy winter clothes, and a storybook, and some crayons, and whatever else he wanted — within reason, of course.

Without looking at me, Tanguy said, "We're doing the show again Saturday and Sunday."

"You found the money to pay for the hall?"

"A loan."

I told him that was great and this weekend they'd have to turn people away, just wait and see. But he wasn't really listening.

"Know what the guy at the Center told me? That I should write a comedy. That's what draws crowds; people want to laugh. My play bores them to tears."

"Not if they understand."

I felt the dark force I had come to sense in him start to

rise, changing his voice and his face. On his balcony the other day it had been the same, and then he'd booted Missile over the edge. I had the feeling he lived for his play, and at the same time it was killing him.

"You'll see," I told him. "The Other is going to show up for you. What do you want to bet?"

He crouched down in front of me; I was curled up in the fetal position on Pauline's stool, my back to the fire and arms around my legs. Everything here wears a girl's name: Pauline's stool, the Horsewoman's mug, the Princess's chair. It's more alive that way.

"You're a strange one, Cecile."

His eyes had cleared. I looked deep into them to let him know he wasn't alone, and suddenly I felt all funny and weak. He really had a fantastic face, an actor's face.

"But I like you," he said, breathing a bit more heavily, moving his lips toward mine. I jumped to my feet.

"How about something to drink?"

He burst our laughing. Then he pulled a watch from his pocket.

"Haven't got time."

It looked like a woman's watch, round and old. Like the ones ladies used to wear around their necks. Something froze inside me. He'd already put the watch back in his pocket. I wanted to see it again, and at the same time I wished I'd never seen it at all. No, I was being silly. I was just imagining things.

I walked him out to his motorcycle. I couldn't think of anything to say; I felt cold.

"Thanks for the working fireplace," he said.

When I didn't respond, he tried to look at my face.

"What's the matter?"

"I was just wondering who you are. When you get right down to it, I don't know you."

"Just passing through," he said.

He pushed his bike through the gate, looked around.

"It's quiet here. Do you have many neighbors?"

"A few. We're friends with the people across the road. We call the man Roughly Speaking because that's his favorite expression."

"Like 'Roughly speaking, I'm glad we met?' " he asked.

I kept looking at him. I couldn't help myself. I wanted him to reassure me, but he didn't know I was afraid, since he leaned toward me and, through his scarf, pressed his moist lips against mine.

13

Another Wavelength

HOW I'D WAITED! To be talked about the way my sisters were, with the same lilt in the voice: Claire's beauty, Pauline's irresistible eyes, Bernadette's perfect body. I waited, and nothing happened. I was the Pest, the afterthought, the baby. No, I really hadn't gotten past the baby stage.

At school dances, I waited for boys to come up to me, single me out. I would have put my arms around their necks; they would have put theirs around my waist, and we would have swayed together, cheek to cheek. That's how you discover you're not pretty: one night as the music plays, standing against a wall, watching other girls revel in their beauty, with their eyes, their hands, their mouths. You find it out the night you tell yourself you don't really like to dance, you don't feel like going out.

"But I like you," Tanguy had said.

He had said it looking me in the face. Desiring me. I wrapped a scarf around my face, touched my parted lips to the mirror above the fireplace. And he'd kissed me. Handsomer than Paul, Stephan, and Antoine rolled into one! All the girls must be after him. And he wanted me. I wanted it to happen all over again. I'm on the stool, he comes over, bends down. I feel the fire on my back. We look deep into each other's eyes: "But I like you." I feel warm all over now. His eyes change. His breathing quickens. He brings his lips close to mine. Why did you have to get up, you dummy? What if he gives up on you? But no, there it was again, out by his motorcycle.

It was eleven o'clock. I tossed and turned in my bed. Turned the light on and off. Now the replay was centered in my chest, not my head; my chest tightened and expanded until I thought I'd burst. To think I might never have known him! Such a near thing. It had all started in church. "What can I do to help?" I had asked Jean-René. "Go to the theater for me," he had said. He'd hit the mark without even knowing it. Now I would fight that dark force that rose in Tanguy, that was called loneliness. And what if I tried to be that Other with a big *O,* the biggest? Tanguy . . . like the tang of sea salt, the waves pitching and rolling inside me, crashing over me. I was choking, sinking. If I didn't talk to someone, I would drown.

I went downstairs without turning on any lights, so as not to wake anyone. I put the phone behind a pillow because of the little click it makes when you pick up the receiver, and I dialed Melodie's number, ready to hang up if a grown-up answered. But no, it was Mel herself. Her parents were out at a dinner party. She sounded kind of groggy. "Do you have any idea what time it is?" "Time means nothing when you're in love," I told her, and yes, tonight I was in love. I told her all about it. Exactly six hours and twenty-five minutes earlier, the lips of a man to die for had touched my lips.

"What about Missile?" she asked. "Don't you care about that anymore?" I cared more than ever. I could explain.

Now Melodie didn't sound a bit sleepy. She felt kind of blue. She wished she could fall in love, but all the boys she met were dopes. She offered me the Pill: her mother never quite finished her month's supply, and over the last three years Melodie had accumulated quite a stash.

We said goodbye reluctantly about one in the morning when she heard the elevator stop outside their apartment door. This time I fell right to sleep. Now it was Melodie's turn for insomnia. The true meaning of sharing.

I woke to the sound of rain. I knew right away I couldn't go to school: too much to think about. In his bed, Benjamin was flipping through his English storybook, singing quietly. Sometimes I felt as though he understood everything, and it scared me. I gave him a piggyback ride down to breakfast. I told Mom the teachers were out on strike that day and to avoid a potential inquisition I changed the subject to Mrs. Lamourette. "Is she still in the hospital? Has she recovered enough to give them a description?"

Mom didn't know much except that the poor old thing didn't want to go home. She'd probably end up living with her son in Pontoise, and she'd always been so proud of her little house.

"You must be able to tell by a person's face if he's capable of doing something awful like that," I remarked. "It's got to be written all over him."

"Don't kid yourself," Mom said. "Every day I see convicts who've done even worse things. And they don't look any different from you or me. When you talk to them, you simply can't believe it."

At that point — as I tried not to think about the watch Tanguy had pulled out of his pocket, the old pendant watch, the lady's watch — at that point the phone rang. The call we had all dreaded but knew would come: Paul.

He was calling from the Riviera. Had been trying for days to call home, with no luck. Did we know where his wife and son were?

Mom was perfect, calm personified, neutral voice. Yes, Pauline had left on an assignment with Beatrice and we were taking care of Benjamin for her. Mother and son were both fine.

I tried to get my ear close to the receiver, but Mom gave me a dirty look and a little shove. No, she didn't know where Pauline was or how long she'd be gone. It had come up all of a sudden. That was all she could tell him.

There was a pause, a few words I couldn't hear, then Paul hung up.

Mom didn't move for a minute, or say anything, or even seem to notice I was there. I had a lump in my throat. Without using names, to protect the innocent, who was eating a strawberry yogurt without missing a bit of the conversation, I quietly asked a few questions. What would the father do now? Would he show up and take the son home? Was abandonment grounds for divorce, and if so, who would get custody? Would we still be able to see the child? Without mentioning his unfit mother, of course.

Mom looked up at me, and now her calm was completely blown.

"Just stop asking me stupid questions and go get to work, would you?"

I got the picture. Once again, I was nothing but a pest.

14

No More "Horsewoman"

MIND YOUR OWN BUSINESS, you little pest," Pauline was saying. "Don't you realize I knew he'd call? Let him stew in his own juices. Who's to say he wasn't with *her* when he called? So don't breathe a word. You promised."

"OK, but just be glad you don't have to live here."

Pauline paused. I could see her. I wanted so much for her to be here — for me!

"Come home," I said.

"Not yet."

"I have to talk to you . . . about something important. Very, very important."

Then she started laughing.

"That won't work on me, Pest. I know you. You're just doing a number on me. Paul got to you all with his phone call. But no way."

I hung up. If she needed me, she knew where to find me.

Three in the afternoon on the streets of Neuilly. What time was it on the little round watch in Tanguy's pocket? On a narrow street, a modern building that already looked as though it was falling apart. The walls inside the elevator were covered with nasty scribbles. Fourth floor. I rang the bell.

"Hi there, Pest!" said Bernadette. "What a nice surprise! Cutting class, or what? Hey, what's wrong?"

All of a sudden I'd had it up to there, and my eyes just started gushing.

"I'm sick of being called the Pest."

"But that's what we've been calling you for eighteen years! I thought you liked it."

I gestured toward her tiny living room.

"And for fifteen years we called you Horsewoman. How would you feel if I called you that now?"

She grabbed my shoulder.

"Come on in."

Inside, lamps were already on. That's winter's game: stealing the light. Every day it quietly swipes a few minutes more, leaving you in the dark, the mud, the dumps. And now, since the day before, the Oise was rising. If it didn't stop, it would wash Germain away. We'd find him belly-up among the barges.

Bernadette shoved me onto the couch. Through the clutter of toys on the floor, you could pick out a few inches of carpet.

"The girls are at school, so we have an hour. What would you say to an Irish coffee?"

"Great! And heavy on the whisky."

Drinking, smoking, taking drugs — maybe even scorching an old lady's feet — are a silent scream, as in dreams when your life is in danger but when you open your mouth nothing comes out. It's awful.

I let my sister cater to me and took a look around so I'd feel better. On the bedroom wall, opposite the bed my parents gave them, the blowup of Germain with three girls on his back. Their names are Bernadette, Pauline, and Cecile, and they're laughing their heads off. Claire, in the background, is working on her tan.

In a corner of the mirror, an off-track-betting stub. That was new! Stephan? I went back into the living room. At night, the twins' beds were rolled out here. Other than that, a pocket-sized kitchen and bath. And other than that, out the window, a preserve of concrete. Not much better than Tanguy's view. But I still couldn't picture Bernadette here. She loved the country, the wind, adventure. She practically used to sleep with her riding boots on. Was this where love got you? Trading space for four walls and boots for slippers?

Here she was, gingerly carrying two tall cream-topped glasses. She handed me the fuller one. It smelled strong, hot, but most of all out of the ordinary: finally, a whiff of freedom.

"What's on your mind?" she asked.

"You! I've been thinking you must miss the horseflesh."

"You bet I do. Every night I dream that I'm riding. And the smell! You have no idea how I miss the smell of a stable."

"Isn't there any way you can get back into it?"

"When?" she asked. "And what about the money? A law clerk doesn't exactly make millions. Six years of college, and it's almost minimum wage. I wish I could strangle whoever said money can't buy happiness. If I had the dough, I'd get someone to take care of the girls and the house and everything, and I'd ride, ride, ride. . . ."

She broke off. "But you didn't come over just to hear my tale of woe. What's going on with you?"

My glass was half empty and my head was starting to spin. I hardly knew where to begin. Too many things: Tanguy, Pauline, Mrs. Lamourette and her scorched feet, the stupid old watch I couldn't get out of my mind, the neighborhood vigilantes . . .

That was the easiest place to start. Bernadette approved. "Tell them I'll sign up for the weekends."

We talked about violence. She knew what it meant. And from both sides.

"When Stephan comes home at night, full of himself and his day's work, I feel like strangling him because my arms and legs are itching to move, as if it were all his fault — the twins, no money . . ."

She readily admitted that society wasn't always fair, that certain people did have an excuse, "Some, but that doesn't mean all. And some are just plain bad apples, whether you like it or not. Evil does exist. There are bad horses, too — nothing works except putting them out of their misery." Of course, at La Marette the four of us were superprivileged, loved, handled with care. But she demanded, and would never give up, her right to defend herself if attacked, and that was that.

She drained her glass and slammed it down on the coffee table. Now that was more like my sister! And besides, no slippers for her: bright socks and sexy leg-warmers.

"What else?"

"Paul called from the Riviera. Looking for Pauline."

"Did you talk to him?"

"No, Mom did."

"What did she tell him?"

"That she's out on a job with Bea, no idea where."

"And you're all worked up over that? You can't say he doesn't deserve to worry. What's good for the goose . . ."

"But I know where she is."

I must say it was exciting to see her reaction. Her mouth dropped open for ten seconds. "You know where she is? And you haven't told anyone?"

"I promised Pauline."

She got up and paced the room to digest this bit of news. This time I needn't worry that she'd tickle it out of me. That kind of treat is reserved for La Marette. At home, we return to "go." It was like a game where we shared everything: the good and the bad, laughter and tears. We each got a turn to throw the dice or deal the cards, but we were all going in the same direction. The object was to find who was It, and little did we know that would mean the end of the game.

"Act One," said Bernadette, looking out at the rain and packing her pipe, "Pauline finds out Paul is having an affair. Act Two, she splits. If I were you, I'd wait for the third act before I spilled the beans."

"And what if the third act is a divorce?"

"People get divorced when they stop loving each other. Or at least one of them does. I wouldn't say that's the case here."

That very second, my heart felt a hundred pounds lighter. *To talk* is the world's most wonderful verb when it's truly conjugated.

"Speaking of acts," I said, "You know that play I went to see last weekend? Well, I met the guy who wrote it. Stars in it too. His name is Tanguy, he's neat. I'd like to have you meet him. To see what you think. Soon."

I'm way behind Mom when it comes to the neutral voice, the cool face. Bernadette slithered over to me like a gigolo, eyebrows arched.

"Would our Pest be showing an interest in the opposite sex? And none too soon."

"Maybe the opposite sex hasn't been interested in me."

She kneeled in front of me and brought her face right up to mine, almost as close as Tanguy had.

"Well, if I were a guy, I'd go for you. I might start out looking for Miss Universe, but once I wised up you'd be my type. You're the real thing. And the guy who ends up with you will never be bored."

I wasn't sure how to take it, but it wasn't far from what Tanguy had told me. "You're a strange one, but I like you. . . ."

My heart swelled: Tanguy! The blue of his eyes never the same, his moist lips through silk.

"Anyway, I'm coming out for the weekend. Then you can introduce me to the object of your affection."

She looked at her watch, sprang to her feet. Four o'clock already! Time to pick up the girls.

As we combed our hair in front of her bedroom mirror, I pointed to the exacta ticket.

"Stephan plays the horses?"

"No, I do."

And suddenly she froze. I knew that look. It was the one she used to wear when she jumped her horse. She took the ticket, turned it over and over, incredulous, as if seeing it for the first time.

"Damn it! This stupid thing is what I've been counting on to change my life? A lucky number, a windfall! I've been reading up on the horses in the paper and going down to the café to bet on the fastest one instead of riding and spurring one on myself!"

With the same black look, she calmly tore up the ticket.

"Thanks. Pes . . . Cecile. You made me see the light. I'm going to do something. I don't know what, but I will. You've got to make your own luck, take the bull by the horns, not wait around for things to change."

The rain made the pavement shine, and the smell of it struck some familiar chord. When we passed a tree, I touched its trunk.

Bernadette stared straight ahead at some unseen goal. If only I could help her, find an idea.

"Till further notice," I told her, "no charge for baby-sitting."

She twirled around and looked at me without replying. She was streaming with rain: wet hair, cheeks, and eyes. At least one sister wouldn't say I was stingy.

Other mothers waited for their offspring on the steps of the school. Women with raincoats, dressy boots, handbags, makeup. Proper Neuilly ladies, nothing like us Mareuil girls.

Soon the door would open and the children would pour out. Two little girls, so alike, fair-haired and blue-eyed, would wrap themselves around their dark mother, bent down to absorb the shock. Bernadette would disappear beneath then, and once again I'd feel a little bit lost.

"Can I ask you something? Until further notice, and I mean to tell you when, don't call me Horsewoman either."

15

Unexploded Bomb

SUPERB, CENTER STAGE, he let loose. Words spewed from him like fire from a volcano, like lava that would snatch those who had not come to listen from their homes, their laden tables, their televisions, snatch them from their restful, comfortable Saturday. He cried out for the Other who would not come, for a mad world, for hatred, for nuclear winter. He cried out and went unheard.

Only a handful of people in the little theater, including Bernadette and me. A flop. He was crying in the desert.

I wanted the play to be over, the curtain to fall. I hurt for Tanguy. Once, as a boy, he had held an unresponsive crowd spellbound. So what if he'd been labeled a reject for it later? He'd told them off. Today he was being rejected in a different way. They simply didn't show up. And his cry turned back on himself and consumed him. This was what I'd felt the other night at La Marette: to live, Tanguy needed the theater, and the theater was eating him alive.

I took all of him with my eyes: I took the child I never knew, the adult he was today, the bad with the good, I didn't care. I willed myself to be the whole audience, all eyes and ears. But tonight he didn't see me. He looked beyond me, at the closed faces, closed ears.

It was the end. He was alone on the stage. "There is no Other." I heard church bells. Saw Jean-René lift his eyes. The Other might be God. "Which side is the prison?" asked Tanguy. He had asked me that a few days before, and I hadn't been able to answer. Leaning forward in her seat, Bernadette listened tensely. Tanguy's voice grew lower, almost inaudible, as if he was speaking now from far away, to himself, in himself. He was saying that inside us, past all the things we grasped at every day to block out, deep inside us, the two eyes watching us, we were still ourselves. The Other was us. Alone. Goodbye. . . .

The curtain came down, rose again. The worst was yet to come: a chorus of boos. They echoed from the back of the room. And not even from those too old and hardened to understand, but from a small group of young people. They booed Tanguy, shouted insults. Immobile, he stared out at them until the curtain came down for good.

I was on my feet, facing those imbeciles, and I heard myself shout. Why had they come? Why hadn't they just stayed home with their machines, the ones that distracted them with pictures, noise, speed, the equipment that saved them from thinking, from wondering just once before they died who they were and what they were doing here. They hooted and answered that they were here, right here. Did I want them to prove it? I yelled back that they didn't scare me. For me they didn't exist.

"Enough," Bernadette barked. "If they don't exist, then stop it."

She pushed down on my shoulders. I fell back into my seat. Only the two of us left now. I refused to cry.

"What's your problem?" she asked. "They didn't like the play, that's all. When you perform you accept the consequences. He attacks, they respond. Only normal. And you'll never get people to pay to come hear they're a bunch of jerks and the world is going to blow up in their faces."

"They didn't understand. It was fantastic."

"We'll discuss that later, if you don't mind. I thought you were going to introduce us."

She looked determined, as if this was something serious. That made me feel better. I guided her backstage. What would I say to Tanguy? I'd never find the right words. I felt small and useless.

His door was closed, of course, but light shone through the bottom. We knocked: nothing. I called his name: silence. "Wait," said Bernadette. "Let's try down there." Down the hall, an office with the light on. The three other actors were there, still in costume. The conversation stopped when we walked in.

"Looks like it didn't go too well tonight," my sister said, not mincing words.

They all burst out at the same time. They weren't letting themselves in for that again. They'd stop before they got any deeper into debt. Besides, they'd never thought much of the play. A play? More like a monologue. They were just the fall guys, never knowing what would hit them next. It couldn't work. In any case, they hadn't made a cent. They were quitting.

I went up to Maryse, who'd joked with Tanguy in his room the week before. They'd seemed to get along pretty well.

"But you're suppose to go on tomorrow. You can't just give up like that. He can't do the play all alone."

She looked me over and laughed. "You can have my part, then. You'll see how much fun it is."

"Anyway, the whole thing was starting to turn bad," added Manuel.

My heart skipped a beat. Turn bad? What did that mean? I was about to ask for an explanation when Tanguy walked in.

He'd changed, removed his makeup. It seemed to me that he was very pale. You saw nothing but his eyes. He stared at us: we'd stopped talking, felt sheepish, small, weak. And he started laughing, the laugh of someone who finds out he's been abandoned and says that's fine with him, just fine, and besides he has everything he needs.

He laughed and brandished a bottle.

"Champagne," he said.

Bernadette stopped the car along the road to the house. She hadn't said a word yet. Neither had I. And anyway, I knew what she was going to tell me. I was ready, but it wouldn't change anything.

She took hold of my wrists: "Stop seeing him. He's dangerous; he'll hurt you. I don't know why or how, but anyone can see that from a mile away. Nice wrapping, but the package is ticking, and it could blow up in your face any minute."

"I love him."

She shook her head.

"That's not what it's called. He's the first guy who turns you on, he's great-looking, and you're ready. Plus, he's given up on life and that's like bait to you. I'm sorry, but desperate cases always did appeal to you. We should have named you Saint Bernard."

"He doesn't have anyone. I can't give up on him."

"See! And have you ever wondered why he doesn't have anyone? He must have had a mother and father like everyone else. And they obviously sent him to school; he knows how to talk and act. Let's say they kicked him out. That still leaves friends."

"They don't understand him."

Bernadette was quiet for a moment. In my mind I looked for Tanguy, the one I'd pushed on the swing, not the one who made us drink a champagne toast to the death of his play, his hope.

"If you refuse to speak other people's language, to put yourself in their shoes, if you speak a foreign language to them, how do you expect them to understand? Can I tell you how I felt?" she said.

I couldn't answer; I was too afraid for my love.

"He hates people. When he talks about war, you feel as though he hopes it will happen. 'I'm going, and I'm taking all of you with me.' "

I protested, "It's only a play. He feels alone, that's all. He needs to meet someone."

"And that someone is named Cecile Moreau, I suppose?"

I saw him standing over me, his eyes on mine: "But I like you. . . ."

"Maybe."

"Tell Mom and Dad about him."

"I couldn't."

"Then at least promise me one thing: be careful. Love him if you have to, but from a distance. And if you have problems, call."

"Call . . ." I didn't tell Bernadette that for the last week, in a way, I had felt I was calling, in vain. But you can call out very quietly, on purpose, so no one will hear, because you're afraid of the answer. I saw Missile sailing over the balcony, and Tanguy's eyes when he erased you, when you stopped mattering. You can call out but gag yourself first.

Another thing I didn't tell my sister was that when we stopped in front of La Marette, with its lights on, with its heart beating inside, for the first time I felt almost like a stranger there.

"He'll hurt you," Bernadette said. He already had: "Which side is the prison?" A swift kick to my heart.

16

The Orchard Treatment

As WE WERE ALL having coffee in the living room after Sunday dinner, through the window I suddenly saw Benjamin dart toward the gate and out of my line of sight. I changed windows.

A low-slung car pulled in. I turned to the family.

"Well, folks, here's Paul," I said.

Within a second there was total silence. All eyes were on me.

"Alone?" Claire asked quietly.

"Who were you expecting?" Bernadette asked. "Elizabeth Taylor?"

She turned to Daddy, who was hastily packing a pipe.

"No reason to panic. He's not coming in yet; Benjamin's got him."

The little boy jumped into his father's arms, hugging him with all his might, as if he wanted to get inside him. Paul let go of his cane to hug him back.

"Act Three," my sister whispered in my ear. "Return to the fold. I told you we should just let things take their course."

The air in the living room seemed to thin out. The Princess, who hates scenes, looked at us anxiously.

78

"But what will we say to him?"

"We'll ask if he's had lunch," said Mom, calm as anything. "There's plenty of lamb left."

He hadn't eaten a bite. He'd left Saint-Tropez at dawn and driven straight through. He thought maybe Pauline would be back, that she'd be here for the weekend. . . .

Mom set a tray of food on the coffee table in front of him. He spoke in a hoarse, tense voice. Bernadette was right: there was love in it. He seemed shrouded in a mist of love and guilt. Benjamin, perched on Paul's lap, couldn't take his eyes off his father. When Paul took a bite, Benjamin swallowed, taking nourishment with, or from, his father.

"You haven't heard from Pauline?" Paul asked.

"Not yet," my mother answered.

And she added, "This assignment must be keeping her very busy."

She looked genuinely sorry. She was. She doesn't like to see anyone suffer, whether or not he deserves it. Not hard to guess where I came by my Saint Bernard side. And throw in a doctor father who wouldn't keep a gun for self-defense . . .

From my father, not a word. Men get less practice telling white lies, skirting the truth. Fortunately there was Benjamin's chatter to fill the silences.

"All done on location?" Bernadette asked. "How did it go?"

Daddy turned to her, looking nervous. But her voice was as normal as Mom's, her expression as calm. Paul studied her a few seconds before replying, wondering what she knew, whether Pauline had told us. What you don't understand, Paul old boy, is that sisters don't need to be told. They guess. Growing up together sharpens your antennae.

"I was ready for it to end," he said.

I could guess what Bernadette was leaving unsaid: "And the affair?"

"And are you happy with the results?" Mom rushed to add. "I mean, satisfied with the film?"

"I've only seen the rushes," Paul said. "They seemed all right. At any rate, it's faithful to my book."

Faithful! He could have chosen his words more carefully. The chill passed. At the window, his back to us, Antoine looked out at the grounds. What did he see? He was standing very straight. How much a man's shoulders say about him! They told me how his mother left him when he was a boy and that he also picked up signals when it came to love and abandonment.

Paul pushed his plate away. He'd hardly eaten anything, didn't feel hungry after driving all day. But he agreed to a cup of black coffee.

"What's this story she and Bea are covering?" he asked, bouncing Benjamin on his good knee.

"I'm not quite sure," said Mom, beginning to fidget.

"And you don't know where she is, either?"

Daddy shook his head no and sighed.

"Really?" Paul persisted.

He looked at us one by one, at the end of his rope. His eyes were rimmed with red. Suddenly I had a series of numbers on the tip of my tongue; an area code, seven digits, and then Pauline's voice on the line, his wife, my sister, daughter number three of this couple looking so uncomfortable, unhappy.

"Really," Bernadette said firmly.

I swallowed my dialing instructions. Just a year ago, I couldn't keep anything to myself. But I'd matured. Now I could lie and cheat like everyone else. Was that why I felt I was in prison? Tanguy was right: we all are. We're our own jailers. Tanguy! A couple of miles away, in the projects, were an empty stage, rows of unoccupied seats, darkness, silence. And Tanguy? Where was he? Where had he gone to nurse his pain?

I got up and walked out of the room. Bernadette found me putting on my parka in the front hall.

"Going for a walk? Good idea. Getting too hot in here with all these people. Where are we heading?"

Not to Tanguy's! We'd walk in the woods full of rustling silence: one huge banked fire. In wintertime a forest makes me think not of cathedrals, but rather of cemeteries. They both tug at your feet with their layers of leaves years deep; they keep reminding you that they'll still be counting springs when you are not.

But that was apparently not how it made Bernadette feel. Head thrown back, eyes closed, mouth open, and nostrils flared, she breathed in the forest as deeply as she could.

"You see," she told me, "it would've been too easy if you'd told Paul all you know. Don't forget that Pauline is the one to decide, not him. And he may be hurting, but it's not as though he doesn't deserve it."

"Have you discussed this with Stephan?"

She looked surprised.

"Of course I have. I tell him everything, even when I feel like strangling him. Otherwise, what's the point of living together? And besides, I wanted to see how he'd react in case it ever happens to us."

"Well?"

"He thinks the worst thing would be to act like it's the end of the world."

She laughed. "So I said, 'Then if I were unfaithful, you wouldn't think it was the end of the world?' And you know what he said?"

"I have a feeling you're going to tell me."

"He said, 'Don't do it. Don't do it, my love.' "

No more laughter in her voice. Something like pride.

Night had fallen when we headed back. A night not quite like any other. Sunday night. Paul's car was still there. As we took off our boots in the front hall, Claire came to find us.

"Mom and Daddy gave Paul the orchard treatment, a little over an hour of it. They were so cold when they got in that Antoine prescribed hot buttered rum."

The "orchard treatment" is Grandmother's specialty. When she has something to say to someone, or something to get out of them, she always suggests a tour of the fruit trees. Everyone knows what that means. We've all had a turn; it's become a family tradition.

"Anyway," Claire said, "the atmosphere is improving."

In the living room, drinks and games. The kids were playing house. Gabriel was the mother, the twins were uncles, the house was under the dining room table with its tablecloth almost touching the floor. The chair legs were trees, and the grown-ups were wild animals in the forest. I sat down near their house and set my cup of tea on the roof. Tasty little children, beware!

Pine honey goes best with black China tea, I think. A voyage in a cup. Paul came to sit down by me, holding his hot toddy.

"Thanks for taking care of Benjamin," he said.

"No problem . . . by the way, what happens now? Can he stay?"

"A few more days, if it's all right with you. I'm not really set up to handle him alone. And Pauline will be back soon, don't you think?"

He was begging me to say yes. He wasn't asking me to tell him what I knew, just to give him some hope. And deep in his eyes was a darkness, a cry, something like Tanguy's. A lump grew in my throat, and not just because of the honey. Sophie had crawled under my chair, daring the monster to strike, then scampering away when I growled.

"There must come a time when you're ready for a story to end, too," I said. "Have you told Benjamin you're not taking him with you?"

"Not yet."

He got to his feet. "I'll tell him now. Do you know where he is?"

I knocked on the table. "Under there, is my guess."

If Gabriel was the mother and the twins were uncles, Ben must be the father or the son. I'd just peeked under the tablecloth when he appeared in the living room doorway.

He had his jacket on and had put up the hood for good measure, hiding half his face and half smothering him. He was dragging his suitcase along behind him, new clothes, books, and toys bursting from every zipper. He walked through the momentarily paralyzed crowd of "wild animals" without a glance, walked up to his father, came to rest between his legs, and looked up at him as if he understood that Paul was about to leave him behind.

"When are we going home?" asked Benjamin. "I want to see Mommy."

17

Till Death Us Do Part

I TOLD PAULINE that her son needed her. And Paul did, too. He'd come looking for her this afternoon. I described his voice, the way his eyes had changed color, and all the loneliness that had seemed to surround him, the despair. I knew about that now. How you feel lost in a crowd of people when the one you care for isn't there. It may not really be his fault, but he's stolen a part of you, and you miss it.

I was in the living room, where the fire was dying out, like this Sunday night that would fade into Monday in less than an hour. On the card table, a game of solitaire Claire had left unfinished; here and there, a stray glass; toys all over the place. We'd clean up in the morning.

Before going up to bed, Daddy had banked the fire and replaced the screen. Little chores make you feel better: things you've done in better times, things you'll do in better times to come. Things written on every page.

I asked my sister to imagine her two men in Paris: Paul with his limp, Benjamin running to the bedroom, hoping he'd find someone to call Mommy. Kids are like that, imagining so hard that they believe in miracles.

"Did Paul really seem upset?" she asked when I'd finished. "You're not just saying that to make me feel better?"

"He looked like there was permanent damage to his psyche and not just his leg. Does that make you feel better?"

He had looked so bad that I'd almost told him all I knew. Bernadette had stopped me. I told Pauline it looked like the next move was hers. What did she think?

"Hold on just a minute."

She put down the receiver and I heard her walk away. I thought I heard her talking to someone: Beatrice? If Pauline was planning to follow *her* advice, I might as well give up and go to bed. She came back after what seemed like a century.

"We still have so much to cover. Tomorrow we're doing the cheesemaker I told you about."

"I guess you're more interested in cheese than in your son."

She hung up. That was when Daddy walked in.

"Who was that?"

No anger in his voice, or even blame, or suspicion, the things you'd expect from a father when you're clearly hiding something important. Only a deep fatigue. I also read it in his eyes. They'd grown pale, not with pain but with age. His fatigue, his rumpled pajamas, the slippered feet that you could see were also beginning to fail him — all this, and on top of it Beatrice, that bitch, wrecking other people's families because she had never had one herself — meant I no longer had the strength to lie.

"It was Pauline. I called her."

He settled down beside me on the couch.

"This afternoon I could tell you knew something."

I nodded. He smelled of toothpaste. The bathroom is just above where the phone is; he must have heard me talking.

"I promised not to tell."

He put a hand on my shoulder.

"If we're to help your sister, don't you think we need all the facts at hand?"

"Absolutely."

I looked him in the eye: "What were you two grilling Paul about this afternoon?"

A flicker of a smile. He stood up. "Come on!"

Not the right time of day for the "orchard treatment," so he led me to the master bedroom. Mom was in bed, wrapped up in an old sweater because we lower the heat at night. Better for your health, for the pocketbook, and for the teeth: the freezing water in the morning is an early-warning system if there's any problem. My father took his place next to his wife, without getting under the covers (I appreciated his delicacy). I sat down on the foot of the bed.

"You've had this bed for more than thirty years," I said.

"Right," Daddy said. "It was a wedding present from your grandmother. She told us it was made to order so we could stay together even if one of us got sick."

I was born in July. Not many people take vacations in November; in all probability, then, I was conceived right here where I sat tonight. That put things in a different light.

"Have you ever changed the mattress?"

Mom looked puzzled, studying her husband, then me. Had we called this midnight meeting just to discuss bedding?

"Cecile knows where to find Pauline," Daddy explained.

He turned to me. "As far as Paul is concerned, we told him we knew about his affair with the actress. We also told him we don't think Pauline has left for good, that she just needed a break from the pain."

Mom turned away, but not before I saw the tears in her eyes. If there's one thing I can't stand, it's seeing my mother cry; it ages me a hundred years in a minute. Would I be the one to console her someday? Even take care of her? Be a mother to my mother!

"And what did Paul have to say?"

"That it was all over with that woman."

"Until the next one?"

"It wouldn't be fair to ask that."

"What else did he say?"

"That he loves your sister. That she was . . . his only future."

I saw Paul's red-rimmed eyes and his muted suffering. Like a storm inside him that might sweep him away. His only future?

"So we tried to make him see that if he was staking his future on her, he should try not to undermine it," Daddy said. "And that when you love someone you try to avoid hurting her."

His voice made me feel good: the voice of a man who knows what it is to love truly. He laid his hand on the sheet and I noticed he was holding my mother's hand, hidden underneath.

"Still," I said, "don't you think it's time you admitted that today a couple's future lasts fifty years or so, and no matter how much they love each other, being faithful is a strain?"

"It should still be what you aim for," my mother said.

I felt myself grow. It was strong.

"Can I ask you something, since we're on the subject?"

Daddy exchanged a look with Mom and they both sat up a bit straighter.

"Go ahead."

"Is it true that men need sex more than women do?"

Suddenly I saw Tanguy bringing his lips close to mine, breathing more heavily. I'd felt a sort of violence, a command from his body to mine, something imperative and beyond control. And I'd turned to mush. I'd felt afraid. Run away.

"I do believe that in the majority of cases," my father said, "the need is both stronger and more frequent in men than in women."

A warmth spread through me. I like it being that way, with men both strong and fragile in the face of life, life summoning them to us. I felt precious.

"And Pauline?" my father asked quietly. "You don't have to tell us where she is, but how is she?"

I told them everything: her letter, the lake, the phone calls. Mom grilled me, eager for news of her daughter: was she feeling, doing, eating all right? I apologized for my lack of information on her diet, but apparently she was surviving; she was interested in her story, which was a good sign.

"She'd be better off showing some interest in Benjamin," I remarked. "If she doesn't want to come back to her husband, she should at least come back to her son. That's what I called to tell her."

"It wouldn't do Ben any good to have his mother come back against her will," Daddy said. "For him to feel good about it, she has to feel good. And Paul, too."

"I think I understand that now," I told them.

They promised they wouldn't take any action before talking it over with me. And I shouldn't feel I'd betrayed my sister. Sometimes you ask people to keep a secret without really wanting them to: an indirect call for help.

It had never occurred to me to think of myself as a Judas. When you betray someone you don't feel so good about it, so light. It may well have been true that in swearing me to silence Pauline was appealing to the whole family. I'd been calling for help with Tanguy, too, but so quietly that no one could hear.

Mom and Daddy looked completely worn out from their long day. I said goodnight and walked out. Halfway up the stairs, though, I couldn't resist the urge to check on them one last time, and I went back to poke my head through their doorway.

The good doctor was now under the covers. His wife had her light out, but not he. She was leaning on his shoulder and the two of them were staring at the ceiling.

"So 'till death us do part' is still a good deal?" I asked.

I ducked out before they could throw anything at me. Falling asleep that night, I wondered if I'd ever be able to make love in the bed where I'd been conceived without feeling like a criminal. Doubtful! And yet, in a way, tempting. Perversity?

18

Drawing the Sun

AND THEN IT'S SUDDENLY TIME to open your eyes, leave the warmth of your bed, grope your way to the window shade, and get hit in the face with Monday and a horror-movie wind, a garden in tears.

Just yesterday, in the room next to mine, a little boy in need of confidence was waking up at this hour. So you sang to him, out of tune at first, but warming up eventually. Now there was only an empty room, forgotten toys, and on the blackboard a drawing with a house, the sun, and a tree. Benjamin really was gifted.

"I have to talk to you," Melodie whispered.

Our classroom shone with sinister fluorescent lighting. Four more months to go before we worked in natural light. Sixteen girls and five boys bent over blue books: an exam on social-work law. Sticking out her tongue, Melodie filled the pages; she'd get a good grade. I stared at the paper. I was the one who'd wanted to study here, and now I wondered . . . words, sentences, ink on paper. And all the while, a short ride away, pain grew, loneliness spread. Noon in the snack bar with Melodie. We'd ordered grilled cheese sandwiches; the gooey center is the best part. At the next table, three guys joked and try to flirt with us. Strangely, for her, Melodie wanted no part of it.

"Have you heard what happened yesterday?"

"No, fill me in."

"There was a fire in the Center. In the auditorium. They got to it just in time. It was in the paper this morning; my father showed me the article."

Melodie looked at me. We were both thinking the same thing.

"It could have been a cigarette butt. No one said it was arson." No reason we should assume the worst.

"What time did it happen?"

"Yesterday afternoon."

I had been walking in the woods with my sister. I'd felt Tanguy calling me; but it was easier to let Bernadette keep me from going to him. Yesterday afternoon he was supposed to be performing. The hall was rented. But his friends had deserted him. So had I.

"Remember at the beginning of the year," I asked her, "when Blackhead asked us to describe a delinquent?"

Blackhead was what we called our favorite teacher.

"We thought they'd all look the part," Melodie said with a half-smile.

"This morning during the test I wondered what I was doing in school," she said.

"Me too," I said.

She looked at me, surprised, relieved.

"I don't know if I'll be able to go out and do it. Maybe Blackhead is right. We've all been too sheltered; we'll never get used to it out there. What I like is studying," she told me.

I laughed. "I'm just the opposite. I want to get out and work. I get the feeling that what we're learning is beside the point. We're in school, and the world is bleeding from its wounds."

"I can't stand the sight of blood," Melodie admitted.

There was a crowd around the pinball machines. Nothing but guys. Having a great time. Doubled over laughing, like kids. No problem. I thought of Ben's drawing on the blackboard: the house, the sun, the tree. With colored chalk, I'd shown him how to put curtains on the windows, draw a smoking chimney. He liked that. One day he'd draw himself next to his house, and then he'd be able to go on to other things.

I thought of Tanguy on the stage, crying out for no one but himself.

"Aren't you finishing your sandwich?" Melodie inquired.

"Take it. I'm full."

I left enough money for my share and stood up.

"Where are you going? It's not time yet."

I wasn't so sure. Sometimes a boy sketches windowless houses, empty skies, dead trees. People look at the scene and boo. So you set it on fire. It was as clear as that. I was on my way.

19

Looking into the Well

H E WAS ASLEEP. The door wasn't locked or even closed tight. Whatever he may have done, he wasn't trying to hide.

He was curled up on the bed, fists under his chin, disarmed, as if he'd fallen there, with his boots and jacket on. The room was dirty and smelled of wine. It looked as if everything had been swept in piles against the walls. Nestled in a sweater, near the heater, two luminous slits riveted on me: Missile.

"Love him if you have to, but from a distance," Bernadette had warned me. Was it loving or dreaming? I looked at him and had no idea. It was easy when he was on the stage: tall, blond, handsome, and passionate. It was easy at La Marette with my good, solid walls around me. Now we were really face to face: him with no stage to stand on and me without rose-colored glasses. "Put on your rose-colored glasses," Grandmother would say when I was little and out of sorts.

I slid down against the wall, onto a cushion. Grandmother: at her house in Burgundy there was a well I used to be really scared of. I'd lean over the edge and drop stones into it. Fall with them. It took so long to reach the water. Why was that well appearing to me now?

I picked up a book, big, bound in red and gold, a storybook. Inside the cover, a childish hand had inscribed a name and address: Tanguy Le Floch, Conflans Sainte-Honorine. I'd been there, a town not far away where we sometimes went to the outdoor market, full of colors, odors, hustle-bustle down by the river with barges, side by side, forming something like a moving village. "He had a mother and father like everyone else," Bernadette had said. Mr. and Mrs. Le Floch. Why didn't he ever mention them? What had they done to him?

I put the book back and took a look around: several radios, a vase, a jewelry box, a . . .

"Taking inventory?" asked Tanguy.

My heart leapt. He stared at me ironically through barely opened eyes.

"Of you."

"And what's the verdict?"

"When you're asleep, you look young."

His eyes shut again. "I don't remember inviting you over."

"I didn't invite you when you came to La Marette, either."

He propped himself up on an elbow and began to laugh. I didn't like his laugh.

"I'm never invited," he said. "I'm not presentable."

He leaned over and grabbed a bottle of wine, drank from it, held it out to me. I shook my head. He put it down. I loved him, and now I didn't feel a thing.

"The fire in theater yesterday, was that you?"

"What fire?" he asked. "What theater?"

I pointed to the stuff piled against the walls.

"And where did all this come from?"

He just smiled without answering. It seemed as though I was the accused.

"And the watch you had in your pocket the other day? The little round one?"

That was the most important question, along with the others I didn't dare ask: "Were you alone? Are you capable of torture?"

"First the inventory, then the third degree!" he said. "Are you going to read me my rights?"

I murmured, "Why?"

"And why are you a good little girl who's never stolen anything in her life?"

His smile had vanished, and his voice was icy: he had nothing but scorn for that good little girl.

"Now can I ask you a question?" he said.

I nodded.

"Why did you come here? Just to give me shit?"

I turned toward the window. There was some sun now, but it only showed that the glass was filthy.

"I imagined you . . . all alone."

I got up, found an old rag in his booty, and went to wipe the window. At least I would have done that much for him. He'd see a little less darkly through it. And then goodbye, since I was only giving him shit.

Missile came out of his sweater-nest, stretched port and starboard. If he kept living there, it meant he wasn't treated so badly. That he was fed, sometimes even stroked. Cats are no masochists. According to my father, they're the only animals that have domesticated man. Whole novels could have been outlined in the dirt on Tanguy's window: black humor.

"Come over here," said Tanguy.

His voice was no longer the same. He patted the mattress beside him. I finished my corners, dropped my rag, and went over to him. Yesterday I'd been afraid to come here; I had been afraid on the way here today. That was over. Fear is for before and after, not during. I sat down

95

on the mattress, back to the wall, like him. And then he did something that threw me completely: he lowered his head onto my shoulder; he was the child I'd surprised in his sleep. I put my arm around him: I was the mother of this child.

"Stay," he murmured. "Don't go back to your nice big house. Don't go back with them — stay with me."

It was as if something jammed in my brain. Stay? I couldn't, and he knew it. Why was he even asking?

I leaned my cheek on his hair. "*You* come live with us. There's plenty of room. We'll help you. I'm sure my parents . . ."

"Shut up."

He stood up, shoving me away. I didn't dare look at his face. I'd just refused to be the Other for him. But I finally understood. The futile search in his play, in his life, was for the one who would share his windowless house, his dead tree, his empty sky. And all that I could give him, he could never take because he was locked inside his house, just as I was in mine: "your nice big house." There was no road from one to the other.

He got up, turned his back, paced. He hadn't said a word since I had turned him down. Bernadette was right. I never should have come. But not to protect myself — to keep from hurting him.

I got up, too, and walked to the door. He headed me off and grabbed my arm.

"No," he said. "That would be too easy."

He pulled me over and threw me down on the bed. Now fear was for during, too. He no longer seemed aware of what he was doing, or of who he was, or who I was.

"Too easy," he repeated. "Just too easy."

His face touched mine, and I smelled his breath.

"You come over here to mess with me, but you keep your white gloves on. You get a rise out of me and now you're going home to put it all on paper, right? Your girlfriend told me about your school. What is this, a field trip?"

"No," I said. "No!"

He took both my arms and nailed me to the wall. He was hurting me.

"Did I ask you to come? Did I go after you? I don't need you."

In his eyes, despair. He was right. I came with my nice little life and my easy conscience, I messed around, I stirred in him something I couldn't respond to, I offered him what he couldn't take. When he said "Stay," he was calling for help. The only way to help him would be to say yes and to try to pull him out of it, but there was really no way.

"You come, you go. What is it with you? Don't you like me? Or only from a safe distance?"

Yes, from a distance. When he was on stage, so handsome, using words so well, both soft and loud. And when I pressed my lips to my bedroom mirror, dreaming of his. And still from a distance when I had combed my hair in the stairway this afternoon, to look nice for him. I had asked for this moment when he suddenly pressed against me, tried to kiss me, to slip his hands under my sweater, when his breathing grew shorter, when the tension I had seen the other time rose in his eyes again, the expression I'd thought so much about, with such emotion. "Spend too much time looking for the bottom of the well, and you'll fall in," Grandmother always warned. "Why don't you go play with the others, Cecile?"

I liked the dizzy feeling I got leaning over the well: death winked at me and I answered no. Playing with the other kids had never attracted me that much. What I liked was spying on the grown-ups: from high in a tree or behind a fence, I never tired of watching, waiting breathlessly to glimpse their mysteries. So I was asking for it the afternoon

I saw Uncle Alexis trying to kiss Therese, the girl who came to tutor my cousin Gaston. I was asking for the strange despair that washed over me: the feeling of cracks growing in the walls of the stronghold that cradled me, safe and warm.

All strongholds are fragile, and you muster what defenses you can to master your fear of living. Now, in Tanguy's expression, like the water deep in the well, I read falling and death. I read that despair and violence are the same: it begins with despair. I stopped struggling. I felt the tears trickling down my cheeks.

"I'm sorry," I said. "Tanguy, forgive me."

He let go of me as if I'd hit him, and looked at me, and pushed me away.

"Get the hell out of here," he said. "Get out. And make sure I never see your face again."

20

The Green Thumb

M Y MOTHER WASN'T HOME. She was at work. Volunteering with convicts. They created their own prisons, too, it seemed. It took a long time for them to open up. It was fascinating to help them find what was best inside them.

My father wasn't home. He was working. He took care of people's sick bodies, but often, he said, the illnesses they suffered from came from their minds, their souls. Their problems expressed themselves in pains, ulcers, rashes. For some of them, all my father had to do was smile and reassure them, and they felt better already.

My sisters weren't home. They were living their lives that were no longer mine. Now when they said "home" they meant a house where I didn't live. And that was as it should be. For me, too, one day "home" would no longer be synonymous with La Marette. And it would be my turn to be called Mom.

God wasn't there. He was in church, in the plaster statues, the lame old ladies, the prayer books. He'd left me. At Tanguy's place, no inspiration or light. No signal.

I filled the tub to the top and spent a long time in the warm water. I was back from a trip. I was dirty, tired. My arms and legs ached, my lips stung. I'd taken myself on a rather dangerous tour of the land of loneliness. I was lucky; I could leave there. I was back home.

I closed my eyes. The steady whacking sound from across the way, the sound of sparks, was Roughly Speaking's ax chopping wood. It pulled me out of the water. It summoned me.

With evening coming on, the fog was gathering and smoke came out of Tavernier's mouth. He stopped working when he saw me walk up.

"Already done with school?"

"I didn't go this afternoon. My heart wasn't in it."

He nodded. "I know what you mean. A little boy can leave a big space behind him."

He started chopping again. It was his weeping ash tree, another casualty of last year's frost. I liked it when the blade took in the wood, the ax and log lifting together before it split, and the thin spray of wood, and the smell. I picked up the logs he'd already cut.

"Don't you want gloves?"

"No thanks."

I'd say my goodbyes bare-handed to this tree that had once thrown a lacy shadow. I piled the logs good and straight on the woodpile at the back of the garage. They wouldn't be burned right away; they were too fresh, in a way too alive. Meat is better when it ages, too. And then, in the lean-to near the house, everything was already laid in for the winter: the thin, sticky beech kindling gathered in the forest, the gooseberry trimmings that get a fire off to a rousing start, and the oak to make it last. I wish I could have been an oak tree. Instead, I'm some short species that branches outward instead of upward, gets tangled up with others and keeps them from breathing. All I needed now was to turn into the weeping kind! I furtively touched my lips to a log: sweet branch, when you burn, what will

Tanguy's story be? I'm always getting the urge to do things like that, because the future is written everywhere but we're too shortsighted to read it.

Night was beginning to fall in earnest when Roughly Speaking put down his ax. There was no feeling left in my fingers; they might as well be sausages.

"How about 'closing up' with me?"

"Great," I said.

The ceremony began. Every night before dinner Roughly Speaking had to make sure that each tree, plant, or flower was where it should be; and in the morning, before breakfast, ditto. Tonight things looked pretty good.

"What exactly is a green thumb?" I asked him.

"Well, roughly speaking, there are two ways to love plants — for themselves or for show," he answered. "People who garden for show usually ask too much of plants, and they can't respond. But if you love them for what they are, they feel it and give you their best shot. That's what a green thumb is. It circulates from you to them, like waves. You young people call it vibrations."

He pointed out a handsome shrub with red berries, which he called his Christmas bush because it flowered like hope in the snow.

"For me, my plants are a little like my children, so a green thumb is also a father's love."

"Does that mean parents are sort of like gardeners?"

"Just the same. And the seed they've sown doesn't always turn out as they'd expected. If they're not careful, they can ruin it."

I turned toward the housing project. From Tavernier's garden you couldn't quite make it out, but the gray pressure inside it still rose like a scream.

"Then there's the soil," he said. "Cities have never been the best place for plants.

"An image sticks in my head," he said. "Listen . . ."

101

In a certain city in wartime, the streets were blockaded with bags of sand. In the spring, the bags began to bloom.

We went in through the kitchen door. The women were in the living room with the television on. We were quiet so it would be just the two of us. While Roughly Speaking rinsed his hands, I looked at the photograph on the sideboard, of him and his old dog Quince. A yellow mongrel, a bit scruffy around the edges, a long story.

"Why did you get rid of old Quince?" I asked.

"He started to bite."

"Rabies?"

"No. We never knew why; he just turned bad."

In the picture, Quince was seated at his master's feet and looked up at him as only a dog can; giving his all.

"Was it hard?"

It took him a minute to answer. "At least I killed him myself. I wouldn't have wanted to leave that to someone else."

It was my turn at the sink. I ran warm water over my breakfast links. It felt both good and bad; I couldn't say whether I liked it or not.

"He could have been beaten when he was little," I remarked. "It happens. Then it's not their fault if they go bad."

"He'd never been mistreated," Roughly Speaking said. "The vet told me it was just in him."

I wiped my hands. Something throbbed near my thumb. I showed him: a sliver.

"I know I was asking for it. . . ."

He laughed. "Next time you'll take my gloves."

We sat down at the table, under the lamp, and I looked away while he tried to get it out.

"Do you think it can be the same for people?" I asked. "That they just start biting, and there's not much you can do about it?"

"It's not the fashionable thing to say," he answered, "but I do think it happens. You try everything. It never works. There are just some bad apples."

He showed me the little piece of wood on the end of the tweezers, the sliver of beech. He squeezed to get a drop of blood out. Then he wiped it with alcohol.

"Not so much as a sigh," he said, smiling. "You're a brave girl."

I felt tears welling up. I went to the window. No problems seeing out here. Just to the left of the house, a foot and a half under the ground, was his famous bomb shelter. And like the sandbags during the war, it bloomed.

"I have a friend who named his cat Missile," I told him. "Don't you think that's a little strange?"

"It could mean he's afraid of the bomb," he said.

"And are you afraid of nuclear war? Is that why you built that?"

He came over to look out with me.

"I thought that if the day ever comes, there will have to be people if we want to go on."

I pressed my forehead to the windowpane: "Go on." I felt something tremble inside me, a kind of sob: my own fragility. It told me that I was alive.

Roughly Speaking slipped his arm around my shoulder.

"I have a problem," I said. "I can't tell you about it yet, but it's a bad one. It really hurts."

"Whenever you're ready," he said.

We looked over at La Marette. We could see the living room window, the two armchairs by the fire, the coffee table. I'd left the light on to say I'd be coming back.

"You know," my old friend said, "when something hurts like that it means new ground is being broken. And when it's over, things grow bigger and better than ever."

21

A Promise of Fresh Air

THEN, WEDNESDAY NIGHT, the phone rang. For once, Daddy answered; I usually got to it first. It was Pauline. I could guess from the sudden pause in his breathing. He turned toward the wall; all I could see was his back, stiffening. In a very soft, very measured voice, as if he feared that anything too emphatic would make Pauline hang up, he asked how she was doing, if she ever remembered she had a family that loved and missed her. When would she be back?

She was speaking from deep in the Jura Mountains. She talked for a while, with my father turning briefly to wink at me. "What if we came to see you?" he asked out of the blue. "What do you say?"

"We"? Now it was my turn to gasp. The two of us? Daddy and I? The response was apparently favorable. Daddy's voice was transformed, full: a minute more and he'd start to sing. He wrote down the address and read it back to her: "Hotel Les Terrasses, Malbuisson, Doubs." I was home free: Pauline would never know I'd betrayed her secret one night when I was feeling low. Now Daddy was telling her that Mom sent her love, the Pest did too. He hung up, came back over to me with his holiday smile —

happiness with a twist of disbelief, he'd never quite gotten over fathering four daughters — and proposed, "Would you do me the honor of joining me for lunch in Malbuisson on Saturday, Miss Moreau?"

A huge wave washed over me. Daddy and I. It felt good. "And if things work out, we'll bring your sister home with us."

I jumped up and hugged him. It was too strong. A minute more and I'd burst. He laughed and hugged me close, waltzing me around the couch in the bargain. Oh, Lord, to get away! To breathe! Was this how Pauline had felt when she said she needed fresh air, as she headed for the train station? For her it was Paul. For me, Tanguy. Smothering. I'd wanted to hold her back. Now I understood why she'd needed to run.

"What about Mom?"

We looked at each other, half smiling, half sad. Much as we loved her, it would be so good with just the two of us. We turned toward the kitchen, where we could hear her unsuspectingly fixing dinner for two future deserters.

"Maybe she'd like to come, too," I said.

"Well, let's go ask her," Daddy decided.

A wonderful aroma of leeks rose from the soup kettle.

"Who was that on the phone?" asked Mom.

"Pauline!" we both blurted out. Mom set down her wooden spoon. She looked at Daddy, then me, to try to see whether the news was good or bad.

"We're going out to see her on Saturday. In the mountains. What would you say if we brought her home?"

Mom lowered herself into a chair, her face aglow.

"You should have told me to sit down first."

I took a turn stirring. "Daddy told Pauline he'd be bringing me along. If you'd like to sign up, too, now's your chance."

"Obviously, we'd love to have you," Daddy added.

Mom looked at us for a minute — one, then the other. I seemed to feel her smile.

"Three of us would really be too much like a delegation! I think I'll let you two lovebirds go by yourselves."

Besides, she reminded us, on Saturday Bernadette and Stephan had a cookout to go to; she'd promised to have the twins over for the day. Not to mention that everyone was coming to Sunday dinner at La Marette. Everyone? The silence filled with images. I would have bet that all three of us were imagining the same scene: Pauline climbing out of our car, her reunion with Paul and their son.

"Soup's on," said my mother.

And that's how a simple bowl of leek soup can suddenly feel like a vacation.

Thursday I listened to the weather report: cloud cover, rain over all of France. Flooding in several areas. I prayed it would last. Not the flooding, but the mild temperatures. If there was snow or freezing rain, caution might keep us home. Like Benjamin, I had my bag ready to go. Something would come up, I was sure, and when Mom came home Thursday evening in a bad way, I thought it had happened.

One of the convicts she worked with, Alain Denis, twenty, had slashed his wrists the night before. They'd found him just in time. And yet that day everything had seemed fine — well, normal. They'd talked; she'd lent him a book of poetry. It was apparently a cry for help. Alain hadn't really wanted to kill himself; he'd wanted to remind them he was alive and hurting. It was probably blackmail, too, Mom explained in a tired voice. "His girlfriend's been coming to see him less and less; he's letting her know that if she dumps him she'll have his death on her conscience."

Mom, still in her coat, was on the couch, on the verge of tears. Charles put his arm around her shoulder; she pressed her forehead to his jacket. For the first time I realized that this work she found so compelling must be terribly hard at times. Showing up full of fresh air and freedom in a universe of shut-ins is no mean feat.

"I could have stopped it," Mom said. "I should have felt something. I'm afraid he'll try again. What can I do?"

"No matter how much you do for him," said the voice of wisdom above her head, "you'll never be able to be his mother, his girlfriend, his friends, his freedom. Would you rather we didn't go this weekend?"

She said no. In bed, that night, I saw flames in an auditorium. A cry for help? Setting fire to what represented his only hope, wasn't Tanguy burning himself?

"What can I do?" Mom had asked.

I hadn't done anything for Tanguy. And now my only thought was to get away, far away, to get him out of my mind.

"I'm afraid he might try again. . . ."

There was still one question I'd sworn I'd get an answer to before we left. So it would have to be tomorrow. Tomorrow or never.

22

Champagne

I TOLD MELODIE I had a dentist appointment, and at lunchtime I rang the bell beneath a sign that said "Moving and Hauling": Lamourette's, in Pontoise.

A truck with the same lettering was parked in front of the house. A woman answered the door. Her housecoat did nothing to conceal her delicate condition. I asked her when the blessed event was expected. In three months. She asked me what I was selling; she had all the baby equipment she needed. I introduced myself: Cecile Moreau, from Mareuil, a friend of her poor mother-in-law's. It was so nice of her to take her in. I'd come to see how she was doing.

"I wish you'd said so right away. I'm in the middle of getting my husband's lunch."

The Mrs. Lamourette I was looking for was in bed, a tray in her lap, picking at her food. I recognized her immediately, though she seemed to have shrunk. She recognized me, too, from the time I went on the quiz show to get money for Germain. In my own small way, I'm a celebrity in Mareuil.

As soon as her daughter-in-law left, Mrs. Lamourette pulled a little notebook out from under her pillow, wrote my name in it with a check next to it. She leafed through the notebook.

"Your mother has been to see me twice," she said.

News to me. But there could be no doubt: there were certainly two checks by my mother's name. And a lot of other names with or without checks. I saw that she was computing her visits, counting friends.

I gave her the box of cookies I'd picked out of the cupboard at home: the ones we buy for the kids, soft enough for them to chew. While I was at it, I had brought a bottle of champagne, too. We always have some extra in the cellar, gifts from Daddy's patients. He never turns it down.

Mrs. Lamourette clapped and pushed away her tray with a disgusted look. She opened the box of cookies while I worked on the champagne, with the cork under the quilt so it wouldn't attract any other takers when it popped. I suggested that she eat her ham and mashed potatoes first; it smelled so good. She wouldn't hear of it; if I wanted to eat that slop, I was welcome to it, then "she" wouldn't catch her. I quickly obeyed her wishes; it's nice to do someone a favor, even when it's to your benefit. With her denture glass, we had the two containers we needed for the refreshments. Mrs. Lamourette had her own method: she dunked the cookies in the champagne until they were good and soaked, then popped them in her mouth. Between mouthfuls she asked me questions about Mareuil, and when we talked about her house she had tears in her eyes. It was all boarded up, and on the fence was a For Sale sign. She'd lived there forever with her late husband, and it was like selling her past. But what else could she do? Now she'd be too afraid to stay on alone. And besides, they'd taken all her savings. The money from the sale would keep her from being a burden to her son.

Very quietly, glancing toward the door, she explained

that she was trying to be as little trouble as possible so they wouldn't put her in a nursing home. She seemed terrified at the thought of it because when you're in a nursing home you're forgotten, like someone left behind on the platform of a train station with the train leaving for another continent.

Certain people sparkle when they drink champagne, but not her. It came out her eyes. The more cookies she ate, the more she cried. I wasn't doing much better: one night, one pervert, one ruined life. I felt guilty somehow. I promised her that before she had to go into a home, we'd take her at our house.

I heard the truck pull away out in the street. That brought me back to reality. It was getting late, and I still hadn't asked my question. I didn't know where to begin, and yet there was only one place.

I pointed to her feet under the covers and asked, "How are they doing?"

She wiggled her toes to make sure they were still there, still working.

"The feeling is returning, slowly," she said. "So slowly. Not that I was in such great shape before."

"Did you see the guy who did it?" I asked, my heart pounding.

She put a hand over her face. "He had a scarf," she said.

And then as my throat constricted she said something fantastic: "The other one, too. I don't understand. I'll never understand how they could do it. They must have a mother, too."

She said "the other one," "they," "them." I'd heard right: "the other one," "they," "them." I picked up the bottle, kissed her soundly on the cheek, her skin like worn flannel beneath my lips. She didn't understand why I was thanking her. She looked at me warily, as if I'd stolen something from her.

"You'll come back, now, won't you?"

I promised I would. But not right away. This evening I was leaving with my father on a quick trip to the Jura Mountains, to a beautiful lake like a mirror of the winter, where we'd feast on sausage and cheese.

She'd never been to the Jura, but she'd tried the sausage and cheese. Loved them! I promised I'd bring her back some.

"They" and "them" . . . all afternoon I heard those words. If Tanguy had assaulted her, he hadn't been alone. He might not have been the one who decided to use the iron. Maybe he'd even tried to stop his partner in crime. He could even have just been the lookout. Maybe. Maybe my fear that something was coming to a head, something I could still stop, was unfounded. Such a useful word, *maybe,* like *probably, after all,* and *so what.*

"Maybe on Sunday the whole family will be back together," Roughly Speaking said with relish when I stopped over to say goodbye.

It was quarter to six. My bag was in the front hall, next to Daddy's; he should be home any second. He'd change in a flash and we'd take off. Claire and Antoine were spending the night at La Marette so Mom wouldn't be alone: to each his own kind of crime watch.

Our hotel reservations were all set; we'd stop near Beaune, the wine capital of Burgundy. We'd sleep surrounded by vineyards. The hotel served dinner until eleven. We'd eat when we got there: like "lovebirds." I'd put on a little makeup to make myself look older, and I was wearing my hair up. I'd act the part of my father's girlfriend so that people would look at us tight-lipped, thinking, "He ought to be ashamed of himself, the old goat." In a way, Daddy would feel as though he was out with a younger woman. I could give him the pleasure of feeling flattered, with all due respect to Mom.

Later, in our room, tucked in our twin beds, we'd talk for a while. It's easier to say things in the dark, but the next day you're embarrassed, you feel exposed. I'd try to talk to him about a boy I knew, who might be dangerous. Should you turn someone in when there's a reasonable doubt? I bet he'd say no. No! In the end, I wouldn't talk to my father about Tanguy. Eight hours of appointments, four on the road, another long stretch the next day, and a daughter to convince it's her duty to go home . . . I didn't have the heart to add to the list. And besides, I knew the good doctor always zonked out the minute his head hit the pillow.

Now I heard the gravel crunch under the tires of a car. The clock would soon strike six. Grandfather clock, if you only knew! Tomorrow night when you count to six I'll be off gazing deep into the eyes of a lake called Saint Point.

23

The Bells
of the Sunken Church

THE LAKE WAS A HARD BLUE, like a storybook sky; the evergreens, dark and dusted with white; the hills, rounded; the peace and quiet, profound. Hard to believe all this had existed, all this had been waiting for me when I was stuck in a plastic, fluorescent classroom, writing answers to a test beside Melodie. Or when I rode through the lonely concrete of the projects. Or when I took refuge at La Marette: cocoon, tenderness. Had it really all been here, crackling, shivering, biting the nostrils, the hands? And had there really been this big, warm dining room opening onto this landscape, this breathtaking, soothing scenery?

I looked at Pauline and I understood. She'd put this wall of evergreens between herself and her suffering; she'd let this snow fall on her pain, had drowned her sorrows in this lake, with the light of the landscape, its calm, somewhat sad eye, its reflection putting things back in their place. A philosophical lake.

"I'd love to go for a dip!"

Daddy laughed. "Certainly, darling. Just the thing after a lunch like this."

It really was a feast. I had my pick of the regional

113

sausages, with names like Morteau, Brési, Jésus. We washed it all down with Brise-Mollet, the local wine. More than one glass and you've had it. Bea had downed three. She was snoozing on her boyfriend's shoulder; Martin was also a photographer and a television cameraman to boot. It was thanks to him that we were all there, since the owner of the hotel, which was closed for the season (meaning open only for family), was Martin's uncle and godfather. Martin filled us in on local history as we dug into a mountain of fritters.

"Any idea what might prick you if you did take a dip in the lake?" Martin asked mysteriously.

"Do tell."

"A church steeple."

"Really?" my father asked hungrily. He loves legends: in each one, he says, is a grain of truth. It's our job to find it. Bea roused herself to listen. Once upon a time there had been a happy and prosperous village. One day a woman arrived with her baby, asking for food and shelter. All the doors closed in her face. Mother and child perished. Later that year, a flood submerged the town.

"The tears of the woman and her child," murmured Pauline.

"So that was it," said Beatrice. "On the shore the other day I thought I heard bells ringing at the bottom."

Martin's uncle brought us coffee. In the window, I watched the reflection of my sister's face. We hadn't been able to talk yet, and it almost seemed as if we'd come just for the pleasure of spending two days with her.

"Are you doing all right?"

She nodded without smiling. The last time I'd seen her, her face had been defiant, full of anger and pain: full of fire, in a way. Now something had gone out in it. Childhood?

"Later," she murmured. "Not now. It's so good to be together."

"Any idea when we'll see certain young ladies' bylines in print?" Daddy asked enthusiastically.

"We're still collecting material," Bea replied. "What we want to show is how mountains like this have everything: all the softness, all the strength, all the joy, and all the sadness in the world rolled up into one place."

"I've noticed," Pauline interrupted in a very small voice, "that scenery responds to what's on your mind: it takes on the same colors. And here . . ."

Here? She trailed off. Everyone was looking at her, but I sensed she was through. I just hoped that her mind, her inner landscape, reflected not only the dark shades of evergreen but also the color of cascading, singing rivers, the colors of hope. In her expression I thought I saw some sunken thing, and my heart ached for her. It isn't all over, is it, Pauline? Can't Paul, Benjamin, and you start over again?

24

The President

THEY CALLED IT THE PRESIDENT. Every year, tree experts came to record its measurements ceremoniously. Today it was a hundred and fifty feet high, five feet thick at the ankle. At two hundred and fifty-odd years, it was the oldest tree in the forest preserve.

This forest had been here all that time too. With its dark army of packed trees standing at alert, head in the clouds, feet in the snow, uniforms soaked.

Like everyone else, I pressed my palms to the giant's trunk. What was still alive beneath this thick crust where tourists had tried to carve their initials to mark their puny passage, to take the tree as a witness when they'd no longer be around — I mean on this earth?

"And all that for light," Charles marveled, looking up.

Not all the trees found it. Some of them seemed resigned to growing outward instead of upward. There were also the condemned ones: a white slash on the trunk meant they were slated to be chopped down, the weak ones, the wounded, the sick, like the one with a huge growth on it. Or simply the ones that needed to be cut to make room for their neighbors.

"They plant them close together at the beginning," Daddy explained. "To give them protection in bad weather. Then they select the strongest ones when they're big enough."

From time to time a packet of snow fell. There was hardly any left on the branches: it was at our feet, dirty, clogged with pine needles. Snow is only pretty as it falls, or in children's books.

Pauline's boot kicked hard at a rotten old trunk. It burst into moist splinters: inside, it was hollow.

"Why should I go back home and sulk?" she said suddenly. "Where would that get us? And anyway, no matter what you two say, there are some things you never forget."

So we were careful not to say anything. She turned her back to the President and walked off without even making sure we were following. The path was crisscrossed with tractor tracks — easy to get bogged down. We walked along the edge.

"It seems that 'that's the way it is,' " she continued. "That I'm free, too, and that it doesn't affect 'our love.' Sounds easy, huh? But what if I don't want that kind of love?"

"You'd be absolutely right," said Daddy.

Pauline whirled around, amazed. Charles preaching revolt? But as he reached out to her she took off again, looking like a little girl in her old parka, her ski hat pulled down to her nose, her woolen socks up to her knees. It was true that it sounded easy for Paul. A wife for continuity, comfort, home. All other women for adventure, for fun.

"Why does a guy like Paul get married in the first place?" I asked.

"Because I asked him to, why the hell else!"

When Pauline swore, it was a bad sign: her way of punishing herself. Or us. When Daddy couldn't find a comeback, it was an even worse sign. Silence. Just a sound of water all around us: above, below, water flowing, weeping. And where had the birds gone? Where were the wild boars hiding, the deer? My fingers felt frostbitten. My socks were wringing wet. Daddy had told me so: you can't walk in the woods in winter with zippered boots. I started to fantasize about the farmhouse we had passed a while before, with its overhanging roof, its wall of logs, its smoking chimney. A stocked and fortified place: let the wind blow, the snow fly — the house was ready. But Pauline hadn't been prepared for rough weather. She'd gone to Paul with only the defenses she'd learned at La Marette: warmth, tenderness, joy. Not the stuff soldiers are made of. The first cold made us shiver, the first rude blow floored us. And if someone cried out to us for help — someone called Tanguy, for instance — we beat a hasty retreat.

"I know he's hurting," Pauline said, out of the blue. "All right, it's over with that cheap actress. It really got to him that I left. But I know he'll do it again. And I have no intention of spending my life waiting for him to come home."

"That would be out of the question," Daddy said.

Pauline whirled to look at him again.

"Does that mean you don't think I should go back?"

"Of course I think you should go back. But differently."

Now Pauline stopped dead. She murmured, "What do you mean, 'differently'?"

The tremble in her voice was hope. It was also what lit her expression as she looked up at Daddy. Was that what she'd been waiting for, behind her stubborn, I-don't-care attitude? For someone to give her a good reason to go home, to lean on the "bastard's " shoulder, and, while she was at it, mention that she loved him in spite of everything?

"I'd go back to fight," said Daddy.

He took his daughter by the shoulders, pulled her face close to his.

"I'd make the jerk understand what's good for him," he rumbled. "I'd make him get it through his thick skull that just because he had a leg shot off at eighteen is no reason to go through life like an emotional cripple, ruining his chances for happiness and other people's in the bargain. I'd prove to him that no matter what his handicap is, he can live and be happy like everyone else."

Wide-eyed, amazed, Pauline contemplated Daddy's anger. The last thing I would have expected, too. Not a word about Benjamin, responsibility, reason, patience. Not even a word about her own happiness or her pain. Daddy gave her a man, her man, the one she had wanted absolutely, and God knows how she had driven him and Mom crazy with "I love him" as her response to all their objections.

"His leg . . ." — "I love him." "He's not stable" — "I love him." "The fast lane . . ." — "I love him, I love him, I love him." Daddy showed her this man of hers and said, "Save him."

A kind of warmth invaded me. So that's what a father is: an emergency exit, a life preserver, guardrail, retaining wall, bridge. In his own way a sort of "President," seeing everything from a height, and full of surprises. Where you feel like carving your name. And never mind telling me that growing up means realizing that the President, bridge, wall, guardrail, life preserver, door is something you have to find for yourself, without relying on your parents to go on forever.

"You took him, Pauline," he said. "You knew what his faults were, and you bought the whole package. You can't leave him now; you have no right. Do you know what he said to your mother and me? 'She's my only future.'"

"His only future?" Pauline echoed.

"And you know what that means," Daddy continued. "Don't cut him off from his future. Don't let him go back to his old ways. Keep him going in the right direction. You can do it."

"You think I can?"

He hugged her to him. She leaned against him. There were only the two of them now: the father and daughter, the man and woman.

"A strong and beautiful woman like you? Of course you can," he murmured.

What had been submerged in Pauline's eyes surfaced again. Confidence. Trust. And the light I'd been looking for earlier: her childhood. Then her eyes flew beyond Daddy's face, came to rest in the distance.

"Look how much better you can see the President from here!" she said.

From where we now stood, it was true, you realized that it towered above all the others. Did Pauline, like me, somehow think of Charles as she admired the tree? So many years . . . and suddenly, inexplicably, I felt afraid, and cold; I wanted to run, get back. Believe me, when our tall pine was felled, there would be no counting the damage.

"I don't know if you've noticed, kids," said Charles, "but night is on its way, and I have no intention of camping out."

We hit the trail. This time Daddy led. Pauline seemed to dawdle. She was just discovering that things were worth a look around, that she was alive and had better things to see than the toes of her boots.

We began to sense the edge of the forest in the distance. It was like peeking through curtains.

"Have you ever seen such a wonderful forest?" Pauline asked importantly.

"Thanks for giving us a chance to see it," Daddy answered, smiling to one side.

"Well, most of these trees were here before you were born," she explained. "You may not be aware of it, but in these parts you plant things not for yourself but for your grandchildren."

"Planting things for my grandchildren *has* occurred to me," Daddy said.

25

The King of Cheeses

AFTER THE PRESIDENT of Evergreens, we met the King of Cheeses. Because, of course, we got lost.

Following Pauline's directions, with her eyes focused on her future, we lost track of the path mere mortals follow, and when we emerged from the forest there was no trace of our car, no point of reference: before us stretched a huge white plateau where the sky, hurried along by the wind, displayed its various shades of blue, changing them to gray and black.

Daddy took charge of the operation. No question now of backtracking through the forest: it would be completely dark before we got out again. Follow the road until we found our car? Chancy. Pauline was sure we should try to the left, and Daddy was just as sure it was to the right. The only solution was to head for the village we could see in the distance, its church steeple looking like an over-turned flower. A village church meant people, help.

We walked across the expanse of white. To keep our spirits up, the good doctor described the herd of handsome spotted cows that gorged on sweet grass in milder weather right where we were stepping in snow. Imagine the warm milk they gave, the cream . . . and he wasn't just imagining things, since, confirming his story, the first house we came to, half stone, half wood, topped with a big brown roof, was the village cheesemaker's. Pauline pushed open the door.

We were in a huge tiled room. Against the wall, piles of big iron pots. In the center, three enormous copper vats. Beyond them, in wooden hoops, a sort of white cake. The smell was so strong it took our breath away. The smell of life — cool, with warm currents.

Bent over one of the vats, a man was pulling out a heavy sack of gauze full of something like thousands of grains of milk. He wore an apron as white as his hair. His face, however, was red, and deeply grooved, like an old forest path. He glanced over at us.

"Be with you in a minute."

We went closer. We didn't dare say a word for fear of disturbing him. The two other vats were full of a thick mixture that a woman was stirring. Now the man heaved his sack onto a wooden slab, spread it out, confined it in a hoop. His gestures were slow, deliberate; you wished he could touch you like that, lovingly; you could guess that this was his life's work and that he was proud of it.

When he finished, he straightened up and considered what he had done.

"Sorry . . . but there are times when it's better not to interrupt what you're doing."

"Nice job," Pauline murmured.

She'd gone to his side, my sister the writer, and looked at him as if waiting for him to say something. The man's eyes took her in: neither woman nor child but a wet dog, a lost dog.

"Tastes good, too, I hope!" he said. "Anything worth doing is worth doing well, don't you think?"

He introduced himself, and Pauline followed suit:

"Pauline Démogée, my father, Charles Moreau, my sister Cecile."

"You don't look old enough to be married," he told her.

"But I am," she said hoarsely.

Daddy coughed discreetly. The man turned to him: "What can I do for you folks?"

Charles explained that we'd lost our car on the road below the forest. All he knew was that we'd started out on the Nozeroy side.

"And you came out the Champagnolle side," the cheese-maker said with a laugh.

He looked at the three of us: poor lost city mice.

"Just let me finish up here and we'll go find that car of yours. I doubt it's gone anywhere."

He went back to his cheese. Now the woman was cleaning the vat he'd freed up. She'd rolled up her sleeves; her arms were pale, creamy. The copper shone like a moist sun. Outside, night had fallen completely. Pauline took Daddy's arm, pulled him aside.

"I have a favor to ask." Her expression was grim again.

"Yes, ma'am?" Charles asked cautiously.

Pauline turned away. She looked at the cheesemaker, who was covering the curd with a piece of wood and slowly lowering a press onto it.

"First, I have to tell you that I'm out of cash," she announced. "In fact, I've been sponging off Beatrice for the last week."

"So long as your father is solvent, that doesn't seem particularly serious," Daddy said, completely unruffled.

She pointed to the cheese that was being made. "Paul loves this stuff. Couldn't we bring some home? It's too good to pass up, and a bargain, too."

That was how she informed us that she was coming back with us, and to the end of my days I'll always think the Jura cheesemaker had something to do with it. Daddy kept his cool. He said that comté cheese was one of his favorites, too, and practically galloped over to ask whether we could buy some. "If I didn't sell it, the cows would have to go on unemployment," the man told us.

We followed him down to the cellar. It was like an underground chapel. Like enormous holy wafers, the wheels of cheese rested on the shelves. A life's work, a life's love. A freshly cut wheel lay on a table. The man picked up a knife and delineated a section.

"Would that be about what you're thinking of?"

"More," said Pauline.

Daddy looked at her. She looked so hungry all of a sudden. He winked at her and pointed up to the shelves.

"We'll take a whole one. We're a big family. It'll last us the winter."

Daddy knew how to make a woman feel special. We left with a wheel of cheese that weighed about the same as Pauline: a hundred and ten pounds, fifteen gallons of milk, enjoy, enjoy!

We had no problem finding our car. We'd just gotten turned around the wrong way. Forests fool you, keep you looking up; you lose your sense of direction. We did have a bit of trouble getting our extra passenger in the trunk: it almost ended its career in the snow.

It was six o'clock when we got back to the hotel, where the porch lights were on to greet us. Bea ran out to the car; she thought we were goners. We showed off our purchase.

"You can use it for a spare tire," she joked, "but I wouldn't count on it for an air-freshener."

It made the car smell like a barn. The Princess would probably never set foot in it again.

Comté has a rough rind, Emmenthal's is smooth, as Pauline recited from her research. The milk is from Montbeliard cows. Nine months to cure.

"I have to get a shot of this for my personal collection," Bea said, posing us.

Daddy partially unwrapped the star of the moment, and Bea started shooting. "If my journalist colleague could smile, the pictures would look a lot better," she said.

That's when Pauline started making a strange sound. It came from inside her, scraping through her throat before it came out, half laughter, half barking. "What's the matter?" Bea asked, worried, walking up to her. Pauline touched a finger to her best friend's lips.

"Now don't say a word, don't say anything. I'm happy; I'm going home."

She added quietly, "I love him." The President may not have heard, though; at his age your hearing isn't what it used to be.

26

Child's Play

MY SISTER AND I across from each other, the water up to our necks. "Brrr!" squealed Pauline as she leapt into the tub. Join the club! I was frozen, too, and I'd dreamed of this moment. I took my rightful place facing her and we let the water run full blast. It was like when we were children, playing the cold game, as we called it: naked on our beds, in the dead of winter, we would inch the covers up the better to enjoy the sensation of warmth: up our feet, legs, thighs, stomach, shoulders . . . now the hot water seared our chins. We were in heaven.

"Have you ever taken a bath with Paul?"

"Once. On vacation. He booked us into a suite with a sunken bath."

"And did you . . ."

Pauline gave me a look of mock indignation. She slipped a little deeper into the water, up to her nose, and blew me a bubble: "Yes."

If thoughts could turn into pictures, what a sight that would be! I looked at her, so slim, dappled with dark. If I were a man, I'd feel almost like breaking her when I took her in my arms.

"Do you think I'm too fat?" I asked.

She opened an eye to check me out.

"You're the round type. Any thinner, you wouldn't look good. And lots of guys appreciate curves. You'll see."

There was no window in the bathroom. Its papered ceiling made me think of being inside a wrapped present. My head swam. I seemed to be floating outside of time. First one out of the water would come back to everyday life, break the spell.

"Do you mind talking about Paul?"

"Not at all."

"What did Daddy mean about 'his only future,' then?"

Pauline looked through me. "Before me, Paul wasn't in such great shape."

"Elysabeth?"

"Among other things." She hesitated. "Do you swear you'll never repeat this?"

"Cross my heart."

"Before we got together, Paul was into cocaine. Not heavily, but still . . . it was the big thing with the creative types he hung around with. They said it gave them ideas and the energy to express them."

"But it's so dangerous!"

"You bet it is. First you can write better with it; then you can't write without it. A vicious circle. You're screwed."

So those were Paul's "old ways." And here was his strength, splashing in the water alongside me. This little bit of a thing who barely took up a third of the tub. I closed my eyes. And I had always pictured Paul as a winner. Growing up also means seeing illusions crumble.

"When I met him the first time, in Montbard, he was trying to get away from all that. It seems I helped him. Somewhere inside him, he realized that I was his chance."

His chance. . . . That twisted inside me. I asked quickly, "And now? Now what are you going to do?"

She shrugged her shoulders. "First, stop feeling sorry

for myself. It takes all your energy. I'm going to try to remember: I fought hard to get him. And I got him, didn't I?"

"And vice versa."

She smiled: "And besides, now there are two of us."

So now Benjamin was back! When everyone had given up reminding her about him. I looked at her. Paul said, "come back," and she said, "Yes." *She* wasn't afraid. Even though a drug problem is serious. A kind of violence, an assault. Not much different from arson.

I whispered, "I wish I had your courage."

Her eyes darkened. "It's not courage. It's love."

Something overflowed in me. The way she said it! Not just with her heart, but from her deepest, most private parts. I think I was jealous, and I resented her. I'd only made up the magic. What the hell were we doing here in this bathtub? What was I trying to do? Bring back the dead? "Two little sisters of days gone by, awash in the warm waters of happiness, come in please." But they'd never be that way again. And they knew it. Ignorance, innocence were things of the past. Pretending to have them was as sad as a funeral. I'll never take another bath with you, Pauline. We're grown up now; we'd better get used to the idea, it's for always.

"What's the matter, Pest? You crying?"

"Of course not." I splashed my face with both hands. "Just a little afraid."

"Of what?"

"That I'll never be able to love someone the way you do. Give everything."

I had thought I was in love, and when push came to shove, there was nothing. Or rather, there was disgust and fear. As always, I had chosen someone it could never work out with. When I was little, it wasn't much better: I had imaginary friends — that way there was no danger. All I was good for was for kissing my mirror, or at best a pair of lips through a silken scarf.

"The rest of you were all experienced when you were my age. I can't even say it's virtue that's holding me back. I want to, but at the last minute I freeze. I must have a father fixation. Typical! The overprotected baby of the family. People shouldn't have children so late in life. I just hope I don't turn out to be frigid. That would take the cake!"

Pauline maneuvered. With her toes, she stroked my shoulder.

"Don't you know we all go through what you're talking about? Every girl is afraid she won't meet Mr. Right. And one fine day he appears out of nowhere, and all your questions fly out the window. You're submerged. You don't think anymore. You give everything, and it's not enough. You wish you could turn yourself inside-out to give even more."

I shook my head. "But there have to be exceptions. I think I'm one. And besides, doesn't it have to be mutual? You can't expect miracles."

"Yes you can," said Pauline. "Absolutely."

"Well, well, don't let me disturb you . . . ," Daddy's voice boomed.

He'd just appeared in the doorway. We slid back under the water. Intrigued, yet cautious, he surveyed the landscape: his daughters, socks on the radiator, clothes strewn everywhere.

"Aren't you supposed to knock before entering a lady's room?" Pauline inquired.

"When a lady leaves her key in the door, it's an invitation," Daddy retorted. "Do you have any idea what time it's getting to be?"

"It must be late. We were talking. We forgot about dinner."

"The fondue is about to boil."

Fondue or no, Charles seemed to be enjoying the show. He sat down on the edge of the bidet.

"How do you expect us to get out if you stay here?" said Pauline. "Cecile has enough of an Oedipus complex already. You should go call Mom while we get dressed for dinner. And let me talk to her. I have something to ask her. Something important."

~ 27 ~

No One for Me

BEATRICE was in rare form. She was matching people to cheeses. Comté was perfect for the Moreau family: home cooking, grated toppings, white sauce, soufflés. "And why not, if that's how we like it?" Pauline protested. "And besides, you can always add spices or wine." Martin, she put in the "runny" category: Brie, Camembert, flavorful and smooth. He was supposed to take it as a compliment, apparently.

"And what kind are you?" Daddy asked Bea.

"Roquefort, Gorgonzola, blue cheese."

"I think I'd say a dry little goat cheese," said Martin. "From a goat that fought the wolf away until dawn. The cheese is hard as a rock, but once you taste it, other kinds lose their flavor."

It sounded suspiciously like a declaration of love. Could that be a blush on Bea's cheeks? She quickly changed the subject: "How about Cecile?"

"Pepper cheese," Pauline said amiably.

"For Cecile, it remains to be seen," Daddy said, smiling at me. "It's ripening slowly but surely."

"I want to be the whole cheese department or nothing! I don't like labels."

Naturally everyone burst out laughing. It would never occur to them that I might really mean it.

This was the best part of eating fondue: the bottom of the pot. The cheese turns the bread brown; the taste is more intense, concentrated. Tough luck for the gluttons who rush into things; by the time they get to the best part, they've already given up. The local wine was going down easily. We were on our second bottle. Daddy was happy as could be. Mission accomplished: tomorrow he'd bring the lost sheep back to the fold. He planned our route home. We'd leave at dawn, head straight for the source of the Loue River. After the President of Evergreens and the King of Cheeses, there was nothing left to do but go and salute the queen of rivers.

The source is a mountain spring that cascades from cliff to cliff, tumbling down to a calmer flow through woods and meadows. Charles collected stories of the legendary Vouivre. The Loue was the haunt of the winged dragon that appeared only once a year, on Christmas Eve, a carbuncle set in its forehead. The person who plucked it out would find the pot of gold.

After the Loue, Charles had one more stop in mind: St. Claude, the pipe capital of France. With our permission, he might even treat himself to one or two. No other pipe, it seemed, could compare for flavor.

Then straight on to La Marette, where Pauline wanted to check in with Mom before going home to Paris. Pauline was laughing. Her eyes shone. Bea looked at her, her and Daddy, and her face darkened. Her own father had never come to claim her like this. She'd always been free, and freedom, when you don't know who you are, is like too much of the sun: it blinds you. My sister turned to her friend.

"You shouldn't stick around here too much longer, either. Don't you think you have about enough pictures? Maybe it's time to work on the proofs. My story will be ready in a week, all right? And besides, what will I do in Paris without you?"

Bea couldn't believe her ears. Then my sister took her by the shoulders and planted a resounding kiss on her cheek. Her friend pretended to push her away in horror.

"Hey, don't go getting ideas. I know you've had a rough time with men, but . . ."

The fish course arrived just in time to keep things from getting out of hand. It was a salmon trout caught in the Loue, with a garnish of chanterelle mushrooms that had been gathered at the edge of the forests, in the wooded meadows where the Montbeliard cattle grazed. For me the Jura Mountains would always mean these flavors: earth and fresh water.

Suddenly a strong gust of wind shook the bay window. "The north wind through the mountains," remarked Martin. Loneliness comes out of nowhere, like the wind. It was Beatrice's cheek on Martin's shoulder. It was the light named Paul that shone in Pauline's dark eyes. It was also that constant presence surrounding my father, behind everything he did, felt, thought: a woman. And for me, no one. Cecile, all alone.

"Stay with me." Suddenly, I wished Tanguy was there, no matter what he'd done, even if I was no longer sure I loved him. I needed someone to need me. I was tired of functioning for nothing, looking out at emptiness, shooting blanks. I needed a man to teach me that I was someone besides Dr. Moreau's number-four daughter, nicknamed the Pest, divided between longing and disgust, between impulse and inhibition, between me and myself. This must be what they mean by an "awkward stage": when you're not anyone yet.

I forgot to mention that earlier in the dinner I lost my piece of bread in the fondue pot. According to custom, I had to kiss the person who found it. They all pretended to look for it just to make me feel good. But no thanks to fatherly, brotherly, social kisses. I wanted a man's lips to lead me far. I wanted, like Pauline, to say "I love you" from deep inside my body. I wanted someone to feel alone without me, just as, without knowing who he was, tonight I felt alone without him.

28

The Pact

I WOKE UP in the middle of the night: horribly thirsty, my mouth like cardboard. Somewhere in the hotel a shutter or door kept slamming in the north wind. Next to me, Pauline slept: a gentle breeze. Daddy and Bernadette do the snoring for the whole family. I got up quietly and went into the bathroom to drink two big glasses of water. Only ten after twelve. Downstairs, the steady slamming continued. I anticipated it with each pause, and it was exasperating. We were used to these things at La Marette. We all counted on someone else to get up and fix the problem, so everyone would end up not sleeping a wink.

A night-light lit the hallway. It smelled like a hotel: one third each polished wood, wool carpeting, kitchen odors. The best part would be the smell of fresh coffee and toast waking the place up. And the end of the hallway was the stairway leading down to the lobby. Halfway down was a landing with a lavatory. There it was: the shutter on the window was flapping. I opened it and fixed the latch. The silence was like a white well where the wind swirled. I closed the window before I caught my death of cold, and I was heading back to my quarters when I noticed a light on downstairs.

It came from the lounge that also served as the bar and TV room. Had someone forgotten a lamp? I have a mania for conserving energy. I went down.

A stranger was sitting in an armchair by a window. Twenty-five, thirty? At his feet, a huge backpack, a pair of ski socks. He had brown hair, fairly short and sticking out all over as if it had just been towel-dried. Dark eyes. He leaned over to look at me, or rather to look at Enrico Banana.

Enrico Banana, the character on the T-shirt I use as a nightgown, is of course a banana. On the front of the shirt, Enrico, half peeled, sways to the music of a band of his peers in the shade of a palm tree. I should add that this garment comes halfway down my thighs and that, not expecting to meet anyone that night, I hadn't bothered to leave on a stitch under it.

The stranger was studying Enrico Banana, whose phosphorescent yellow must have signaled my presence in the darkness. Before he had time to decide that I was an apparition, I said, "The hotel is closed for the season."

He was speechless for an instant and then smiled. "Then what are you doing here?"

"They make exceptions for friends."

He lifted a hand and swung a room key from his fingertips.

"And suppose they made one for me, too?"

I saw how ridiculous I must seem. All there was left to do was to go and hide my humiliation and my slight hangover in my bed. But to do that I would have to make the heroic decision to turn around and show this man, who obviously didn't take me seriously, the equally phosphorescent Enrico Banana on my back, serenading a bunch of swooning bananas.

He spoke before I made up my mind.

"Have you ever felt this way? When I get to some new

place, even if I've been there before, I always need to take a moment to adapt. You can tame a place, the same as an animal. The best way is to sit down and get used to it, without forcing things. That's what I was doing."

"I always feel like that," I said. "Even when I come home after a trip, it takes me a minute to feel right. And I know every square inch of the house by heart."

"Have you been here long?"

"We got in this morning and we're leaving at dawn. Doesn't leave me much time to tame the place."

The north wind shook the window. In the forest, which I already felt like calling "my" forest, it must be sweeping the last packets of snow from the trees, bowing the tip of the President. Tomorrow I'd be far away. The sight of the forest would swell the hearts of other hikers. It would be deep, and high, and majestic without me. I felt almost sick. I didn't feel like going home, back to Melodie, Tanguy, my life. Impossible. I was fed up with all that. I tried to breathe deeply, and it made a strange sound. No air could pass.

"You're upset about something," the stranger said.

That made it even worse. It was the last thing to say to me. Those were the words I'd been waiting for weeks for someone to say. I might have expected them from my mother, my father, or Pauline. But no. The Pest was always just fine. If she had problems, she took care of them on her own. It all came swirling up again. I didn't know I had been carrying such a weight. That I was so unhappy.

"No, I'm fine," I said. "It's just that a flapping shutter woke me up. And on top of that, the wine they serve here . . ."

"I have a cure for that," he said.

He leaned over and fished a tube out of his pack, then went behind the bar. He certainly knew his way around. He filled a glass with water.

"Drink this."

I obeyed. I drank it in little gulps to kill time. I still hadn't taken a step; I was still in the same spot, in the doorway to the lounge. He went back to his armchair. He wasn't especially handsome, or tall, or anything. But the way he looked at you! You got the feeling he was really interested in you. And his voice went with his eyes.

"May I make a proposal?"

There was a new swirling in my chest. I nodded yes: "Yes, well . . ."

"From what you tell me, you're leaving in the morning. That means we'll never see each other again. I won't know your name, you won't know mine. There will only be this moment between us, and that's all."

I nodded again. Yes, this moment. Little more than someone you pass in the street or the person sitting across from you in the bus. And then?

"So, if it can help you in any way, use me."

It took my breath away. Use him? But how?

He pressed a hand just below my collarbone, at the place where so often my breath choked up and sometimes it hurt so much.

"Let it all out."

I turned my eyes away. It started again: the blockage in my chest, the obstructed throat. Next stage: out the eyes.

"I don't think I can use you before I learn to control my own body," I joked.

At home, everyone would have laughed, and that would be that. He didn't even crack a smile.

"You really don't want to sit down?"

I hesitated. Sitting down, in a way, would be a defeat: giving up. And in another way, a victory: over my pride. He looked away to leave me free to choose. Another solution would be for me to disappear: I could be in my bed in a flash.

As in every hotel, chairs circled the round cocktail tables. I chose the circle next to his and lit my lamp to say that I was ready.

"Once," he told me, "when I was fifteen, I was in a bad way. In fact, I wanted to die, I think. Then one day I crossed paths with a stranger. We talked. I knew I'd never see him again. That freed me to tell him certain things. That's all. It helped me."

"I'm older than fifteen," I told him. "I have no desire to die. I'm sure I'll live to be very old and fat, dozing by the fire, alone with my regrets."

I tried to say it with a lilt in my voice, like someone on the radio, but the result was catastrophic. And why bother? He'd never know that I was called the Pest and that I didn't take anything seriously, at least not myself.

"I think what I mean is that I really want to live but I'm not quite sure why or how. The usual, I guess," I said.

"The usual things in life are often the most important ones . . . for instance, the need we all have to love."

I looked out toward the lake. I could not see but could nonetheless sense its sunken town, like an old love. Mentioning love to a girl of my age, he couldn't really go wrong.

"Sometimes you don't quite know how to do that, either," I said. "And maybe you do have such a need to love that you make a complete mistake . . . and really make a mess of things."

I could barely squeeze the words out, especially the word *love*. Just a trickle of air through my throat. I coughed to loosen it. He got up again, but this time it was to come over and put his jacket around my shoulders.

"A cold on top of a hangover is deadly!"

I managed to laugh. His jacket was lined with sheepskin, very soft and warm. I pulled my legs up under me and covered them with Enrico Banana. He waited.

"Ever since I was little I've wanted to help people," I

said. "A real Saint Bernard. The problem is, I choose the wrong ones to help, I guess. And I end up making trouble for everyone."

He said, "You seem afraid of something."

I paused. That was also the last thing to say to me, the one that went furthest. But he couldn't have known it.

"I know someone who's all alone. He's done some dumb things. Worse than dumb, really, but I didn't know that at first. People might say he's no good. What they don't know is that when you get a close look at someone like that, it's nothing like reading about a criminal in the paper. I practically chased him; he didn't want anything from me. But then when he asked me to help him I ran away. And if things turn out badly, I'll be the one to blame."

"Turn out badly?"

"With somebody dying," I said. "And I don't know what to do about it."

He thought for a minute, staring at the thick ski boots in front of him, the kind that give you awful cramps.

"Life is a series of choices," he said. "Call them our paths. And sometimes, it's true, we don't know which path to follow."

"Well, I can drop him completely, cross him out, forget him. That's the easy way, the sensible way. Or else I can try to help him, whether or not he wants help. Then at least I'd keep him from doing any more harm. That must be the brave way."

I stopped. The wind was rising. I saw poor old Mrs. Lamourette, curled up in a little ball, tears on her flannel-soft cheeks. I saw Roughly Speaking's picture with his dog Quince.

"Or I could turn him in before he does anything else."

I pressed my head to my knees. I'd said it. I'd pulled the words out of myself and now I felt a need to scream. Because it was rotten of me not to have turned Tanguy in

141

after what he'd done: stealing the end of an old lady's life is what it really was, all the happiness she had left. And I'd thought I could make it up to her with a bottle of champagne? But turning Tanguy in would be rotten, too: he'd asked me to be his Other. I could be all he had left.

I heard my stranger's voice; it sounded far away.

"Just now you told me you didn't know how to live, or why. We live through our choices, finding the strength to make them. To live up to them."

I used a corner of Enrico Banana, then lifted my head. My confessor was standing in front of the bay window, looking out to leave me some privacy.

"I don't know which choice to make."

"I can't tell you that. It has to come from inside you."

"And what if inside me it's nothing but a mess?"

"Isn't it a little better already?"

"And what if I make the wrong choice?"

"You'll make the best of things."

The ornate grandfather clock struck one. Was it pine? With a little research, I'm sure my father could have found the Chairman of Clocks in the area, too. When the minute hand had swept the face five more times, Pauline and I would get up. She'd ask, "Get a good night's sleep, Pest?" and I'd say yes with a kind of smile inside me. I realized that this moment would remain a precious one in my life. I wouldn't tell anyone about it so they wouldn't tell me I'd been dreaming.

"Thank you," I said. "I guess you were right. I *was* feeling kind of upset."

He smiled. "Don't thank me. I was just in the right place at the right time. When it was getting to be too much for you to handle and it was starting to show."

In Tanguy's eyes, such an unusual blue, sometimes so hard, there was an expression that both called out and rejected: an automatic no. My stranger's expression was

like an invitation: in his eyes you saw yourself next to him.
I felt like asking him where he was from, his name, his
age, what he did, why he was here; but that wasn't in our
agreement.

"If there's something you're having trouble handling,"
I said, "I'd be glad to listen."

Again he smiled. "Listening to you has helped me already. It reminds me that communication still exists. Not
to mention magic."

The President, the Vouivre, the woman in the lake and
her child . . . which one had unlatched the shutter to bring
me here? Under my breath, I said thank you to all three
just in case.

"Doing better now?"

"Fine."

I felt lighter in the chair: my own weight. I'm afraid I
yawned.

"You should head up to bed," he said. "You can't push
magic too far."

"I know."

Push too hard and you fall back into real life. I closed
my eyes for a second. I went down into my deepest inner
pathways. Still painful, but less dim. Between us we'd managed to clear those paths quite a bit.

Tears welled up: I could let them fall. Sometimes, on
the ski slopes for instance, you come to a trail that's really
too hard for you. You know you'll wipe out if you try it.
It's not necessarily cowardly to take a different one. The
hard part is admitting to yourself that you aren't good
enough. For Tanguy, I wasn't good enough.

"Well?" he said.

"I think I've just made my choice. Tell me I'm right or
I'll camp out down here."

"You're right," he said.

I stood up. His open jacket clung to the back of the

chair; I left my ghost in it. He leaned forward and looked at me as if he wanted to remember me. I wanted to cheat and at least tell him my name; he wouldn't tack on "the Pest."

When I got to the door of the lounge, I turned around. "And you really never saw your stranger again?"

"Never!"

"Weren't you sorry?"

He shook his head.

"Remember . . . magic. . . ."

29

Return of the Native

WE GOT BACK to La Marette at five. It was raining. I jumped out to open the gate. Four cars in the driveway: Stephan and Bernadette's, Antoine and Claire's. And what do you know, the Saint-Aimonds' Mercedes! So Bernadette's in-laws were paying us a visit. More and more often now they'd stop by on Sunday, have a cup of tea and a slice of pound cake, and try to tell their darling grand-daughters apart. At first they used to phone ahead; now they just dropped in. That was nice. That was friendship.

There was also a sports car with handicapped plates. That was the one Pauline was staring at, her hand frozen on the handle of the car door. She hadn't seen Paul since he had left her to go back to the set and Nina Croisy. Courage is fine from a distance, but when you come face to face with things, fear is there. She must have thought it would be easier to see Paul again at La Marette. That was probably what she had wanted to talk to Mom about last night. Now she couldn't do it.

"Get back in the car, Cecile," Charles ordered. "I have an idea."

I hopped in. Instead of heading for the garage, he parked at the end of the drive. He turned to us.

"We'll surprise them with the cheese. You two will have to help me!"

We got out, taking care not to slam the doors. Pauline put her hat and scarf back on. Daddy opened the trunk and we tried to get the wheel of cheese out. It had sweated in the trunk: slippery as all get-out.

"I don't think we can do it."

Pauline straightened up. Distress in her eyes, glued to Daddy. We read: "Paul! I don't think I can do it."

"Too late to turn back now," Daddy said with a grin.

He turned toward the Taverniers'. I understood. I headed over there.

Roughly Speaking was in the middle of a rugby game on TV. Overtime. A crowd of fans screaming for a bunch of muddy guys with bashed-in faces to scramble for a ball: another form of communication. As soon as he saw me, Tavernier switched the game off and got up to kiss me on the cheek.

I announced, "Daddy needs you to help carry a wheel of cheese. Right this minute." He was already out the door. It warmed my heart to walk beside him. I tugged at his shirtsleeve. I always feel like touching the people I love. Pauline says she needs to smell them. On the way, I told our neighbor we'd brought him a surprise, but not to let on that I'd told him. He made a face when he got near the car: "Your cheese is good and ripe!" We must have been, too, since we couldn't smell it anymore. Footnote: the three of us would never feel much like eating comté again.

We girls let the two men get the offending object out of the trunk. Then all four of us hauled it across the lawn. The yard was in sad shape, with its sodden pathways, half-dead grass, too-dark trees with too-heavy branches, overflowing pond. A lighthouse above the flood: the house, with light in three windows, two in the living room, one in the kitchen. Behind the curtains, it was bursting with life.

The two on the bottom side had a rough time of it getting up the front steps. I had the thing under my chin. At any rate, Pauline couldn't get away from us now! I said to her, "I can see the headline now: 'Cheese kills two.' " She had a fit of nervous laughter.

We'd made it through the front door. Loud voices and laughter from the living room; apparently no one had gotten our scent. Daddy turned the knob, pushed the door in with his foot, and, cheese to the fore, we made our triumphal entry.

Everyone rose in a single movement: the adults by the fireplace, the kids with crayons and paintbrushes at the dining room table.

"Full speed ahead!" Daddy said, leading the way, his deckhands stumbling behind.

Once everyone got over the shock, the noise was stupendous. Someone had the sense to clear off the coffee table so we could put down our tank's worth of milk. High time. Then came the usual round of hugs and kisses.

Over by the fireplace, Paul stood still. He looked at his wife as if he wanted to let her decide. She looked away, as if she didn't have the strength. The twins and Gabriel had gotten into the swing of things. They were treating their grandfather's legs like trees, trying to climb to the highest branches, and Charles, busy kissing the Countess of Saint-Aimond's hand, was nearly bowled over.

"How strange you all smell," remarked Claire, her tone more affectionate than critical, but with her handkerchief glued to her nose.

Mom hugged Pauline, still hidden beneath her hat and scarf. Hervé de Saint-Aimond was next in line: "We all want to hear about what you were doing in the mountains!"

My sister's lips trembled. He managed to add, "But it must be nice to be back with your family."

"Especially the sensitive souls," Bernadette interrupted, dragging her father-in-law away.

The Saint-Aimonds weren't aware of the situation. Grandmother's principle: "The more you let out about heartaches, the harder it is to pick up the pieces."

I spied Benjamin the same minute Pauline did. Like father, like son: he didn't budge either. Glued to the dining room table, crayon in hand, he waited, petrified, to see what would happen next. He looked at his mother, then at his father, with that expression of his, so serious for his age that you want to shake him. Pauline looked at him, and suddenly her face crumpled. She groped in her bag for a huge pair of sunglasses and slipped them on.

Then Paul finally made his move. He came over to her. I'm describing the scene in slow motion; in all, it couldn't have been more than two minutes since we'd walked in with our fragrant cargo. Paul came over to his wife, who looked more like his daughter, trembling and lost. He didn't take her in his arms, as might have been expected. He simply reached out and took off her sunglasses. No need to drive to the source of the Loue River to see gushing torrents.

We all looked away. Luckily the Saint-Aimonds were preoccupied with the twins, who were having a competition to see who could give the cheese the longest lick. The Countess was trying to explain that the rind was not edible, to the despair of the twins. They thought it tasted terrific. We all pretended to be interested but couldn't help glancing over our shoulders. Paul touched his lips to Pauline's closed eyelids, one, then the other. Once that good job was done, he unrolled her scarf, unzipped her jacket. We dared hope he'd remember where he was; if not, we'd have to form a screen between the young couple and the Saint-

Aimonds. Now he was removing Pauline's jacket. They still hadn't exchanged a word. Their silence was nerve-racking. Stephan's parents started to crane their necks around, too.

With sudden enthusiasm, Daddy began to tell the Count in minute detail about the manufacture of pipes in St. Claude. And we were flabbergasted to hear Mom ask after the Countess's mother, who'd been dead for three years. Then, after an eternity that must have lasted two or three minutes, Paul and Pauline let go of each other. He took his wife by the shoulders, she took her husband by the waist, and they went over to their son, who'd gone wild, laughing and crying at the same time, and ran to hide behind the table until Pauline caught him, scooped him up in her arms to kissing height, hugging height, grown-up height. Quite a picture.

It seemed like enough for one day. But no one had noticed that Roughly Speaking had slipped out, until he reappeared, diffidently bearing two dusty bottles. He'd spent a vacation in the Jura Mountains once. To go with the cheese, he'd like to offer us this wine he still had in his cellar. Arbois wine, also known as Brise-Mollet.

~ 30 ~

By the Name of Tanguy

WE WERE JUST LOCKING THE GATE, Daddy and I, after everyone had left, when we saw Cadillac and Ferré coming up the walk. They were all excited: glad we were home. There was news.

It had happened the night before, about seven o'clock. Some people in town had noticed a light on at the Belons': a weekend place they use mainly in the summer. It looked like a flashlight, dancing around the ground floor. They'd alerted the neighborhood watch right away. It was the first time they'd been called, and everything worked to perfection: ten minutes after the first alert, a dozen-odd determined citizens had silently ringed the house. In the meantime, the police had also been called.

Unfortunately, careful as they'd been, the intruder must have spotted them, because he'd gotten away on a motorcycle parked out in back. It was a young man, they could tell that much even though they hadn't gotten a good look at his face, wrapped up to the eyes in a silk aviator scarf.

"He didn't get anything," Cadillac said. "Except a gun. A revolver."

"We wonder if it might not be the same guy who broke into poor Mrs. Lamourette's," said Ferré.

150

"There were two of them at Mrs. Lamourette's," I pointed out.

It was hard to talk. A revolver! Ferré looked at me, amazed. "They may not always work as a team," he said. "Anyhow, this time, thanks to us, the police have a lead."

"A lead?"

All three of them turned to look at me. Fortunately it was too dark to see much. The only lighting was an old streetlamp that cast a weak, orangy glow. A bit like stage lighting.

"We got the license plate number of the motorcycle," Ferré explained. "It belongs to a guy from the projects, and there's a possible link to the fire in the theater there about a week ago, remember?"

"What kind of link?"

I should have saved my breath, I knew it, but I couldn't stop myself. It was stronger than me. It was also as if someone else were speaking in my place, living through all this. When I saw them walking up to us, I had known right away. They were going to mention Tanguy. Something had been put into motion that I was part of, that I could do nothing to stop now.

Daddy leaned close to me: "What's the matter? Have you been watching too many police shows?"

I managed a smile. "I want to hear about the theater. I saw that play there three times, remember?"

"Three times!" Cadillac exclaimed. "You must not be much of a critic. I heard the play was a disaster from start to finish."

"The disaster was that nobody understood it."

There was a silence. Cadillac looked mad, and my father, upset. He asked them to come in for a minute, but they turned him down. They still had a few people to call on. They were afraid the thief might strike again. This time they'd get him for sure.

151

"After last night, do you really expect him to?" my father asked. "I'll bet he's already taken off."

"Maybe not," said Cadillac. "He seems to be looking for something around here. He was sighted this afternoon, apparently, but without his motorcycle this time."

We said goodbye to them. They walked very close to each other, still talking and gesturing excitedly. In a way they seemed rather happy with things. I saw the bloody faces of the rugby players and the cheering crowd. "What was that all about?" Daddy asked. "No matter how you felt about the play, you didn't have to be rude to them."

The rain had stopped, and something like thousands of black sparkles rose from the lawn. Mom was cleaning up the kitchen, where the kids had had supper just before leaving so they could be put straight to bed when they got home. La Marette made a handy second home! The only tax: huge amounts of affection. My mother had a happy face: replenished.

"Now that Pauline is back, maybe we can breathe a little easier," she said.

I sat down at the table. I felt awful. A mountain north wind ran through my body. What if it was me that Tanguy was looking for? Mom turned her back to me, rinsing the dishes. Each of the grandchildren had a personalized set, and they all knew which was whose.

"I'm turning in," Daddy said in the doorway. "Any takers?"

"Be right up," said Mom.

I folded my arms on the table and buried my head in them. In the bend of my elbow, it smelled like childhood.

"Someone needs a good night's sleep," Mom said. "Must have been a tiring trip."

"Especially last night," I said. "I stayed up talking."

She didn't ask about what or with whom. She was tired, too; she must be in a hurry to be alone with her husband, whom we could hear singing in the bathroom, a sign that all was well.

She still had enough energy to talk to me about school. She'd noticed that I hadn't been working half as hard lately. I didn't argue. She didn't ask if there was a reason.

As we headed up the stairs after checking the lights, the thermostat, the fire, she turned to me: "Someone by the name of Tanguy stopped by yesterday afternoon. He wanted to see you. I told him you'd be back tonight. Sleep tight, now."

31

To Stop Death

HOW COULD I SLEEP AT ALL? With this fear in my stomach, this enormous weight on my chest: the sensation that the world had stopped, was holding its breath before the explosion. Just what Bernadette had said about him: nice wrapping, but the package could blow up in my face. And instead of listening to her, I'd told Tanguy, "Come live with us: there's room for you at our house." And he'd come. And now in Mareuil everyone was waiting for him: the police, the crime watch. And tonight, where was he? And tomorrow?

Forget . . . block it out . . . last night at the mountain hotel I'd believed that it was possible to choose. It was already too late. Life was waiting for me around the bend, what people call life when it's going badly: the tunnel, last stop, dead-end side of life. You're free in your choice of paths only for a brief moment. One step in the wrong direction and it's all over. "Make the best of things," my stranger had said. But how?

First solution: forget him. Second: help him. Third: tell everything; go down to see my parents, wake them up. "I know the guy who tortured Mrs. Lamourette. Set the fire in the theater. Broke into the Belons' Saturday. I asked him to come live here. He's looking for me." What choice would my parents make? Silence? The police? Cadillac and Ferré?

It was still dark when I got up. And still raining, still windy. Winter is a well. To the east, not even a day's drive away, in a village with a rounded church steeple, with roofs drooping down to house windows, by the white-dusted tips of a forest, in front of the deep gaze of a lake, there was a hotel. And in this hotel, the kind of place you dream of when you can't stand things anymore, when you're smothering, when you feel like running away without knowing where to, there was a man who'd been able to read me. He'd asked what was upsetting me. No one would ask me that question today. And if they tried to, I'd find a way to stop them.

Melodie was waiting for me in Pontoise, on the school steps. "Tell me everything! Did your sister come back with you?"

Yes, we'd brought her back with us, and she was fine. I'd tell her all about it later. It was time to go work.

It was a psych class; I liked psych. I'd even been in love with the teacher for a few days because I'd imagined that his profession had taught him how to figure people out, but when I talked to him I could tell he was the same as everyone else: still working on himself. He spoke calmly, a practiced speaker. He spoke from above, like people who for the time being are not in pain. "Certain children," he said now, "are deprived of all hope, sure that they are soon to die; they then do everything they can to bring it about more quickly." You couldn't hear anyone breathing, just papers being shuffled. Next to me, Melodie underlined his most important points in red, with a ruler. But everything was important, vital, urgent. "Deprived of all hope . . . sure that they are soon to die . . ." I stood up.

"What's happening?" my friend whispered. "Where are you going?"

I gathered up my notebook and pens, put them into my bag. My heart was pounding hard. "Deprived of all hope." He'd laid his head on my shoulder and said, "Stay."

"Are you crazy? You can't just walk out."

I walked across the classroom. The teacher had paused: the whole class looked at me. "Sure that they are soon to die, they then do everything they can to bring it about more quickly."

The rain had stained the walls of the projects black. At La Marette, the soil drank the water; here, it found nowhere to go. It spread in puddles between the houses; it ran along the sidewalks; it was pathetic. Tanguy's bike was not in front of his building. In the vestibule, all the mailboxes had been pried open; there were shreds of junk mail on the floor. His door was locked. I knocked: no answer. Same when I called his name. Maybe he'd gone back to his parents'. Then maybe he wasn't the one who had broken into the Belons' on Saturday? But I didn't believe in maybes anymore. An excuse for not making choices.

As I walked back down the stairs, two men stepped out of the shadows: "Police." I froze. My head swam. I'd been expecting something like this. They'd arrest me, handcuff me. "We'd like to ask you a few questions."

I showed them my ID. College student, father a doctor, living in Mareuil. They exchanged a glance. Mareuil? I could read their minds: Mrs. Lamourette. The Belons'.

They asked me how well I knew Tanguy Le Floch. Why was I coming to see him? Had he asked me to meet him there?

I heard myself reply that I hardly knew him. I'd just seen his play two or three times. I'd stopped by to say hello; no, he hadn't asked me to come.

"Have you seen him recently?"

I'd been out of town for the weekend, Malbuisson, in the Jura Mountains, they could check with my parents. Their voices softened. They believed me. It must have been perfectly obvious that I was a nice, clean-living, middle-class girl. Besides, before they let me go they wanted to warn me to be careful: Tanguy Le Floch might be involved in some nasty business. Did I know whether he used drugs?

"I don't think so," I said.

As I got back on my moped, one of them asked me where my helmet was. I'd forgotten it. They said they'd let me off this time. I smiled at them. I made myself sick.

Riding back to La Marette, I felt my freedom sitting on my shoulder, like a bird, perhaps a dove, both precious and fragile. I'd come to warn Tanguy that he was in danger. He'd been to see me on Saturday. There was a witness: my mother. I knew what he'd done, and I hadn't turned him in. That was called being an accessory to a crime.

The first time I smelled death, I was eleven. It was on a friend dying of leukemia: Jean-Marc. Next I recognized it on Gabriel, another boy I tried to save but couldn't. It was a smell and it was an absence: life lost its colors, sounds had a strange echo responding from the depths of the unknown.

In psych class I had learned that inside each of us is the life force and forces of destruction. In the majority of cases, the life force wins out. For a few people it's the other way around. Did I attract death? Without really knowing it, was I looking for death?

It was there in my chest as I rode home. I recognized it. And just as with Jean-Marc, and then with Gabriel, it seemed to me that there was nothing I could do to stop death.

32

"She": My Mother

I'VE BEEN EXPECTING YOU," said Mom.
She grabbed me by the elbow and steered me into
the living room, slamming the door closed.

"Sit down."

It was an order. I took a seat on the edge of a chair; she
took Charles's armchair, opposite me. She didn't look so
young anymore: a hard, tired face.

"Where have you been?"

"At school . . . a teacher didn't show. . . ."

I was afraid. What was up? The police? Tanguy?

She looked at me for a few seconds, pityingly.

"Your adviser phoned. You walked out in the middle
of class, with no explanation. And now you're lying."

I breathed again. She didn't know anything.

"I can't take it," I said. "It's words, words, words, and
in the meantime life . . ."

"Life means having respect for other people, too," my
mother said in a quavering voice. "It's taking at least some
things seriously. This isn't the first time you've cut class,
she tells me. Your grades are poor. You're aggressive,
insolent: they're not sure they want to keep you."

"Good," I said, "because I'm not sure I want to stay."

158

I'd realized just that minute that I didn't want to go back there. Mom breathed in deeply. She was trying hard to stay calm. I could see it in the tendons of her neck. In a way I would have preferred to have her yell at me.

"Just whó chose this school?" she asked.

"I did," I said. "I admit it, and I still think it's the kind of work I want to do. But in school all they do is give you words to learn by heart, and to hell with people in trouble. . . ."

"What people?" Mom asked. "Who are you talking about? Everything begins with words, you know. And here's another word you ought to think about: try *lazy*."

Lazy! How could she possibly say that! My mother really didn't understand anything. She wasn't even trying. Before, ages ago, when all four of us were at home and she was a full-time mother, she had been better at listening. Claire could tell her, without Mom having a fit, that she was pregnant and didn't plan to get married. When Pauline fell in love with an older man, she understood. She had the time, the desire.

She stood up. Blood had rushed to her cheeks. It happened to her often these days: hot flashes. That was all we needed: menopause. She opened the window, and I heard her breathing. She had tired shoulders, because of me. Last night, how happy she'd been! I was spoiling everything for her.

She closed the window and came back over to me.

"You've never accepted the least discipline. You've always had to do things your own way. We hoped that you'd become more responsible as you got older, but you haven't. In fact, you're still just a fresh little kid."

I felt like screaming. A kid! I hated her for saying that. It was humiliating. Two days earlier, in Malbuisson, someone had seen me differently. He'd tried to give me strength. She was taking it away.

"You know," I said, "that it isn't always easy to choose. Everyone makes some mistakes."

"And everyone needs to listen to advice, not just go on thinking you're the only one who's right."

"Maybe other people don't know how to listen either."

My stranger had looked at me and understood my call for help. He hadn't needed words to know I was hurting. My mother saw only one thing: I wasn't doing well in school. My adviser had talked to the dean. I might be asked to leave. But she hadn't even asked me why I had walked out in the middle of a class. My own mother! It must be just a whim. There couldn't be any serious reason. And this morning, when I couldn't eat a bite of breakfast, she had blamed the fondue, fish, wild mushrooms, white wine I'd no doubt had too much of in the mountains. And last night, in the kitchen, when the words were on the tip of my tongue . . . no, my mother was no longer with me.

She looked at her watch and sighed. She was running late because of me. Her inmates . . .

"Your inmates," I said. "You're willing to listen to *them* for hours on end. To understand everything they've done, no matter how horrible. But your own daughter . . ."

"How could you?" she screamed.

This time she couldn't control herself. She stood up and brought her face close to mine. I no longer recognized this woman: I refused to recognize her. There was such anger in her eyes.

"They haven't had a family . . . they haven't had affection. Most of them never had anyone to listen. You have no right to compare yourself to them."

When your mother looks at you like that, it kills you. I stood up.

"Affection," I said, "family — all of that can be worse than anything. It makes you blind."

I slammed the door and went up the stairs. My legs were

trembling. I couldn't breathe. I locked myself in my room. She'd better keep out. "She," not "my mother." "She." I sat down on my bed and looked around me. This is what I was to my parents: a stupid Donald Duck poster, a pile of scratched records, a musty collection of seashells, mindless fan magazines, an old cardboard puppet theater. It all added up to the Pest. And because my name was Moreau, and I lived at La Marette, and they fed and loved me, I was supposed to be well adjusted, follow their straight and narrow, neatly record in my notebook how children had wanted to die, underline it in red and blue, file it away after I learned it by heart, and not feel like saying screw it all.

Below, I heard the front door shut, then the car door. The car pulled away, the sound it made blending into the background noise. Well, she wouldn't be *too* late. Her daughter could wait.

I stood up. My head swam. Since last night, I hadn't been able to eat. Good for the figure. Too bad it wasn't bathing-suit weather. I opened the window and looked out. So this was what my village looked like on a Monday while I was in class. Quiet, a little dead. Because I shouldn't have been here, and also because I was suddenly terribly afraid of losing it, I felt as though I was watching Mareuil stealthily, like a thief.

I saw the hand of the town-hall clock reach two, and it rang out loud into the distance, into the landscape and into my memory. I saw a woman leave her house, lock the door, and walk over to the bakery for a little chat with the always willing Mrs. Cadillac. I saw Roughly Speaking, armed with a broom and dust rag, go behind the shrubs and down into his bomb shelter. The caverns of the apocalypse get as dusty as everything else, I suppose. My eyes came to rest at last on the church. Lest we forget, Jean-René was the one who had sent me to Tanguy. But the church was locked up. Jean-René was only there on Saturday and Sunday. "You have to find God in yourself," he would say. Only, most of the time God was silent. And when you had the feeling He was talking to you, like earlier that day in the classroom, when He was telling you, "Go on! Someone cried out to you! Someone has asked you for hope to keep living, and you're abandoning him . . . ," then the police got on your case, not to mention your own mother!

I closed the window, went down to my parents' room, and dialed Bernadette's number. Aude answered, Stephan's sister; she was watching the twins. Bernadette would be back around six. Aude's voice was warm: "What's new with you? How are you doing?" Quickly, while I still could, I answered, "Just fine." Could Bernadette call me back? As soon as possible?

I hung up. On the nightstand, on Mom's side, there was a picture of the four of us, back when she had ears to hear us. In the end, I pitied her: not one single time would she have asked me, "What's the matter?"

And plenty was wrong: I was exhausted, I felt sick to my stomach. To forget . . . I buried my head in the pillow and went far away, into the pine trees, to a hotel where someone who didn't even know me, to whom I meant absolutely nothing, had listened to me so well. And I told him everything.

It was almost five when I woke up. I felt better. Hurry, Bernadette, call back! In the meantime, I got an apple in the kitchen, cut it in two, and filled the core with honey. Delicious. Our orchard had done great work in the apple department this year. We had even had to borrow bushel baskets from Roughly Speaking. Eating apples, apples for applesauce, pie apples — the least ripe give the best taste. I picked out three nice ones for our neighbor. A trip to his shelter would help pass the time. Six o'clock: I'd let Bernadette make the choice for me. I'd pass the buck.

But my choice was waiting for me here. Here and now. I was almost at the gate when I heard my name. I turned around. The voice came from the basement. We have three rooms down there. The finished one is Bernadette's old room. No carpeting, a tile floor; she could go right in with her riding boots on, handy for her. The second room has the boiler, the gardening tools. In the third we keep wine, canned goods, and so on. We'd taken the wheel of cheese down there the night before.

That was where the voice had come from; and the two eyes looking out at me from the basement window were Tanguy's.

33

The Bottom of the Well

HE WAS SITTING ON THE FLOOR, back to the wall, in the dust. I turned on the light.

"Watch out," he said. "The neighbors . . ."

His voice was hoarse, brutal; I turned the light off again. I'd seen his torn jacket, his unshaven face caked with dirt, and his eyes with their black flame of loneliness and violence. He laughed a strange laugh: "See! It's never too late to take someone up on an invitation."

Yes, I'd invited him. And my choice, the choice that had led me to this instant when I was so afraid and felt so empty, was one I'd made long before: the day I'd seen him onstage, handsome and desperate, and wanted to love him.

"It's not easy to see you alone," he remarked. "It's a real zoo here. God, what a racket you all make!"

Not a racket, Tanguy — a joyful noise, though I could no longer see it. I murmured, "How did you get in?"

"The key under the third step, remember? You're the one who showed me, that day on the swing."

"How long have you been here?"

"Since last night."

Last night we'd brought the cheese down after cutting huge chunks of it for my sisters. Daddy had put it up on

164

a shelf above the apples, wrapped in cloth. He'd said, "Apple pie without the cheese is like a kiss without a squeeze," a favorite saying of his, and we had all laughed — not that it was so funny, but when you're happy you make noise for no reason, to prove you're together.

"I slept in the boiler room," said Tanguy. "Would have frozen my ass off in here. But I like the smell of cheese better than the smell of heating oil. Won't you come in?"

I took a few steps forward. I wished, hopelessly, painfully, that he would leave, that he'd never come, that I'd never known him. That was all I felt in me; no more love or pity. Rejection.

"Anybody up there now?" he asked.

I shook my head. My eyes were adjusting to the dark. He was curled up on old potato sacks. At his side, two empty bottles.

"What do you want?"

"Money and clothes," he said. "I've had the cops on my ass for the last three days. Yesterday I stopped by my place, and they took my bike. I almost didn't get away. It's because Manuel squealed to them."

"Manuel?"

"They brought him in for questioning after the fire in the theater. He was scared shitless. Gave them my name, the bastard. Maryse told me about it. The heat's on me."

"The heat's on you here, too."

That's what I'd gone to his place to tell him: to beg him not to come back to Mareuil. I told him everything: Cadillac, Ferré, the crime watch, the whole town on alert. He'd been sighted yesterday. The cops still had his room staked out.

"Good. I hope they stay put."

He was smiling. From the beginning he'd worn this unsmiling smile; and I was shivering, from the cold, from nerves. What had I done? That time by his side in his room

165

at the projects, I'd thought of the well at Grandmother's: "If you look too long, you'll fall in." I was falling. I couldn't see the bottom.

"Scared?"

"Yes."

"And you'd just as soon get rid of me, right?"

I turned away. He could tell I was deserting him, like everyone else.

"There's not much money in the house," I said, and I had a deep, throaty voice I didn't recognize. "But clothes, no problem. How are you going to get out of town?"

I didn't want them to see him, catch him, find out what I'd done.

"On your moped. You can say it was stolen."

"Where are you going?"

"First I have some business to take care of in Pontoise. Then I'll disappear."

Some business? My heart was pounding. I didn't want to ask the question. I wouldn't touch the sore spot. I wouldn't hurt myself looking for the truth. I wouldn't be the Pest. I just had to get him out of here, and fast, that was all that counted. The rest was none of my concern.

The words came in spite of me.

"What business?"

"You think I'm going to let that asshole get away scot-free?"

He tapped his pocket, and I heard Cadillac the night before: "A gun, a revolver." I wasn't surprised when he pulled the gun out. I saw it as I asked my question, and a sort of gray, heavy water without light spread through me; this must be what they call despair.

Again I heard my voice, as if from a distance.

"You're going to kill him?"

"We'll see."

"If you do, you've had it. The cops will get you."

"Which side is the prison?"

I started to cry. It was the third time he had used that phrase, and it tore me apart. And I'd been right about words. Some of them are liars. When a well-dressed teacher standing behind a lectern dictates them to you, words like *despair, loneliness,* and even *death* become almost beautiful, like black pearls. They light a sort of flame inside you that allows you to take the measure of your own good fortune. But if they slam you in the face and your protective film breaks, then despair, loneliness, and death are simply dirty, sordid, squalid, intolerable, and you wish you could be a child again.

"What's wrong with you?" he said. "Stop crying!"

"I can't help you," I said. "I can't help you do that."

He got up and walked toward the door. He was still holding his gun.

"Would you rather have me just leave and shoot the first person who tries to stop me?"

I knew he'd do it, and I touched bottom. So this was death. Someone holding a little black tool and saying "I'll shoot" without thinking of the person who'd fall.

"Why not start with me? What makes you think I won't turn you in?"

He looked at me a minute before replying, still with his smile like a goodbye, though I still didn't know to whom.

"You haven't yet, and from what you tell me you've had plenty of chances."

I heard the hall clock strike half past five. In half an hour my mother would be home.

"What kind of clothes do you want?"

"Now you're listening to reason. Pants and a sweater, as neutral as possible. Dark glasses, if you have any."

He stopped: "Wait. . . ."

People were passing by in the road. Several of them. The crime watch? We could hear them talking. Without a sound, Tanguy went to the basement window, pressed his face to the bars. I went to the window, too. We couldn't see because of the stone wall, but they'd stopped and were discussing something. The light from the streetlamp bathed our four chestnut trees in orange. Lined up along the gate, they'd been spaced so each would have room to grow full. In great forests, like the ones in the Jura Mountains, many trees were condemned to die because they were too weak to reach the light. They either fell on their own or were felled. There wasn't enough light for all of them.

The people walked away, and I sensed Tanguy's sigh: "It wasn't for us," he said.

"Us?" I looked at his blond hair and narrow shoulders. Is this what a killer was like? Fragile? Like me in some way? Finally, oh Lord, finally something moved in me besides fear and denial. What was left for Tanguy? No more friends, no theater, no home, no future, no sort of sun. He had only his gun, and me, for a while more. And I suddenly felt so sorry for him that it was a kind of love.

He looked at me out of the corner of his eye. "Done crying?"

"Thinking," I said. "Not sure what's happening, and wondering about the Other."

"Let's just say we didn't make it."

I touched his sleeve. "Tanguy . . ."

A moment's hesitation. Then he shoved me roughly away.

"What are you waiting for? Do you really want to keep me here?"

His voice was nasty. Walking to the door, I felt my body like a target.

"And make it fast," he said. "Waiting is the worst part."

34

The Choice

I WENT up to my parents' room and opened the closet. To the left, my father's suits. I knew them all by heart: the old ones he wouldn't get rid of despite my mother's pleas; the ones he wore every day; a few reserved for special occasions; the new one he hadn't been able to bring himself to wear yet.

"As neutral as possible," Tanguy had said. What he needed was jeans or corduroy slacks, just like the ones over there on the chair, the ones my father had worn in Malbuisson.

"No!" I recoiled. Impossible. That was a choice I couldn't make: I couldn't give Tanguy my father's clothing to go kill Manuel. Not that.

I fell onto the bed. My throat was so dry! I could hardly breathe. I couldn't stop myself from shaking. Impossible to think, think things over. Nothing. Nothing but this word inside me: *Quick.* My mother would be coming home. He'd tortured old Mrs. Lamourette. He'd set fire to the theater. *Quick!* But I was as good as sending him to kill Manuel. *Oh, Lord, quick!* And what if he killed my mother? I had to do something, right away, fast. He'd start to worry, come upstairs. I heard someone sobbing. It was me. I couldn't let him leave here with his gun. I wanted to die.

Outside, a barge passed on the Oise. Night was here. I heard Roughly Speaking's voice that day: "When you're ready to talk, I'm here." Now!

He was still in his shelter, with the huge steel door propped open. At the back of the main room, on his knees, he was sorting books. I went to him. "Quick," I said. "Quick." But now I couldn't even get the words out. Just a strange croaking noise. I took his shoulder: "Quick, quick . . ." Tanguy could have seen me leave the house, run. *Quick!* He stood up. "Forgive me, Cecile," he said. I saw his hand fly and felt my cheek sting.

"Now talk. What's the matter?"

I told him everything.

He'd closed the door. I was alone in this underground room, sitting on this white chair like the ones you see in hospitals. All I had to do was wait. He'd take care of everything.

I had to get hold of myself. I could take my hands off my ears: I wouldn't hear anything. No police sirens, no shots, no screams. The shelter was made for this: so that outside the world could fall apart without you hearing it. There would just be a slight quaking, it seemed. The furnishings were designed to withstand it. Five minutes to six! Ten minutes since Roughly Speaking had gone up. I'd refused to wait in his house. It was perfect here.

I looked around me. I no longer felt like crying. I felt hard as a rock, but it hurt. Across from me were the beds: three very wide bunks, sleeps nine — nine bodies. To the left, the kitchenette: table, chairs, sink, stove. The other room was a dormitory, with nine more beds. Last year Roughly Speaking's relatives had visited, and the kids had slept down here. They'd loved it. Six o'clock. The police must be on the way.

I stood up. My legs were like lead and yet I felt empty,

devoid of myself, of everything, of my past as well. As if what was happening had erased it. I was the fourth daughter in a happy family. I'd had a fairly uneventful life. "And make it fast. Waiting is the worst part." What had Tanguy meant with his dark looks and his smile? Waiting for what?

I paced the room. He'd pressed his forehead to the bars on the basement windows and looked out at our yard, our good fortune. I'd finally made my choice. It had taken me a long time to turn him in. "At least I did it myself," Roughly Speaking had said about his vicious dog. "I wouldn't have wanted to leave that to someone else." I was leaving it to others. I'd shut myself up where I wouldn't see anything. Six-ten: Mom had to be home by now.

I went to the closet and opened it. White clothing, a special material, suits for after the explosion, with hoods and gloves, on the hangers. Over there on a high shelf were the masks; I counted twenty. Roughly Speaking had calculated generously. Counted us in. "There will have to be people to go on," he'd said. I didn't want to go on. Not interested anymore. I only wanted to stay here and never leave. What would the police do? "You haven't turned me in yet," Tanguy had said.

Accessory to a crime. At what point had I become his accomplice? When I'd spotted all the stolen goods in his room? When I'd seen Mrs. Lamourette's watch in his hand? Accessory to everything. Lies to the police. They'd arrest me, too. It was almost six-thirty.

Mom had told me that in prison one of the things the inmates can't stand is the sound of the guards' keys clanging all day on the bars to make sure they haven't been sawed through. All day, clang, clang. I didn't mind going to prison, but I felt bad for my parents. My father said the fifties were a time of harvest. Pauline, now me — he was having a great one this year.

171

By the bed, there was a picture on the wall: Madonna and child. I went over to them. I said, "I don't believe in you anymore. I don't believe you exist, but help me."

At around seven the door opened. Tavernier came in first, my mother and father behind him. The police weren't with them. I was stretched out on the bottom bunk, in back, against the wall. I rolled to the edge, stood up, and waited. All three of them were very pale, and Daddy's eyes were blue-ringed, like when he had problems at work.

My mother came closest. We were the ones with something to settle; after all, we'd just been talking. I looked away, but I was ready. She could even hit me. She took me in her arms: "Sorry," she murmured. I wasn't prepared for that; it was worse than a blow.

Seeing Bernadette come in, I understood that they all knew and that it was good, because I wouldn't have been able to live with this weight and now they'd have to talk to me about it a lot and they had really, really better not try to gloss things over.

Bernadette came to me. To make a joke, I wanted to ask her if Pauline and Claire were coming down, and why not bring the kids, but it wouldn't come out.

"It's over," she said to my parents. "They've taken him away."

"What's over?" I asked.

Roughly Speaking told me the first part. He said "your friend," talking about Tanguy, which was wonderful of him and incredibly painful. Then my father took over. He didn't let other people handle the parts that hurt; he said things to your face and you knew there was nothing hidden. While he told me this horrible thing I looked at the legs of the chairs and counted them. It seemed to me that as long as I could do that, I wouldn't fall, I'd hold up. Bernadette didn't say a word: a red-letter day. Mom also looked away, and I don't know whether it was back at my childhood or toward tomorrow.

"Now it's time to go," said Daddy.

I shook my head no. I couldn't. I wanted to stay, come out a long time later, when outside things had cooled and I could breathe again, perhaps even enjoy things — but not now. It was as if there would never be another spring.

"Look at me, Cecile," said Charles.

I couldn't do that, either; it was impossible. I couldn't bear to see in his eyes the hurt I'd caused him.

He took me by the shoulders. What were they all waiting for? I wanted to be alone again.

"A little courage, now," he ordered. "A little dignity, please. Look at me."

So I managed to raise my eyes, and in his there were tears, an immense fatigue, but not a trace of anger or blame.

"Let's go," he said.

Outside, there was a strange smell, and my eyes stung. There were a lot of people on the road where it's usually so quiet. We headed straight for the police car. It wasn't the same men I had seen at Tanguy's.

"This is the girl who came to tell me," said Tavernier. "She heard him when she got home from school, and she's still in a state of shock, roughly speaking, as you can see."

They barely looked at me and didn't question me since I didn't know anything, since, quite simply, when I got home from school I had heard something in the basement and gone straight to tell my neighbor.

Late in the evening, despite the winter cold, people stayed on the road to sniff the odor and to look at the doctor's house. They told the story of what had happened over and over. When someone new arrived, they jumped on him. Words had become words again: the flame of fear and pleasure leapt from chest to chest, from mouth to mouth, and I understood their excitement. It had happened to me once when there was a department store fire in Pontoise; I couldn't tear myself away from looking at the flames and the men fighting them. Their shouts had concerned me, their courage had gone straight to my heart. They were saving me, too, and that day was warm with something besides the fire — a greater warmth. We had all felt like survivors.

Yes, what had happened today could have happened to anyone in Mareuil. Violence was everywhere; no one was ever safe from it. The world, society, unemployment, justice, values, principles.

But I'm afraid no one said either *despair* or *loneliness,* although those words were the heart of the matter.

All in all, it was a simple story, the kind of thing that happens every day. It would be in the morning papers, a few lines in the section reserved for local news.

Sometime before 7:00 last night, an alleged criminal sought by police was found hiding in the home of a doctor in Mareuil, near Pontoise. Alerted by a neighbor, the police were on the scene within minutes. The suspect, implicated in several local burglaries and a possible arson incident, was considered armed and dangerous. The house was surrounded; tear gas was used. There was no reply to police orders. By the time they entered the basement, it was already over. When cornered, Tanguy Le Floch, 22, unemployed, had turned his stolen handgun on himself.

35

The Other?

FOR THREE DAYS the snow fell. The sky seemed to lie flat on the garden, the barges plied the silence that closes again in their wake; I had the feeling that the hands of the clock were moving for no good reason. It was December.

Finally, I went to see Mr. and Mrs. Le Floch in Conflans-Sainte-Honorine. Melodie came with me as far as their door. She insisted that she wanted to go in, afraid of I'm not sure what. I wouldn't let her. I had to take a few steps without a crutch.

The house faced the street and was prosperous-looking. Tanguy's father answered the door: tall, thin, with cropped hair. He was a career soldier, retired. He showed me into the living room, where his wife waited.

She wore a gray dress, and her hair was pulled back as if the better to expose her suffering. She motioned to a chair beside her.

On the phone, I'd introduced myself as a friend of Tanguy's. I needed to talk to them; it was important. I told them forthrightly that I had liked their son very much and that it was hard for me to accept what had happened. I wanted them to help me understand.

Mrs. Le Floch began to cry, although it seemed as if her eyes had already given all they could.

"Tanguy left home two years ago," her husband said. "We won't be able to tell you much."

"Well, can you tell me something about what he was like before?"

"What good will that do you?" he asked.

"Easy, now," said his wife.

She got up and motioned for me to look at the photographs on the mantel with her. Most of them had been taken in foreign countries, North Africa, Germany. A military man has to move a lot. There were three children, two boys and a girl. The older son, Bruno, appeared as a cadet next to his father in uniform. The daughter, Agnes, was married, with children. Tanguy was the youngest.

She picked up a picture of him at ten or so.

"He 'lacked internal controls.' That's what the doctors said when he was a child. At times he'd seem to go berserk. He caused us a lot of trouble. We had to move several times."

I murmured, "What kind of things did he do?"

She turned away. "Awful things," she said. "And for no apparent reason."

Then I picked up the picture. He was standing on a sand dune in the desert, looking into the distance. An indifferent, empty expression.

"Maybe it was because he couldn't find the Other," I said.

Mrs. Le Floch didn't seem to catch on. "What do you mean by 'other'?"

"The one who'd really understand him, love him."

"But we tried everything!"

She started crying again, as if I'd accused her. I felt very little pity. I had the feeling that I was fighting, for Tanguy and for myself.

"Then maybe he was looking for God or something like that."

"He didn't believe in God," his father said. "He claimed it was nonsense, that afterward there's nothing."

I walked over toward him. He held himself almost at attention in his chair, and I felt his pain, buried like a sword straight up through his body.

I asked, "Was he afraid of war?"

He repeated the word *war,* a common one for him: his job.

"He said that we were bound to blow ourselves up, and the sooner the better. I don't know if he was afraid."

"He didn't love life," his mother spoke again. "Or people, or anything. Why?"

I couldn't answer. Because! Suddenly I had nothing more to say. I'd imagined them differently: hard, unbending, responsible, guilty. That would have made everything easier. I could have blamed them. But they were ordinary parents; they probably would have gotten along with my own. They'd done everything in their power for their son and I'd sicced the police on him, and now I had the nerve to show up at their house! Just like I had called on poor old Mrs. Lamourette knowing who'd tortured her.

They asked me how I'd met him. I told them about the play. I told them he had been very talented and that his play had been a success. Now I wanted them to forgive me. They seemed completely disarmed; they hadn't heard their son's praises sung very often.

Before I left, I asked to see his room. The words just popped out. I always have to dig to the bottom, and at the bottom is suffering, like fire at the center of the earth. I must be a masochist. It would have been so much easier to hold on to the image of Tanguy in the cellar, with his gun and his wild eyes.

His room was full of books, pictures of actors, and

posters. Now I'd know the child I'd also betrayed. Curled up on the bed, a black cat purred. I murmured his name, Missile, and got a flash of yellow in return.

"Another girl, someone named Maryse, brought the cat here last Thursday," Mr. Le Floch explained. "He asked her to."

Thursday was four days before Tanguy's death. The police had already had his place staked out: he hadn't wanted to abandon his cat.

Seeing me to the door, they asked me what I did in Mareuil. I told them I wasn't sure yet. I'd been in a state of shock and was still recuperating. Just before Tanguy's mother closed the door, I don't know what came over me, but I kissed her.

The hard part was waking up. Even if I'd had a good night's sleep, I couldn't get up. I asked myself "Why?" and "Who for?"

A few days later I called the hotel in Malbuisson. The owner answered. Of course he remembered me. Hearing his voice, the accent like pine bark but softened with meadows and running streams, I had the whole place inside me, had all that lost happiness. I mentioned a young man arriving late the night before we left. We'd talked. Was he still there? I had something important to tell him.

"Emmanuel?" he exclaimed. "He's in Africa. A doctor with Save the Children, have you heard of them?"

I had, and it didn't surprise me to hear that that was his work. He knew how to sense pain and soothe it. Emmanuel . . . I liked the name. It means, I think, "God with me."

The next morning, Daddy came to sit on the foot of my bed, and he explained to me that I was shedding my skin. That's how it always is when you've been through a rough experience, and unless you want to hide beneath your old skin — which is the last thing you should do — for a time you're fragile. Like an injured finger when the nail falls off. Beneath it, the skin is pink and tender. You have to give it time to grow back.

Daddy told me it would be great if my new skin was ready for Christmas. We'd toast it with champagne, my favorite. I didn't make any promises, but I asked him also to prescribe that no one call me the Pest anymore. That is, if he really wanted me to turn over a new leaf. Did we have a deal? He laughed. He'd been hoping I'd ask him that for a long time, and I could count on him to pass on my orders . . . and anyone who disobeyed them would have to answer to him.

Meaning he'd be there to listen.

36

The Night before Christmas

THE TELEPHONE RANG. It was three in the afternoon: the night before Christmas was starting to fall. It rang and I sensed nothing: inside me, not the slightest signal.

Bernadette answered. She held the receiver out to Mom: "The hospital, for you!" Mom was up on the stepladder decorating the Christmas tree. She didn't sense anything, either. She got down from her perch with her necklaces of garlands and headed for the phone, saying, "I hope your father doesn't have an emergency or something like that."

Bernadette returned to her place at the table with the rest of us. We were wrapping. There was paper everywhere: we measured, cut, folded, taped, tied ribbons. When we were done, we'd write the recipient's name in very small letters: Benjamin, Gabriel, Sophie, Melanie, what a haul! There was a small mountain in the center of the table.

Mom said "Hello," then fell silent. A garland slipped from around her neck and fell; she didn't pick it up. That surprised me, but still nothing alerted me. If we'd had a dog, it would already have been howling, for sure. Pauline, scissors in midair, noticed her sit down very slowly, as if falling in slow motion in a film. And suddenly, in a voice

180

that was not hers and made us all recoil, a voice from her guts, hoarse, shocking, Mom said, "Tell me what's wrong with him. I have to know."

Bernadette got back up and made a beeline for her. Claire glared at Mom: what a way to talk! Pauline grumbled, "What is it now?" Her eyes searched mine, and I felt her fear.

In the same maimed voice Mom said, "I'll be right there," and she hung up. Her face was like wax. She looked at us; she was trying to tell us something, but the words wouldn't come out. Bernadette sat at her feet.

"What's the matter? What happened? Is it Dad?"

Mom stood up, slumped back down. All four of us surrounded her now. Upstairs, the kids were singing full blast, as befits a Christmas Eve, with star-shaped question marks for pauses. Now something was swelling inside me, choking me: denial. I took the pipe, his stupid pipe that he'd picked from a hundred others, with me, in the mountains. I cupped it in my hand, clung to it. He'd hardly broken it in.

"Has he had an accident?" Pauline asked.

Mom sucked in a deep breath. She said, "Cardiac arrest."

"Will he be all right?" Claire gasped. "He'll be all right, won't he?"

"He's never had any trouble with his heart," Bernadette remarked huskily.

I said nothing. I knew. Mom tugged at the garlands; they slipped off her neck, to the floor. Her face was flushed, disbelieving. She looked at us one after the other, questioning. Brusquely, Claire turned toward the window, pressed her forehead to the glass. A kind of violent churning filled me: everything was gray, a ship was foundering. It was called the family. Sinking noiselessly beneath our eyes, with its captain still on the bridge.

I wanted it to be this morning, when my father had left

and I'd run to the door to remind him about the *foie gras:* "Please don't forget to pick it up. They're holding it for us." He was already almost out the gate. He'd stopped and turned around, with his slightly stooped shoulders that made you want to be gentle with him, and he'd smiled at me: "Of course I won't, darling. What would Christmas be without *foie gras?*" And off he went. Off to his death.

"I think he's gone," said Mom.

37

Death of the "President"

HE WAS SMILING. He looked rested, somewhat more than that morning. It seemed as though he was going to open his eyes, see us there, sit up, amazed: "But what are all you girls doing here?" It seemed as though he was still there, that he hadn't abandoned us, his "five women," as he'd say, pretending it was too much of a good thing, but happily, proudly. For someone who hated to hurt people, he'd really gone and done it now.

It was a shiny white room with two beds; the other was empty. He was flat on his back under the sheet, a way he would never lie, not my father — it would hurt his back too much. His blanket wasn't over him but was folded on a chair, beige with stripes.

Mom was sitting right next to him and staring at him as if waiting for a sign. But he'd never open his arms to her again. He'd never again look at her like a child, like a man: a child needing tenderness, a man demanding love.

He'd left the hospital after a quick lunch to go do some errands. It was just after he'd picked up the *foie gras* that it happened. He'd gotten back in the car, turned the key in the ignition, and his heart had stopped, his head slumped on the steering wheel.

"My darling," Mom said. "My darling."

Bernadette stood behind her, at attention. She blew her nose from time to time, as noisily as possible, forgetting that she was a woman, out of fury over all this love turning into water. Claire stared at the wall, hard as a rock; not a word, not a tear since Mom had said "He's gone." Pauline and I were at the foot of the bed; I felt her arm against mine.

The door opened; it was Antoine. He went straight to Charles, looked at him a few seconds to make sure, then took Mom in his arms, repeating, "Oh, Mattie . . ." My word, were those tears? When a man cries, it's violent: rough sand. With us, it's fine sand. When a man cries, tons of words like *strength, pride, manliness* — castles with towers and banners — crumble.

"I just heard. It's horrible. . . ."

Mom broke loose the better to quiz him, corner him: wasn't he a doctor, too? Hadn't he worked with the man lying there on the bed? She asked, still in her disturbing, hoarse voice, "It isn't possible, is it?" And yet she knew very well that it was: you could already read it all over her. But she was fighting hard not to tumble into this night with no end, not even night, not even emptiness: nothing.

Antoine held her tight to keep her from falling. He tried to meet Claire's eyes, but she kept stubbornly staring at the wall as if it would open onto the enchanted gardens in the fairy tales Charles used to read us, full of fountains and palaces. Antoine helped Mom back to her husband's bedside, went over to his wife, and pulled her to him; he pushed her head down on his shoulder, as a father would. For a time he could try to be one to her, but still he would not have watched her grow up. Claire broke loose. Now Antoine hugged Bernadette, who said, "Shit, I just can't believe it," then Pauline, who was crying too hard to talk.

Next it would be my turn. No thanks. I didn't need sympathy. I was lucky: *I* was still alive. Charles was the one we should feel sorry for; he was going to miss out on everything: Christmas, his grandchildren, spring in his garden. "I want you to know I'm here for you," Antoine murmured in my ear. So they say.

People came by: a doctor, nurses. They also checked first to see whether it was true, then with gray faces paid their respects to us, starting with the wife. I tried to see them through my father's eyes: so it was people like these you went to every morning; they were the ones who took your time, sharing it with the patients you cared for so much. I wanted them all to be miserable; I was afraid they'd forget him too soon. There were a dozen of us in the room now, and everyone spoke quietly. High time! My father hated noise: the more his ears failed, the more sensitive they became, and Mom used to tease him about it. We wouldn't have to bother anymore.

"What did you do with the kids?" asked Antoine.

"They're over at Taverniers'," said Bernadette. "They don't know anything yet."

"We'll have to take it slowly with them," Pauline said.

She and I had gone over together to tell Roughly Speaking. Outside, the air was no longer the same and the wind had blown as if for someone besides us. He had come to the door with his holiday smile; I'd said the word for the first time and felt as though I was playing a stupid trick on him. He froze, looked over at La Marette. I saw the blood rise to his neck, flood his face, say no for him. I was afraid he'd choke, so to distract him I'd pointed toward his bomb shelter and said, "You can never prepare for absolutely everything." "Oh shut up!" Pauline had screamed.

Now she looked at the bump the two feet made beneath the sheet. His feet were not his best feature, but we'd take him back with them just the same. Over by the door, Bernadette was still talking with Antoine, reestablishing relations with life.

"I got Stephan on the phone. He's coming. Couldn't reach Paul, of course. He's in for a shock when he gets to La Marette tonight."

"La Marette?" Mom repeated, as if the word had awakened her.

She got up and walked over to them. That morning she'd been to the beauty shop, and her sprayed bouffant hairdo above her devastated face was like a false smile drawn over a clown's lips. She laid a hand on our brother-in-law's arm.

"He would have wanted us to celebrate Christmas anyway, don't you think? Because of the children. But I'd like to bring him back to the house. Do you think I'm allowed to?"

I'm with him in the forest. We're walking in single file. He's wearing his corduroy pants, his boots, his plaid shirt. It smells like snow, pine needles, the pleasure of being alive. We stop to look at the tallest of trees, the one people pick to carve their names into, the one called the President.

And now our President had fallen. Felled with the names of five women on his trunk, and we were just beginning to feel the aftershock.

38

Words Without End

"WHAT ABOUT Grandpa's stocking?" Gabriel asked. "Aren't we going to hang his up, too?"

Twelve stockings dangled from the mantel; the thirteenth was his.

"Listen," Antoine said, "Grandpa had to go somewhere."

"We should still hang it up," Sophie decided. "That way he can get his presents later."

Benjamin looked at his cousins, his face sullen, angry.

"He won't get his presents, because he's dead," he declared.

We all froze. How had he found out? We'd decided not to tell them until the morning.

"No he's not," Gabriel protested. "He went out of town to see a patient, and he'll be back tomorrow to carve the turkey with dressing."

"We don't like stuffing," commented Sophie, "so we get mashed potatoes."

"And gravy," Melanie chimed in.

Now it was us Benjamin scowled at, as if to blame us for trying to fool him.

"He's dead," he insisted. "He's up in his room, and it

smells like church from the candles. He won't be able to give Poppy his hat."

"You're sick, you know it?" Gabriel said scornfully.

Tears welling up, Benjamin waited for our response. Mom opened her arms; he flung himself into them.

"What's this about a hat?"

"Grandpa and I picked it out together for Poppy, so his ears won't get all red," Benjamin hiccupped, "and then the birds won't think they're berries. And to thank him for having me over when Mommy was at the lake. Grandpa promised we'd go over and give it to him tonight: Poppy cried when I told him."

"At this point," Bernadette sighed, "we might as well go ahead."

Mom motioned that she wasn't up to it. Antoine took over; he gathered the kids around him as if preparing to tell a bedtime story and spoke very seriously: "Yes, Benjamin is right. Grandpa is dead. His heart stopped today, but we'll meet him again in Heaven. He's looking down at us now."

The four little ones searched our eyes, to figure out whether they should be crying or if it was still Christmas and in spite of everything they'd be allowed to have fun.

"We'll never see him again?" asked Sophie.

Antoine shook his head.

"Never, ever?" Melanie chimed in.

She almost sang the words. She didn't really know what that nasty word meant, the opposite of *always,* which it resembles like a brother: words without end, nights without dawn, deep holes. And the day they do find out, they'll become, like everyone else, lost children inside, fragile adults, potential corpses.

Meanwhile, the Christmas tree, in front of the window, shone with all its might. My father had picked it out . . . as always. A nursery tree, of course, with the roots, so that after the holidays we could plant it at the back of the yard with its older brothers and feel that we were bringing it back to life. Somewhere church bells rang: no midnight Mass tonight. Instead we'd keep watch here with him.

Benjamin had calmed down. Sheltered in Pauline's arms, he eyed his cousins resentfully. Slightly intimidated, Gabriel raised a finger to ask a question. Claire, still locked inside herself, clenched her quivering lips. Antoine leaned toward his son with all his strength, all his tenderness: "Go ahead, hon."

"Will we still have Christmas dinner tonight?" Gabriel asked.

We had the *foie gras* with toast points, the poached salmon, the *bûche de Noël*. We drew the line at champagne, though. The table was set up, with every leaf added, in the middle of the living room, and Bernadette insisted on the best china and the embroidered tablecloth that's not machine-washable and costs a fortune to have laundered. We managed to talk and make some plans. The children kept us going; we were doing it for them and because he would have wanted it that way, we thought. But I felt ashamed to be so hungry and to eat in spite of everything, especially when Mom seemed to be in another world, somewhere off with him, returning to us now and then with a bewildered expression, as if she'd been hit from behind, saying, "I can't get over it."

When the cleanup started, I went up to see him. I needed to be alone with him, without witnesses, without a role to play. I forced myself to look at him as someone gone, lost. I was attracted: since it has to end that way, why not go right ahead? I told him what was on my mind, that you don't desert people in midflight, you don't break a contract, a contract for life. Now what was I going to do without him? And why was death on my case like this? It hadn't even been a month since Tanguy.

I saw myself talking to him. At any rate, what we say is always for ourselves, but you don't notice it until you're with a dead person. It was just my imagination that his chest was rising, his eyelids moving. It was because of the flickering candles and because he was still alive inside me and I could hear his voice ordering me, "Be quiet," telling me, "Get up!"

The phone rang; someone answered downstairs. I glanced at the extension by the bed and felt like putting it to his ear so there would be one last time. He hadn't had any "last times," and now we were going to have all the first times without him.

Then I told him I loved him, and I said it without any qualifiers, no "so much" or "really." I said it straight, the way a woman does to a man when she wants his protection, his eyes on her, and his two arms to hold her. After that, I touched my lips to his for the first and last time, and at that moment Pauline walked in, sent up to make sure I wasn't committing hara-kiri over my father's body. She must have had the shock of her life. His lips were frozen. Without speaking, she stared first at me, then at him.

"I wanted to do that, too," she said.

After we let the kids check their stockings for the thousandth time, we piled them all into Bernadette's room and came back up to arrange the presents. The twins had asked for tool kits, Gabriel for a doll and doll clothes, Benjamin for books and a calculator. Although their parents had all done their best, there would certainly be some disappointments, but that would teach them about life: if there's nothing left to wish for you get too self-centered, and you're a good candidate for the psychiatrist's couch.

It was Bernadette who hung up Daddy's stocking. She made a big pile of his presents and said, "We'll put them all out and give them to Roughly Speaking."

Then, from Claire's room, there was a strange noise, a

sort of affectionate, surprised complaint. Claire blushed to the roots of her hair. She quickly explained, "My present for Daddy. I couldn't leave him out in the car. I was afraid he'd die of the cold." And as she said the word *die* she turned practically purple, though we all pretended not to notice. Now we heard jumping and scratching at the door. "Bring him down," said Mom.

His name was Prince. Prince Rami, with real royal bloodlines. His father was a great hunter. His mother had carried off blue ribbons in dog shows. There were three signs of his pure breeding: when you pulled back his ears, they reached clear around his head; his teeth were perfect; and his tail was stiff to the end. He was a long-haired dachshund, solid-colored, complete with shots and papers. Only, Claire was worried because for the time being he couldn't be shown; his testicles hadn't descended. If they didn't within six months, the vet would operate. We'd see.

He bolted all over the living room, washed everyone's face (starting with the mouth), gnawed hands all around, scattered the presents. He hid under the table, got his paws tangled in the lamp cord, and burned his muzzle trying to get an ember. He looked at everything as if it all belonged to him, as if nothing was forbidden or impossible. He was young.

"I thought he'd help Daddy relax," Claire murmured. "And besides, I don't know if any of you have noticed, but he smiles!"

And when Mom laughed, reading *Prince Rami Moreau* on the tag on his collar and seeing his mouth part in what did indeed look like a smile, the Princess was finally ready to cry.

39

The Burgundy Contingent

GRANDMOTHER! She got in at four that afternoon,
blind with rage because Aunt Nicole and Great-Uncle
Alexis had made her lie down in back for the whole trip,
complete with pillow, blanket, and hot-water bottle. At
the house, a sad gathering, calling hours, pinching hand-
shakes, and teary kisses. The five of us in a line: one-way
traffic, please. With the arrival of the Burgundy contingent,
the smell of garlic filled the living room: Henriette, the
old family retainer, had packed a lunch.

Grandmother wore the pearl-gray suit that also served
for weddings. She went straight to Mom, took her by her
two arms, looked deep into her, into her heart, and declared, "Thirty years with a man like that is something they
can't take away, Mattie. It's like money in the bank, and
you can live on it, you'll see." Mom answered, in a little
girl's voice, "Thirty years wasn't enough." That pushed
Grandmother over the edge. She turned to those present
and took them as witnesses: why hadn't God called her
instead, well into her eighties and of no use to anyone?
Had he forgotten her? Then she led her daughter out of
the room, and I think it did Mom good to obey.

We'd left the tree up, with its ornaments, tinsel, and big

star at the top. At the foot we put a picture of the departed, and people glanced at it sidelong, wondering whether it was such a good idea. The kids were at Roughly Speaking's. Unloading the presents on him was really hitting below the belt. He'd rather have gone without the handsome turtleneck sweater, the books, the records, the checkered hat Benjamin had picked out. His arms, his eyes overflowed; the thanks were on us.

The funeral was set for the following morning in Mareuil. We had a family plot in the village cemetery, on the good side, not the side that gets fumes from the garbage dump. Lefranc's Funeral Home handled everything; they sent two guys in dark suits who played their role so well that Mrs. Cadillac took them for relatives and expressed her sincere sympathy, which they accepted solemnly.

There would be a religious ceremony. Even if my father hadn't believed in God, he had approved. He'd said that was what was best in us and that it was better to live with your eyes raised upward. Jean-René was on the scene the minute he heard the news, and he put in his two cents: Charles had gone on to a better life. That seemed to make everyone feel better. But I wanted him in this life, right now, in my arms, beneath my lips, the way he was and not only in spirit. With his faded eyes, so tender that you drowned in them, his shattered back, and his heart that had so secretly tired of beating.

"Come here a second," Aunt Nicole said. "I need some help."

I followed her into kitchen. She had taken over the catering department as soon as she arrived, and now there was always something cooking.

"Pile two dozen eggs into this bowl, and try not to break them, will you?"

As I followed her orders, she carefully unwrapped the foil from two fat brown truffles.

"We'll put these in with the eggs, cover the bowl, and tomorrow we'll have an omelet that's out of this world."

And tomorrow came. The family was assembled in the living room, ready to leave for the church, which was already filling up with connections, friends, neighbors, and the medical profession. All five of us were in black. Claire had put on some lipstick. Antoine went to Mom, who looked much nicer now that her hair had deflated; she stood as straight as she could.

"If it's all right with you, Paul and Stephan and I will be the pallbearers. We don't want to leave it to outsiders. Could we ask Tavernier to be the fourth one?"

Great-Uncle Alexis got to his feet so fast that he knocked over his cane.

"So that makes me an outsider, I suppose?"

"*You* will escort my daughter," declared Grandmother.

That was when Bernadette got up and stood square in front of Antoine.

"I want to be the fourth one," she declared. "I'll carry him with you."

Our brother-in-law was flabbergasted. Mom looked at her daughter wide-eyed. Now Claire got up, furious.

"I'm the oldest. It's not fair. I can be a pallbearer, too. I'm certainly strong enough."

Pauline and I exchanged a glance. She nodded. I said "The four of us will be the pallbearers. End of discussion."

Total silence. We heard footsteps up in the bedroom where the subject of the discussion lay. Mom stared at us as Daddy often had: in disbelief.

"Listen," Antoine said calmly. "You'll never make it; it will be too heavy."

"We can still try," said Pauline. "If we can't do it, you can help us."

"But it's something women never do!" Stephan protested.

Bernadette turned on him with a withering look: "Of course not! Women are only good for lighting candles, picking out wreaths, and pouring the coffee."

"You mean," Claire said in a quivering voice, "women are allowed to drive buses, fly planes, even go to the moon, but we still can't carry our father to the foot of the altar?"

"Let them," Mom said. "Please let them."

They would lift our father onto our shoulders, and we would take him into the church where his favorite music was playing. We could do it! We were the ones who had always carried the boat down to the Oise when spring came, before the husbands had come along to play captain. The four of us would carry him to the foot of the altar, before God and man: Moreau, Charles André Maurice, thanks to whom we were alive, and would be for quite a while yet, according to statistics.

"And if people don't like it, to hell with them," Grandmother confided piously to our smiling Prince.

40

Leave La Marette?

TAKE A WHIFF of these eggs now," Nicole ordered, uncovering the bowl, "and tell me if I was wrong."

I ran my nose over the shells. It was true! They had soaked up the smell of truffles.

"Smells great! Where did you get truffles?"

"From Georges. Remember? The fellow from Uzès. He sent me them for Christmas. I heard the whole Post Office smelled of them. They placed bets on which package it was."

Georges . . . one of my aunt's suitors. Too bad she wouldn't marry him: we'd have a lifetime supply of truffles. We'd go gather them near Uzès with the sun and the song of locusts.

The puppy slipped into the kitchen; he questioned us with a wag of his princely tail.

"Do you think I could train him to hunt for truffles?"

Like Georges's dog. With a bit of luck, our take would pay for the trip south. With Prince's breeding, he had to be a good hunter.

Aunt Nicole contemplated our aristocratic midget, who was smiling his widest in hopes of gleaning some goodies.

"You don't need a prince to hunt truffles," she said.

196

"Any old mongrel will do. Want to know how they do it?"

"Oh yes."

I wanted to hear about walks through tall oaks, about good brown soil other than the kind you scatter on coffins.

"You take a jar," Nicole began. "You fill it with dog biscuits and add some truffle shavings, then you screw the top on tight. As soon as the biscuits smell like truffles, you give one to your apprentice truffle-hunter."

"And the dog likes it?"

"He loves it! Dogs aren't dumb. So you give him one biscuit a day until he can't live without his treat. Then one afternoon you wave one under the dog's nose and you go bury it by a green oak. Then you let night fall and the sun rise with the dog's expectations. In the morning, you take him out and show him where to dig for it. Repeat the exercise as often as possible. No more jar; he has to dig for his treat. And one fine morning, what does he find you? A truffle. The smell of his biscuit multiplied by a hundred."

"And he eats it?"

"Certainly not," said Nicole. "A black fungus doesn't look like anything to him. Except for the smell, it's nothing like his dog biscuit. So you take the truffle and reward him with his treat as usual. And there you have it."

"It doesn't sound too hard."

Nicole grinned. "Child's play! And after two or three years, your dog is trained."

She picked up Prince by the scruff of the neck and kissed him on the snout before setting him on my lap. "Unfortunately, this isn't truffle territory, and your royal highness here has to watch his weight."

Ground meat and carrots twice a day. He lapped it down in three mouthfuls and whined at our feet all day for seconds.

"Daddy's favorite way to eat truffles was with noodles."

"A man of taste," Grandmother declared in a thundering

voice, making her entry into the kitchen. "Noodles set off the texture and flavor; only, people are afraid to mix simplicity with luxury, even though that's what makes the best marriages."

She sat down at the table next to me. Prince immediately jumped to the lap of this more comfortable person. True, dogs aren't dumb! We watched Nicole peeling onions for her casserole: everyone was staying to dinner tonight. Now Mom walked in. She'd changed, put on gray pants, a sweater. She'd barely sat down when a knock came at the back door. It was Roughly Speaking. His wife wanted the kids to have dinner over there: there was a program on TV about mountain climbing, and Gabriel was fascinated. We agreed. "Sit down for a minute . . . Poppy," Grandmother suggested. Scarlet-faced, "Poppy" was already at the table. I put some water on for tea fanciers.

Claire stuck her head in to see who was there, disappeared, and came back with Bernadette and Pauline, all three of them looking resolute. Something was up.

"If you agree," Bernadette declared to Mom, "we all want to spend summer vacation here once the kids are out of school. The guys will come out after work. It'll do the kids good to get out of the city."

Mom looked at the three of them, then her eyes returned to her hands, stretched flat on the table.

"And then what?"

My heart seemed to stop. I looked at my sisters, like statues. What did she mean, "And then what"?

"This big house . . . for two people . . . ," she continued.

"Not for two, for twelve!" Bernadette protested. "Don't forget we're all here every weekend."

Roughly Speaking moved to get up. Grandmother held him back with a firm grip on his wrist. He slumped back into his chair and buried his face in his teacup.

Now the husbands walked in from the yard. Dead silence in the kitchen: the only sound was the stream of water Aunt Nicole was running over the onions to keep from crying while she peeled them. The men looked at us without understanding what was going on. Bernadette and Claire were frozen solid; I felt my temples pounding like they do when I'm sick. Leave La Marette? Is that what she meant? Impossible. The house was our roots, our blood, and all we had left of him. My father had loved this house! He'd made so many things: the shelving, the bookcases, the record cabinets. None of which we could use, because no matter how good he was with his hands when it came to patients, as a handyman he was all thumbs.

"Forty-three hundred square feet," Mom continued in a blank voice. "Six bedrooms, cellar, attic, an acre of grounds . . ."

Antoine got the picture. "Don't you think it's a little soon to talk about all this?"

Mom raised her eyes to him; they shone with tears. "Not when I can't stop thinking about it."

"If it's a question of money," Bernadette declared, "we'll figure something out."

"If you're worried about the garden," murmured Tavernier, "I can handle all that, roughly speaking."

"As far as taxes go," Stephan observed, "remember, the house is in your name."

Mom still stared at her hands as if from now on they'd be useless. Paul was the only one who hadn't said a word. He gazed at her intensely, and I had the feeling that inside him he was writing something the rest of us hadn't felt yet.

"Here," Mom said defiantly, "everything reminds me of him."

"I'm glad it does!" I said. "I hope it lasts!"

Mom threw back her head and looked at me. I lowered

my eyes. All of a sudden I felt cold. Why was she looking at me that way? What had I done wrong? What had I done to her?

"I'll sleep in your bed with you tonight if you want me to," Pauline offered in a tiny voice.

"The bed, his desk, the books, the furniture, the walls, the air, absolutely everything," Mom said in the same defiant tone.

Claire's chin trembled. Antoine put an arm around her shoulder.

"Everyone reacts differently to a loss," he said. "Some people need a change of scenery. That doesn't mean they're trying to forget."

"You see," said Grandmother, "with certain kinds of ink, when you try to erase it, it only makes things worse. It smears, it ruins the whole page. I've always thought you can't erase what's been truly written into your life. It will stay with you, whether you're here or somewhere else."

We didn't even hear Alexis come in from his tour of the grounds, mud up to his knees. Now there were a dozen of us in the kitchen, which fortunately was designed for it. According to my father, the most important room in the house — the warmest room, where we had all lived our childhood in some way.

Alexis set his cap on the refrigerator.

"Your garden is looking rather strange, if I may say so," he declared. "There are some plants, you really wonder what on earth they could be and how they got there."

"Don't you know?" said Bernadette with a laugh that seemed to split her chest. "Because Daddy put them there! He mixed everything up, and his specialty was planting bulbs upside down."

"And we were all informed that next spring we'd just have to see what came up," Pauline joined in.

Mom looked at her, then at Bernadette, then at Claire,

then even at me. She seemed to be asking us a question, the way you ask something when you don't want to know the answer.

"If you leave this house," Claire said in a hollow voice, "I warn you that it will tear all our hearts out, starting with yours."

Mom didn't answer right away, but her face seemed to clear.

"I think I needed to hear that," she said. "You understand, it seemed so impractical. . . ."

Her eyes toured the kitchen walls. "He wanted to paint the kitchen. I'll have to get to that."

Aunt Nicole asked for volunteers to grate cheese. There were enough onions in the sink for an army, and despite the copiously running water our eyes stung. Grandmother had more tea over the stated objection of Alexis, whose pipe Bernadette had commandeered. The husbands had helped themselves to beer. Pauline organized an expedition to the woodpile for the living room fireplace. Roughly Speaking, it seemed, had gone off his rocker. He got up, sat back down, promised Prince a yard worthy of his lineage, and laughed too loud, as if he'd had the fright of his life and was now so relieved that his feelings were about to explode and couldn't find a proper way out. He finally gave Grandmother a big hug and exited, clutching his handkerchief.

Then the phone rang. Stephan answered. It was for me, someone named Emmanuel.

~~ 41 ~~

Shattering the Magic

CECILE," he said, "is that you?"
  I answered yes. I didn't remember his voice being so deep; I had been so sure I would never hear it again.

"Where are you?"

"By a lake," he answered. "In an empty, snow-covered hotel where magic happened one night."

I couldn't say a word. I had so many things to tell him. It was too late, too late for everything.

"I hear you tried to reach me while I was away," he said. "In Africa. But that's another story. You said it was urgent?"

"Not anymore," I said. "It's all over. If you want to know, I ran out of choices. Out of paths. But anyway that doesn't matter now. They're all dead!"

Pauline came in with her load of kindling, followed by Stephan, carrying huge logs. I turned toward the wall. On the other end of the line, silence. What was he waiting for? For me to bare my soul again? I was through with that. It only makes you weaker. Pauline and Stephan tiptoed out.

"Listen," he said.

I was crying. I'd been holding up pretty well, and now this jerk was making it all spill out, the same as the night we'd met. His voice brought everything back: the slumbering hotel, the awning slapping at the window just hard enough to make us feel protected, and the feeling of being truly listened to, seen, understood. The warmth. The whole of that fantastic night when I thought I was so miserable and yet Tanguy was still alive, my father was still alive, when I thought I had choices but the die was already cast and the cadavers tagged.

"Cecile, what is it?"

"Who told you my name?"

"Martin," he said. "Martin and Beatrice. They never stopped talking about the Moreaus after you left, about Pauline, the Pest — "

"No!"

I hung up. Everything was spoiled. No more magic. No more dreams. My throat burned. I hated him, for the hope he'd given me, for how much I'd leaned on him since that trip. Every time things went wrong, I'd summoned his voice. I had been glad he worked for a relief organization; it had helped me. I repeated his words: "You'll make the best of things." Only yesterday . . . he never should have called.

The phone rang again. I got Pauline. "Tell this guy I never want to talk to him again." I galloped up the stairs, my hands over my ears.

"Cecile," Antoine said. "Are you in there?"

He paused in the doorway to my room, spotted me in the dark, and came to sit down on the bed, next to me. His hand sought out my cheek. I huddled against the wall, burrowed in the smell of the wallpaper. One image I couldn't get out of my mind: my father coming to Tavernier's bomb shelter to tell me Tanguy was dead. The dark circles under his eyes: he had looked so tired. At his age, deep fatigue on a face looks the same as despair. How I hadn't wanted to go back outside, back to life. How with all the strength

203

of his will, he had forced me to get up: "On your feet now!" How he had carried me.

Antoine's hand persisted, discovered tears:

"Sweetheart . . ." The first time he'd ever called me anything like that. What was the matter with him? Was he going to kill me with kindness?

"I don't need you to replace him," I said. "Don't go to all this trouble. Save your strength for my mother."

"I'm not going to any trouble," he said. "I just wanted to be with you. Any objection?"

"So long as you don't tell me I'll get over it."

I didn't want to get over it, ever. I wanted to keep my father alive in me, burning and painful. I owed him that much.

"When you have heart trouble," I said, "I suppose too much stress is bad for you."

"Your father didn't have heart trouble per se," he said. "And stressful things happen to everyone, no matter how hard you might try to avoid them."

He lit a cigarette. I went to get him an ashtray from the mantel, next to the big pine cone. That was part of our trip to the mountains, too; it was Emmanuel.

"Why is my mother mad at me? Did you see the way she looked at me in the kitchen?"

"I didn't notice anything," he said. "How was she looking at you?"

"As if she was accusing me of something. I wonder what."

"You know," Antoine said, "when something very painful happens, you're mad at the world. Because you realize no one can do much for you."

Downstairs, a regular ruckus: they were getting the table set. It might as well be a holiday. What an idea, to die at Christmastime!

"I've decided I want to be a nurse," I said. "I talked it

over with Daddy, and he thought it was a good idea. I want to start right away. Even if all I do is empty bedpans and change bandages. Can you help me?"

He laughed. "Sure! But maybe not first thing tomorrow."

I looked him right in the eye: "It won't be easy to run La Marette with a widow and an old maid."

He blinked. I surprised him? That's what happened when I stopped acting like the Pest. I picked up the pine cone. When I felt bad, I liked to look at it; it had become a habit. I'd hold it and dream of someone who'd seen me differently, not as a Moreau, not as the Pest. As myself.

"Past time for dinner," Antoine said. "And Nicole says she won't make the omelet without her truffle helper. You're holding everyone up."

He got up and looked me over. I asked, "Are my eyes all right?"

"With a little water, they'll be fine."

He started down the stairs. "Antoine!" He wheeled around. I threw the pine cone to him.

"Do me a favor and toss this thing in the fire, will you? Just another dust collector. You don't even notice that it's dead."

～ 42 ～

Rags to Riches

MOM LAUGHED. Sitting on the rug, she laughed until she cried in front of the open closet, the one where we kept all the sporting gear used only on occasion: skis and boating equipment, wet suits, slickers, fins, snorkels. Behind the row of ski boots, carefully wrapped in a plastic bag, she'd just discovered all the old clothes Daddy had sworn he'd gotten rid of: worn shirts, threadbare pants, an antique bathrobe, sweaters . . .

For three days now we'd been sorting the dear departed's things. Do it right away, we'd been advised, or you end up keeping everything. We made two piles: clothing in good enough condition to be given to friends, and stuff some people might welcome but we didn't dare offer because it had seen better days and they might be offended. Sometimes one of us was a taker. I wanted all his sweaters, but I couldn't swear I'd ever be seen wearing them: wool is what holds odors best.

"It's hopeless, a man like that," Mom said, contemplating the find. "Simply hopeless. It's all here. He never got rid of a thing."

It would take months of convincing to get him to give up an article of clothing. The negotiations began every

206

year at fall cleaning time: "Listen, darling, you haven't even worn this jacket for three years. All it's doing in here is attracting moths. . . ." And Charles, discomfited, would head out, bundle in hand, to the pile of dead leaves at the back of the yard; he said he'd rather incinerate his old faithful servants than throw them out with the household garbage. And here they were again, every single one of them, carefully folded and bundled in plastic.

"He really pulled one over on us," Claire allowed.

"Everything else," said Mom, "I'll be able to get rid of, but this, this useless stuff, I don't think I have the heart."

Pauline rummaged in the pile and extracted a sweater with so many openings that you couldn't tell which way it went on.

"But what was he planning to do with all of this?" she asked in amazement. "He knew he'd never wear any of it again."

"He couldn't throw things away, it's as simple as that," Mom explained. "His family was very poor. They lived from hand to mouth. So they saved everything — they might need it."

"Then how did he pay for medical school?" Bernadette asked, astonished.

"Scholarships. And I think a relative helped him. He didn't like to talk about it."

It was true my father never talked about "before": before Mom, before us, before La Marette. It was as if he'd blanked it out. Sometimes a word or phrase would hint at it, or his horror of wasting food, or the way he looked at the homeless in the streets, a furious look, unable to accept that such poverty still existed.

"If only we'd known," murmured Pauline. "We would have loved him even more."

Sitting on the floor, around stacks of ragged old clothes, the four of us observed a moment of silence, celebrating a wonderful man named Charles. Mom leaned against the wall; she looked straight ahead, at her loneliness.

"The hard part," she murmured, "is all the 'first times.' The first time you open a drawer, or eat something he liked, or look at one of his things . . . the first trip out to the orchard, the first walk. And soon it will be the first spring, the first berries he loved so much. It's a little like being born again, differently, painfully, into a darker world."

Tears ran down her cheeks; her eyes were closed. I felt so bad. I couldn't breathe. I wished I could say "I'm sorry." It was just after Tanguy died. My father came up to my room. Suddenly he seemed short of breath. He raised a hand to his heart. I asked, "Are you all right?" He answered, "It's nothing."

"All right, babe?"

Bernadette looked at me, worried. I was fine! Unlike some, I'd live.

Then Mom put the bag back in the closet. She wiped her eyes, stood up, smiled gravely at my sisters.

"It's been great to have you here with me, but it's time for you to be going home. You belong with your husbands, and I'll have to get used to living alone."

It was Friday; they'd leave Sunday night after dinner, as always. It would be the second Sunday without him. "Live alone," Mom had said. What about me?

Pauline stuck her head into my room.

"Cecile, I forgot something. Bea wants us to get together tomorrow night. We'll meet at her place, go to a movie. How about it?"

43

Emmanuel

I RECOGNIZED his voice right away, in the hallway, without even seeing him: an unusual voice, somewhat muted, almost restrained. Martin's voice answered him. They laughed. I froze: I'd been lured into a trap.

"Hi, guys," said Beatrice. "Everyone's here now but Paul. We've been trying to pick a film. We can't agree."

She led us into the living room. The two of them were standing by the window; he was taller than I remembered, darker, too. They came over to us, and Martin gave me a scratchy kiss on the cheek.

"This is Emmanuel," Bea said, "another mountain man. Martin's cousin. He's a doctor with Save the Children. Take a good look; you won't see much of him. He's always in Africa, and I hear his patients number in the millions."

"He's heard so much about the Moreau sisters that he wanted to meet you," Martin explained.

"Too bad he missed the man of the family," I remarked.

He shook my hand. There was just a small, happy flicker in his eyes to remind me. This was no trap: Emmanuel hadn't told them. No one else in this room knew that one windy night, in the lounge of a slumbering hotel, without even knowing his name, I'd told him my deepest secrets.

I asked Bea if I could use the bathroom, and I locked myself in. I didn't know what to do with myself: out-and-out panic. I wanted to run away, hide, and at the same time I was scared to death of hurting his feelings, even though he meant nothing to me, had disappointed me.

A knock at the door: "Open up," Pauline ordered. I obeyed and shut the door quickly behind her. She looked at me disapprovingly. "What's the matter? Are you sick, or what?"

"I don't feel so great," I confessed. "I think I'd better not go out with you after all."

"Oh no you don't," said my sister indignantly. "You're not going to get out of it that easily. It's not fair to back out on people. You're coming with us, Cecile."

I moaned, "Don't you see how awful I look?"

That was a foregone conclusion: washed-out face, stringy hair, red nose, thick legs. All that was missing was the glasses I'd need at the movie.

"Awful?" Pauline said. "You dope! Look at yourself! You have the world's most beautiful eyes, and the sweetest mouth."

"That's what they say to girls who don't have anything else. You might as well tell me I'm fun to be with."

It didn't get a laugh.

"I'm not the one who says so. It's Paul. If you weren't my sister, I'd be jealous. Do you know he described you in one of his stories? Something like 'superb eyes that both hold you at a distance and call for help, a woman's lips with a childish pout to them . . .' "

"The body of a diseased toad . . ."

This time she burst out laughing.

"Come here, toad."

She pulled me over beside her, in front of the mirror.

I was ten times shorter and weighed a hundred pounds more. I looked at the woman's lips that no man had really kissed yet and the eyes that were probably calling for help because no one had noticed their charms.

"I'd take your chest," Pauline said. "Do you think it's any fun being flat as a board? I'd take your waist and hips, too. I always wanted an hourglass figure. I'll keep my legs, though, if you don't mind. You can't have everything."

"What about my feet?"

"We all got Daddy's feet, and we'd never get a hand for them," she said, "since you seem to need to make a joke of everything. And now, why don't you tell me what's going on?"

I turned my back to the mirror: "Do you think it was fair for Daddy to check out while I was still Daddy's little girl? I'm not sure I'll ever trust men."

The bell rang in the front hall just in the nick of time to spare us a heavy scene. Pauline's face lit up: "There's my man. And if you must know, it was hard to get him to trust me. But I did, didn't I? Now, I'll give you two minutes to clear out of here, or I'll tell them everything."

"What do you mean, everything?"

She left without answering. I tried to clean up around my exquisite eyes, which were looking a little grimy at the moment; I flushed the toilet as an alibi and went back to the living room. In the end, Bea picked the movie. It was showing just down the street. She grabbed me by the arm, wearing an up-to-no-good expression.

"Guess what, little girl? Now that you're legal, I'm taking you to an adults-only movie to celebrate."

It had gotten fairly good reviews, and the theater was full of hypocrites, thrilled not to have to slink in. Most of the time the set was minimal: a room, a bed. Costumes certainly didn't set the budget back much. As for the dialogue, it was "Yes," "No," "Again," the rest in heavy breathing, moans, and cries, depending on what was going on as the lighting and focus changed.

The theater was silent. But I was ashamed. Ashamed of being there, of watching this awful thing, and of putting my glasses on to see it!

I took them off and closed my eyes. Now all I needed was for my father to be in the picture. He came thundering in, as if to ask, "What on earth are you doing here?" It was my first movie since his death and my first X-rated one to boot. "All the first times . . . ," Mom had said. Nice combination.

"Are you all right?" Emmanuel asked.

He tried to look in my eyes.

"I just feel a little down. It's nothing."

He leaned over to Bea, spoke to her, then got up: "Come on!" I followed him.

The decorations were still up along the avenue, oblivious to the fact that people who hadn't had a very merry Christmas had no need of an extension. It was Saturday, the night everyone goes out, and there were people everywhere. The air was icy, but it felt good: breathing deeply, I felt cleansed of the film's moist, hairy, slimy images.

"To tell the truth, I hate that kind of film," said Emmanuel.

"They must be fun to make, but I'm not sure they should be shown."

He looked surprised. I turned my eyes away: my private life is no one's business.

We went into an English pub, long and narrow, with a luxury train decor, and we sat down in the last car.

"What would you like to drink?"

I asked for a Scotch, which earned me another astonished look. He picked his brand of beer, the waiter left, and we were alone again. There were lamps on each table, frosted mirrors, carpeting. Silence choked me. I'd have to wait for later tonight, in my bed, to enjoy this moment and decide whether it had been good. It was always like that; I was incapable of living in the present.

He looked around. "You know, when I'm away, it's hard to believe that a place like this exists."

"Away?"

"Somewhere in Africa, Asia. Where the choices are simple."

Life or death. He started to tell me about his relief work. He spent most of the time in refugee camps. When they got there, most often they found nothing. No hospital, of course, but no safe water either, no food, no medicine: nothing but a rotting, dying corral full of people. So before they could practice medicine they had to act as construction workers, carpenters, welders, electricians. The rest of the time he was a surgeon.

He spoke with a great deal of calm and warmth, looking as though he had hope in spite of everything.

I asked, "Why did you decide to go there?"

A slight smile: "In one of the countries where I work, there's a road the people call the route of hope. It's the one we arrive on. There has to be someone to come down that road."

I looked at his hands. They were very long, slender and strong at the same time. I imagined them inside a body, removing death. I wished they would touch me.

"Now I have a confession to make. Sometimes when you're in the field it's hard to get to sleep, so you call someone to the rescue: your mother, your wife, an actress, a singer, anyone. I didn't call on anyone but a girl who popped up, in a strange-looking nightshirt . . ."

I stuck my nose in my glass. I can't stand compliments.

When I get one, I always feel as though it was meant for someone else.

"A girl named Cecile."

I looked up at him:

"You can call me the Pest. Everyone does."

He stretched out a hand to cover mine. A few seconds earlier I was wishing he'd touch me, and now I wished I was a hundred miles away.

"Beatrice told me about your father."

"Mom is the one it's really hard on. I'm doing all right."

He paused a moment. I took the opportunity to finish my drink, which gave me an excuse to pull my hand away.

"And the guy you were telling me about?"

I said, "He shot himself." He didn't comment. Just as he had that night in the mountains, he waited for me to continue. But that night was over, and so were the days when I was a happy, lighthearted girl. Now, suddenly, I was filled with an immense desire to be back there with him, the same as that night, with open choices, innocence. And the desire to go back was unbearable. I could never go back. I couldn't bring anyone back.

He asked, "Did you love him?" And in a way that saved me. I answered yes, said it was mutual, the real thing. Untouched though I was, I heard myself talking as if I'd made love with Tanguy. I fled on a raft of words, away from these dangerous shores. But hadn't it been love when he'd bent to kiss me at La Marette, when I'd heard him breathe differently, seen his eyes change? It had been, because I'd only have had to say yes. Tanguy had wanted me, as I was; I hadn't had to try, like Pauline had. That was what I wanted to hold on to. It's all right to pick and choose among memories. It was my business if I was holding on to dreams and not reality.

He listened, his face serious, chin resting on his hand. What was he expecting? That I'd collapse onto his shoulder and tell him that I'd killed them both and I'd never forgive myself?

I went on to tell him that I'd promised myself not to forget Tanguy, to be faithful to him. And as I talked I felt as though I was raising walls to protect myself. From whom? From myself?

~ 44 ~

Three Months Already

I THREW MYSELF into my nursing studies. My aptitude tests were promising, my language skills were adequate, and the interview went well. Behind the desk, one of the doctors questioning me had known Dr. Moreau. That was certainly worth a few extra points — thanks, Daddy!

Each day when I walked through the hospital door, the door to a wealth of suffering, I felt I had found a refuge. These walls also protected me. Behind them the world held its breath. Everything seemed filtered through white, sounds seemed distant, things smelled different, even food had a different taste.

In the morning I had classes. In the afternoon we worked with patients: taking temperatures, giving sponge baths, changing sheets. When I went into a room, people's eyes called to me as if from the bottom of a well, eager for a bit of light. I dove into them. I drowned myself in them; if I could have, I would have slept at the hospital.

"Relax!" Pauline told me, concerned. "Slow down a little, babe. We never see you anymore. You're always over there or else hitting the books. What's the story with you? You're studying to be a nurse, not a nun!"

And I liked putting on my white uniform, leaving my

usual clothes in the closet. I became anyone, everyone, no one. Quiet, hospital zone!

Mom was working hard, too. Her volunteer days were over. She was taking an accelerated course to become a medical secretary. In a year she'd be qualified. She had no choice — she needed the income.

At La Marette, the hardest part was mealtimes. We ate in the kitchen, facing each other, and I thought of the old days, when there had been six of us around the dining room table, when he was still around and she would laugh at nothing in particular. She forced herself to talk to me, to keep up with what I was doing. I had trouble answering. I could see that she was in a hurry to get up to her room, too, although no one was waiting . . . no one who still thought she was pretty, perhaps would touch her, call her "my woman" as he sometimes had, sounding like a "shameless male chauvinist," according to Bernadette.

Speaking of Daddy, we learned he had left a letter willing each of us some money. Not a ton of it, but still . . . The will was dated December 6, a week after Tanguy's death; a week after he had clutched at his heart up in my room. Tanguy, his heart, a last will — had Mom made the connection? She must have. Last night I'd felt her looking at me hard: she seemed hesitant to talk. I waited for her verdict to fall, but nothing happened.

Three months already! The days grew longer. Spring hurt. My father wouldn't see it. I preferred the night.

Emmanuel called. I wasn't home. He left his number. What did he want from me? I had nothing left to say to him. I found even the memory of his hand on mine paralyzing.

Melodie found a boyfriend. They made love. She didn't think it was so great, but she hoped things would improve. He wanted it all the time; she didn't. At one time we had done a lot of research on the subject together. We had bought magazines. It had cost us a fortune because we'd buried the one we were really after in a pile of others. We'd worn scarves and dark glasses. We had felt guilty; it was great. Melodie had gotten a magnifying glass to study the important details more closely. An old house has more hiding places than an apartment, so I had had to keep them all. The day Mom almost stumbled on them, I'd dumped our whole collection into a neighbor's garbage can. I hope it didn't cause Mr. Chopin any problems, but his wife sure did look grumpy the next day.

Benjamin had been having problems. He was a loner, anxious, nervous — "asocial," Pauline said, since she likes to be technical. Almost every night he woke up crying; he said he saw death by his bed, a black shape trying to swallow him up. The doctor put him on tranquilizers.

Fear of death, a stage most children go through. Benjamin was just a little ahead of the timetable. But it should abate as he grew older. He'd have less time to think.

I went into town to baby-sit for him while his parents went out for the evening. If death put in an appearance tonight, it would have to answer to me.

45

My Friend Gregory

I HAD JUST turned off the television and was settling down on the couch I call home while I'm baby-sitting Ben, when I heard a noise: high, whiny, electronic beeping. I turned on the light.

It seemed to be coming from the study at the end of the hall: a small room that was more like an upgraded closet, populated with books and files, that Paul uses when he needs to be by himself. Pauline calls it his confessional.

It couldn't be my brother-in-law, because he was visiting friends thirty miles from Paris and wouldn't be back until the next morning. I got up and took a look in Benjamin's room: his bed was empty, so there was my answer. What could he be up to in the confessional when he should have been asleep in bed?

That was indeed where the sound was coming from; light filtered through the bottom of the door. I turned the knob very slowly, in case he was sleepwalking, and went in. His back was to me. He was much too busy to hear me.

He was sitting in front of Gregory, the brains of the household, Paul's computer. Since buying it the year before, Paul had found it indispensable for his work: word processing, accounts, the budget. But it can also be used for fun. Paul and Pauline owned all kinds of computer games, even a few for Benjamin. Anything goes!

Ben was playing one of them. I inched closer. It wasn't one of his own games — computer tennis, soccer, or ping-pong. He'd chosen a grown-up math game, a tough one. Gregory would secretly think of a number; his opponent had to find out what it was by naming another number, with the computer adding or subtracting that one from the right answer. I tried it once: I crashed.

Ben's hands flew over the keyboard: one number after another flashed on the screen. My word, he was confusing the machine with a piano, it was going to short-circuit! I was about to stop him when Gregory began to applaud.

You win, Benjamin! appeared on the screen. *Want to play again?*

My head swam. I was dreaming! He couldn't have won. He was only four, too young even for arithmetic. He hit a key with his index finger: the word *yes* appeared on the monitor. *I'm thinking of a number,* Gregory answered. *Concentrate and get ready to ask me questions.* Ben prepared by closing his eyes for three seconds. Then he raised his finger like an orchestra conductor lifting his baton, ready for his first turn.

"Wait a minute," I said.

He whirled around, saw me, and burst into tears. Total despair. I took him in my arms and rocked him to calm him down. He looked scared to death. And I'm no monster, not death. What on earth was the matter?

"They'll sell him now," he hiccuped. "They'll sell Gregory."

I finally understood. He wasn't supposed to use the computer. Paul had made him promise not to, saying he'd sell it if Ben disobeyed. I promised I wouldn't tell, and he calmed down. Then I gave him my standard sermon: at his age, you might as well do as your parents say, because they're bigger and they always have the last word. It would be better if he stopped doing it. More sobs. He stared hopelessly at Gregory.

"How did you learn that game?"

"I watched Daddy," he said between two gulps. "It's not hard."

"Show me," I said.

He must have won by chance. It happens. He got back on the chair, and again his hands danced. Gregory flashed answers back. Ben's eyes on the numbers had an extraordinary expression, deep and luminous. I felt my heart pound. He barely took the time to think. In fact, it didn't seem hard for him. Gregory applauded. *You win again, Benjamin. Another game?* I was speechless.

Benjamin got down from the chair and came back to my lap. Not a trace of pride in the way he held himself.

"See, Cile, I did it. But sometimes I make mistakes. Gregory never does, and you can try as many times as you want to. Would you like to play a game with him?"

"Not tonight, thanks!"

I didn't tell him that I'd never win, that I only had to look at the monitor to feel a thick fog fill my mental screen.

"Listen, Ben, who taught you to add and subtract?"

He pointed to the keyboard: "Gregory," he said, "and Poppy, too, and Grandpa when he wasn't dead."

"Seven plus nine?"

Instant answer. I asked a few more questions, increasingly difficult. His fingers jumped, his eyes flew to the computer keyboard; he seemed to find his answers there. I didn't dare go too far. I felt dizzy.

"And in school, have they seen how you count?"

Tears again. This time it was the preschool teacher I had to promise not to tell. The other day she had said he was disturbing the class because he was counting ivy leaves instead of coloring like everyone else. She treated him like a show-off, and all the kids laughed.

"She says that's no way to behave," Benjamin explained miserably. "She says I'm always causing trouble and I've got a swelled head."

I told him I wouldn't say anything to the stupid woman. I glanced at the keyboard. If only it were just numbers! I had to face the fact that he knew letters, too. I pointed to the last sentence on the screen. "Read that."

"You win again, Benjamin," he recited. "Another game?"

There was a possibility that he knew it by heart. Some children have incredible memories. At ten, Claire would recite the first four pages of the phone book every time she was told she didn't work hard enough in school.

I told him not to move and went to his room for a minute. There were picture books everywhere, piles of comic books, books in his bed, even. I picked one at random and went back to put it in his hands.

"Now read this."

He sped along: a regular machine. I picked the first book I came to on one of Paul's shelves. I wanted only one thing now: for this to stop.

"That's one of Daddy's books and it's not for kids, so I'm not supposed to read it."

"I say you can, just this once. Go ahead."

The words flowed less easily; he followed with his finger, sounding them out.

"This caused a rift between the two major proponents of existentialism . . ."

He stopped to ask, "What does that mean?"

I promised I'd explain later. I was at my wit's end. I hugged him tight to make sure it was really him.

"And did Gregory teach you to read, too, you big love-bug?"

He stroked the computer's letters with his fingertip.

"They all did: Gregory, Daffy Duck, Speedy Gonzales . . . and alphabet blocks when I was little. Mom gave the blocks to Ali, though. He's sad because his dad loves another lady."

He slipped out of my arms and picked out another diskette to load in the computer. It wasn't numbers this time, but a synonym guessing game. I waited, resigned, for Gregory's congratulations. Benjamin looked happy; he laughed in little bursts. Pauline was worried that he had no friends. She was wrong. He had one: the computer. He had a friend that knew his name, was always willing to play, never cheated or made fun of him, took him seriously, and praised him when he did well.

I waited until he finished his game.

"Listen, Ben, these are grown-up games. Has your mom seen how you can do numbers and read?"

He shook his head no. His face was serious, with an adult expression. I'd often noticed that expression at La Marette. I'd say to myself, "He knows," and I'd feel intimidated.

"My mom is really busy and so is my daddy," he explained. "They need peace and quiet or we won't see their names in print. And I have Monica. She gets to put catsup on her fries but she can't speak French yet."

Monica, the English au pair girl, took Benjamin to and from preschool and fixed his meals. No comment on her; I didn't want to find out that he could speak English, too!

"So no one knows?"

"I read and do arithmetic with Poppy," he told me. "Poppy says I get an A-plus, but he thinks if Mommy and Daddy found out they might put me in another school far away and I'd be sad."

Roughly Speaking had told him that? He knew all this

and hadn't told us? And now he had Benjamin frightened? I was so mad I couldn't see straight. I couldn't understand. I'd have to think.

"What say we get some sleep now? I think I just saw Gregory yawn."

He laughed. That made me feel better. I wasn't sure how to talk to him anymore. On my lap I held both a very small boy and a sort of wizard.

"Can I say goodnight to him?"

I said yes. On the screen, he typed *Good night, Gregory.* The instant reply: *Good night, Benjamin, sleep tight.* For a moment Benjamin sat still and looked at his friend. My heart ached, the way it does when you hear certain very beautiful pieces of music, because somewhere deep inside the beauty there is suffering.

"I taught him to say *I love you* to me, too," he murmured.

46

Kites

ROUGHLY SPEAKING was getting ready for spring. He'd transferred part of his garden inside his greenhouse, and a little of ours as well, the fragile plants, the saplings. Surrounded by pails full of soil, compost, sand, ashes, rainwater, on his "operating table" he was repotting, bedding, grafting, treating. It smelled of life.

"Come to give me a hand?"

Prince was already badgering his legs, and when Tavernier bent down to pet him, the pup turned over onto his back, spread his paws to expose the maximum amount of sensitive surface: the dog had no shame. I told him to sit.

"I came to talk about Benjamin."

I think he understood at once. His back stiffened; he slowly took off his gardening gloves, without looking at me, without comment, and shook the dirt from them. I described the session with Gregory, omitting nothing. I'd gone over and over it all night and had drawn my conclusions: Benjamin was a gifted child, the kind you hear about sometimes on TV, with a brain different from other children's. He might have an important future. What I couldn't understand was how no one had noticed. Pauline had said that his preschool teacher wasn't satisfied with his progress. But I knew I hadn't dreamed what I had seen him do.

"No, you weren't dreaming," Roughly Speaking agreed.

He went to get his tobacco pouch out of his lumber jacket and then returned to my side. He always takes his time with things; that's another reason it's comfortable to be around him. Prince was sticking his nose into every pot, hoping to find something edible.

"He mentioned Gregory. I thought it was a little friend of his. I had no idea it was a computer."

"But it *is* a friend," I said. "Maybe the only friend he has, except for you and me, and I'm his aunt. So you knew. . . ."

"Since the fall. Remember? When his mother took off."

One day, when Benjamin was building a town in the dirt in the corner of the garden that he had given him to play with, Tavernier had heard counting. Benjamin was counting houses, the windows in his houses — and also the trees, the flowers, the stones in the walls, everything he could find. At first Roughly Speaking had thought he was just saying numbers at random, but when he checked them, the figures held up. And it was no coincidence that he found our old calculator in the boy's pocket, the battery fresh out of juice. Another day, while working a crossword puzzle with Ben on his lap, our neighbor had heard him quietly sounding out the words in the newspaper.

"I don't know how to put it. As if it was all in his head already. . . ."

"And you didn't say a word to us?"

I still resented it. I felt as if he'd stolen something from us. He looked me right in the eye to show that he took full responsibility.

"I couldn't decide. Don't think it was easy. I wanted to do what would be best for him, roughly speaking."

He'd observed Benjamin and seen a fragile plant that was growing too fast for its roots. For the plant to make it, above all it must be strengthened, not stretched like elastic until it snapped.

"What do you think his parents will do when they find out that at four he reads and does arithmetic like a ten-year-old?" he asked.

"At least they won't keep him from playing the games he likes. They'll stop treating him like a little kid."

"But he *is* a little kid," he said. "A four-year-old who wants to be like other kids, stay in his school, and make friends. When his parents find out what he can do, they'll want special schooling, they'll send him God knows where, and he won't be happy."

He'd started pacing alongside his tools. They were lined up along the wall, in perfect working order, bristling with teeth, claws, and hooks. It was the first time I'd seen him really angry. Perhaps with himself because he felt guilty for not telling us, perhaps with life for distributing gifts so randomly and constantly presenting challenges.

"You see, Cecile, the first thing in life is simply to be alive. Your two feet planted firmly on the ground. It's like kites. Without string, they don't work. Once you're rooted and you've learned to nourish yourself with what's around you, to smell, touch, see, taste — *then* you can take off, rack your brains about the nature of the universe. But if you take off without a base, you'll never make it."

I pictured Ben in front of Gregory, straining forward, his eyes shining, flying, yes, flying away. It couldn't be stopped.

"Last night I sensed that he has a destiny," I said. "With the right encouragement, he could become a great scientist."

"And a great problem to himself?"

He looked down at me, wishing hard to convince me, and now *I* began to feel angry. Benjamin didn't belong to him.

"At any rate," I said, "it's up to his parents to decide, not us. You shouldn't have told him not to talk about it. Now he's scared."

He lowered his eyes. I'd hurt him. He really loved Benjamin. In a way, Benjamin was his son, the first and last he would ever have.

He pressed his two fists to the table, clenched tight.

"Just what do his parents do for him?"

"They're his parents. We can't do anything about that. And they do love him."

"Leaving him all day with someone who doesn't speak a word of French? Never taking the time to look at him? Believe me, it doesn't take much to see that he's different."

"I didn't see it."

"You've had other things on your mind," he said.

He walked to the door and looked outside at the yard that was now being taken over by night, but gradually more slowly, more lightly as the winter passed.

"It's hard enough to do right by a normal kid, and with one like that it's almost impossible. Because you invest too much of yourself, roughly speaking. Do you think I didn't feel proud when I found out he was learning things all by himself? But at the same time I was afraid for him."

That was what I'd felt. I wanted to crow the news, and at the same time I wished I could hide Benjamin in my arms.

"I don't know what you'll decide, but think about kites and try to forget your pride," my neighbor told me.

He came back to my side. He didn't seem angry anymore. The two of us spent a minute looking at his bulbs, full of unpredictable colors, some of them ready to bloom splendidly and others, no one would ever know why, that would fail to thrive.

"I wish you'd mentioned this to Daddy. He would have known what to do."

"Don't you think he had enough problems already?"

My heart skipped a beat. Yes, enough. And it was clear who had caused them and where they'd led.

I caught Prince by the scruff of his neck. He'd poked his nose into the pail of ashes Roughly Speaking uses to repel slugs, and he looked like a clown. I buried my face in his coat and told him we were going home. Just let him try and cross the road by himself, he'd see what happened! He understood perfectly and grinned at me.

"I'll walk you home," said Roughly Speaking.

The rain had stopped. The trees dripped, whispering. The leaves were polished with light from the streetlamp.

Footsteps sounded different on the wet gravel. I adjusted my pace to his. As we passed his bomb shelter he stopped. I murmured, "Don't even bother telling me, I know." Great scientists were the ones who had discovered the means to blow up the earth a thousand times over, the earth that nourished them with food and joy. Had their string been cut too early, too?

Already, braving my warnings, Prince was breaking high-jump records against the gate to La Marette. "Just wait till I get there," I yelled. Tavernier laughed.

"He's still at the stage where he's trying to train you. That's how puppies are. I'm planting some parsley for him: good for the royal coat."

He ran his hand briefly through my hair, something no one had done since my father died.

"Wouldn't do your coat any harm, either."

We were at the wall. He gestured broadly.

"Tell me, Cecile, is there anything more important than a garden?"

~⌒ 47 ⌒~

Dinner for Two

I STOPPED at the store and bought the ingredients for a special dish: ham and endive rolls. While the endives were cooking with a crust of stale bread to absorb the bitterness, I set the table in the living room and lit a roaring fire.

When they were done, I drained them well, wrapped them in a thin slice of ham, drowned it all in béchamel sauce, scattered a half-inch of grated cheese over the top, and popped it into the oven.

I dimmed the lights and plumped the pillows. My mother was in for a surprise! Usually, when she came home, I was up in my room and didn't come down until she called me for dinner.

I'd ask her whether school was still hard for her. Whether she was used to being the oldest in the class yet, and not the quickest, with rusty work habits and a rusty memory. Whether she wasn't afraid, sometimes, that she wouldn't make it.

I got a tray ready for cocktails, complete with black olives and salted almonds. I felt like getting a head start to bolster my courage, but I didn't because that's how you become an alcoholic — drinking because you need to, not to celebrate with friends.

And I'd talk to her about Ben. Didn't she think he was more intelligent than the norm? In her opinion, was he particularly fragile? Does the fact that you're exceptional — meaning different — reduce your chances of being happy?

Prince heard her pull in before I did and started yelping joyfully. I heard the gate slam. I was already sorry. I wanted to run up and hide in my room, but it was too late: she was inside.

Seeing the place all lit up, she had thought we might have a guest. I announced that she was my dinner guest, for once. She shouldn't move, I'd do everything. She looked at the table set in front of the fire and smiled: a good idea to eat in here. A nice change.

I told her to go up and change, and while she was gone I poured her a little cassis and a finger of white wine. I knew the proportions to the smallest fraction of an inch. It wasn't for nothing that my father had appointed me head bartender at the La Marette Club. I always used to fix his evening Scotch: lots of ice, to the rim with water, and just a drop of poison. . . .

I'd ask my mother if she still missed him just as much, if when she woke up in the morning she still had to make the whole trip over again as she had on those first days because in her sleep and in her dreams she'd erased his death and had to learn it all over again. If she still found, in spite of everything, the daily glints of small joys she was always preaching to us about when he was still around because she only had to catch them from the sunshine she lived in.

She'd put on pants, a loose shirt, and had taken off her makeup. If I had a hard time recognizing her these days, perhaps it was because now I saw her. When Daddy had been there, she'd been my mother, period; a mother, you look at selfishly. Then I'd seen her change into a woman, a widow, and tonight it had been my stupid idea to make her my dinner guest. I passed her her glass and offered the olives. She said thank you. We started drinking in silence, and when the phone rang — Claire — I was relieved; she was, too, no doubt.

They talked a long time; then it was Antoine's turn. He was handling money matters. The government was merciless. It wanted its share of the estate and for fear of being cheated had frozen everything; now the widow Moreau was being bombarded with papers. When they were done, it would be the right time to ask her why Daddy had suddenly decided to write a will. Had he felt tired? Had he told her something? And why just after Tanguy died? I would watch her face closely as she answered. Meanwhile, I felt cold, and I went up to put on another sweater.

She noticed it when she came back to join me after hanging up. It was the first time I'd dared appear in it: one of Charles's sweaters, still smelling of him, especially since it was a turtleneck. She looked at me, as if to ask *Why?* I had the sweater on because I wanted to tell her how my father had worn it in the mountains, in the Joux Forest, how I'd had something like a premonition: I'd thought I saw our tall tree fall, bringing down a whole section of my life, and I'd suddenly felt a chill. She stretched out a finger to touch the sweater. I could really smell the endives now. I headed for the kitchen.

They were almost done. Just a couple more minutes. I stole a moment to splash water on my face. When I was little, I sincerely believed that that refreshed the mind.

My mother loved the dinner. I explained about the stale bread to soak up the bitterness. You can also use lemon if you have one on hand. Prince was very excited by the ham. We chatted with him the whole time.

Over dessert, my mother asked me how things were going for me. The hospital? My spirits? She wished I'd go out more often. Was it her imagination, or was I shutting myself off from things?

That was when I should have told her that things weren't going well at all, that I was at sea, felt like a pest to myself, when everyone had been trying to forget my nickname. That if I never kissed her anymore, since my father's death, it was because that would be like asking her forgiveness, which would mean admitting my guilt, and I couldn't. If she thought I'd had something to do with what had happened, she might as well tell me flat out. I wouldn't blame her if she couldn't stand the sight of me. I couldn't stand it, either, especially when I looked into my eyes. I was even ready to move out, as long as I could come back on weekends like my sisters.

She was waiting for my reply. I said things weren't so bad. It was just a little hard for me, too, all these changes. Had to admit that Dr. Moreau had taken up an awful lot of room in the house, without seeming to, with his smiles, his glances, his tenderness, his bad back, and his practiced gestures reaching for his pipe, his paper, or one of our cheeks, like a man who imagined he had his life ahead of him. But I said all that into the turtleneck that came up to my nose, and my mother didn't hear it.

It was eight o'clock. There was a good movie on TV. I suggested that we watch it together, and she thought that was an excellent idea.

In the old days, when all six of us were at home, sometimes we'd plan dinners in front of the TV. We'd pick a great movie and draw straws to see who got phone duty. Mom would get some take-out food, something unusual, just for a change. Someone would always talk or laugh just when you needed quiet. Bernadette booed the love scenes Claire swooned over. Pauline always went for the strong silent types. I had a weakness for bad guys, I'm told, immediately casting them as underdogs and making excuses for their behavior. Daddy was aggravated into thinking he had the silliest daughters in the world, but most of the time he was asleep before the conclusion, and mountains could crumble, sirens blast, the most beautiful love scenes melt into kisses: a smile on his lips, his head lolling, he was off on a journey of his own.

We would never let Mom wake him up. We'd turn down the sound. Then he'd be a little like our son, and we didn't know that one day you become an adult the same way you become an orphan.

48

The Best of Yourself

I N MY FAMILY," Emmanuel was saying, "there was a 'special' child, too. Sometimes he'd look and look at me, as if to ask why, and I had no answer to give him. It was my brother."

"Was he gifted?"

"He was what they call mildly retarded. Just enough intelligence or sense to realize that he couldn't do the things other people did."

He looked into the distance. Looking at injustice. We were practically alone at the English pub. Past teatime, not yet dinnertime. He'd ordered a hot toddy; I had hot water with lemon. He was surprised: "No Scotch this time?" And when I confessed that I hated the stuff, that I'd ordered it because it was the only British drink I could think of, he burst out laughing.

"Everywhere I went," he continued, "I dragged Hugues along. I wanted him to do as many 'normal' things as possible. I divided people into two categories: the blind and the voyeurs. The ones who ignored him to spare our feelings and the ones who stared at him as if he were a strange beast."

"What did you want them to do?"

"See him for what he was: an unhappy, unlucky little boy. Once, on a train, a woman asked me, 'Is it very hard for him?' I could have kissed her."

"And will it be very hard for Benjamin?"

His eyes came to rest on me, dark and gleaming. Since he'd told me about his brother, I felt I knew him better. I had called him the day before. I'd told him I had to see him right away, about something that didn't have to do with us, concerning a problem with a child I loved. All he'd said was "When?" Today!

"It's always hard to be different. People don't like it. You're alone. Don't expect Benjamin to inspire admiration. Tell yourself he'll annoy people, disturb them, bring out their jealousy and meanness. Look at his teacher. She must realize he's ahead of the others, so she sets him apart, ridicules him."

"So Roughly Speaking is right? I shouldn't say anything?"

The nickname made him smile. At La Marette, we're so used to it we don't even give it a thought.

"Imagine how you'd feel if, instead of winning a math game with a computer at four, your nephew sat down at a piano and played you a superb rendition of a Chopin waltz. Would you close the piano? Would you hold him back with the excuse that he wasn't old enough for his talent? That an artist's life is too hard?"

"I'd find him the best teacher," I said, "and help him become a great virtuoso."

"And you'd be right. Everyone needs to be able to give the best of himself. The handicapped as well as the gifted."

"The best of yourself . . ." Suddenly I could breathe better, more easily. All of us, somewhere inside, have a "best" to develop.

"So you think I should tell his parents?"

"Certainly. And they can consult a specialist. There are

people who work with that kind of child. Benjamin isn't
the only one."

A family had just come in: father, mother, two kids.
The mother helped the younger one off with her jacket.
They took possession of a table a bit as if they were starting
on a trip. What had they come here to celebrate? Life?

"And what about Miss Cecile Moreau?" Emmanuel asked.
"How has she been doing?"

Miss Moreau replied that she liked nursing school. The
best part was working with the patients, even if for the
time being all she did was straighten beds and take temperatures. At least she was of service. I liked the verb *to
serve*. It can have greatness. My father had sometimes said,
"Serve your country"; I had visions of soil and blood, but
it was still grand. The week before, a girl had been brought
in after a motorcycle wreck. She was in a coma. You could
feel that she was a prisoner of herself. Our job was to make
contact, talk to her as much as possible, get her to wake
up. I'd call to her, "Marie? Marie?" Sometimes waves would
flicker over her face. At times it seemed to me I was in
her place. It was me on the other side of an invisible wall.
I called out, and no one answered.

"Cecile, what's happening?"

Once again the spinning feeling, the painful wish to go
back to before, to have it all be just a bad dream, to be a
carefree, lighthearted girl in a hotel by a lake. Why was it
the same thing every time I was with Emmanuel? At
first it was fine. I felt good. Then everything fell apart.
Was it because, with a brother also hemmed in by invisible walls, Emmanuel had learned to read what you can't
express?

He took my wrist, and his eyes insisted.

"Let me help you."

I murmured, "I don't need help." And I added, foolishly,
"What do you see in me?"

237

He sat up straight and smiled: "You're a brave and generous little soldier."

Inside me, a sort of disappointment. What was I expecting? "You're pretty"? "I'm attracted to you"? That's what my sisters would have been told. He was sorry for me, that was it. He must think he was still down in strife-torn Africa. Caring for the wounded.

I stood up. "I have to get home. They're expecting me."

We walked side by side in the street. I had a feeling of emptiness, failure. And yet he'd told me what I wanted to hear about Ben. I could be proud of him. But was Benjamin the only reason I'd wanted to see him again?

We got to my moped. I put on my helmet and straddled the bike.

I'd ride fast, drown my thoughts. Ignition, blast-off!

"Not so fast," he said.

He gripped the handlebars and stood facing me.

"Don't think you're going to get away so easily. I'm not done with you. I want Miss Cecile Moreau to know she has a big job ahead of her: reconciling with someone."

My heart leapt. My mother?

"Who do you mean?"

He didn't answer right away. I lowered the visor of my helmet.

"With yourself," he murmured. "With yourself, my darling. And I have every intention of helping you do it."

49

"My Darling"

M Y DARLING. . . ." What did it mean? Do you call a brave little soldier "my darling"? And this tide rising in me, the wind knocked out of me, the feeling of warmth mixed with fear, especially fear, why?

Because there was some mistake! Those words were addressed to a girl who didn't exist. I'd fooled him from the beginning. Brave? I was anything but, hiding deep in a hole, just as in my dreams, when war breaks out and I cover my ears, close my eyes, wait for the explosion. Generous? I brought everything back to myself: Benjamin, Marie, even Emmanuel's brother. Through them, I looked only at myself.

"My darling. . . ." What would come next? Would he take me in his arms? Kiss me? The *No* knotted in my stomach. There, too, he'd picked the wrong person. I had told him that I'd made love with Tanguy, that it had been great. He didn't suspect he was taking on the only eighteen-year-old virgin for miles around, probably the only one within a hundred miles of Paris who'd never been kissed for real, for good. He had no idea that I was completely inhibited, body and soul.

I didn't love him. If I loved him, I wouldn't have felt

so afraid, of what he had said, of seeing him again. According to Melodie, love made everything easy. You flowed naturally from apprehension to saying yes, from fright to ecstasy. I hadn't really loved Tanguy. Close up, I'd felt disgust. I'd never be in love. Passion wasn't for me. It was my nature. I might as well face facts.

A beat-up car was parked in front of La Marette: Jean-René's. I hadn't seen him since Daddy. Death sends some people scurrying to church, but not me. Just the opposite. Life seemed so tiring that I had no desire to sign up for another tour of duty on high, even if I would have wings. It didn't frighten me to think of leaving for good. What took courage was staying on when the people you love give you the slip, one after the other.

I walked in quietly and went directly up to my room. The mirror had nothing new to tell me. The magic effect of two words had not turned me into one of those girls you see in magazines or on television, where men shower them with cars, jewelry, trips around the world, and lacy underwear. Except for the fact that my wonderful eyes were red from the wind, and my touching mouth had chapped lips, nothing had changed. Reconciliation was not close at hand, because your first quarrel is often with the mirror, and reconciling with your self, even with a capital *S,* means first of all reconciling yourself to a face, a pair of hips, whatever. His "my darling" must have been meant in a brotherly, friendly way, from a comrade in arms to a "brave little soldier," by mistake or out of pity.

Mom and Jean-René were deep in conversation. On his gray sweater, his crucifix pin shone clearly. He said it was radar for SOS calls, that when they saw it, people with troubles came to confide in him. Too bad it hadn't worked on Tanguy.

He stood and kissed my cheek with his luminous smile. Where had I been hiding myself? They hadn't seen me for ages. "They"? The huge Christ on the cross in church and him?

I didn't have the heart to tell him that for now the connection was broken with the force that had once drawn me forward, and that he called God. I said I was awfully busy with school.

We sat down on the couch, and he began to talk about the things that propel kites upward: hope, faith, ideals. I heard Roughly Speaking: "The first thing is to have your feet planted on the ground, to smell, see, feel." I heard Emmanuel's voice: "my darling." I felt it in the secret part of myself that I'd one day have to come to terms with, since it was life. It wasn't proper to think of such things in front of a priest, but no matter how hard I tried to close my ears and my memory, the two words were planted somewhere in me, between my heart and my groin, and they sometimes swelled to the point that I felt my chest would burst.

"Now there's a little smile," Jean-René remarked. "I was beginning to lose hope."

It was because I'd just remembered that the name Emmanuel means "God with us," as if, in some way, the man upstairs had caught up with me after all.

50

A Child in Need

BENJAMIN studied the peas on his plate, divided into several piles. I used to play with them, too, when I was a kid. He tugged at his father's sleeve. All of a sudden he seemed very preoccupied.

"The teacher won't let me wipe the blackboard," he said. "She always has Astruc erase it. And Astruc stole the blue chalk; there were pieces of it in his pocket."

"And why won't she let you, poor little guy?" Paul asked.

"Because I've got my head in the clouds," Benjamin stated. "And if she let me put my jacket on by myself, it would take all week."

Pauline laughed and affectionately ruffled her son's hair. She and Paul were leaving on a skiing vacation in the morning. They were here for a farewell dinner and to leave their boy with us. I looked at the piles of peas on Benjamin's plate, and suddenly my heart was pounding. He hadn't sorted them at random: each pile contained ten. Was this the time to show his parents what he could do? I'd give it a try.

"What kind of game are you playing with your peas, Ben?" I asked loudly.

Benjamin raised his face to me, and once again it wore a luminous expression, as it had the other night.

"They aren't peas, they're marbles. There's a pile for Astruc, one for Emmery, one for Romain, and we'll see about the rest of the kids when they're nicer to me."

"And how many marbles are you giving them?"

"What is this, a quiz?" Pauline protested. "Just let him eat, why don't you? His food's getting cold."

"Open the hangar!" Paul chimed in.

Benjamin looked at his plate, then at his parents, and at Mom too, smiling at him. Then he awkwardly stirred the three piles together with his knife. Peas rolled onto the tablecloth.

"Settle down now," Paul said curtly. "Aren't you old enough to have some table manners?"

As he said those words, I suddenly felt like getting up and letting them have it. He didn't deserve his son, and neither did Pauline. Roughly Speaking was right: if you don't take the time to look, you don't really love. But I couldn't say anything without mentioning Gregory, and I'd promised. . . . Besides, they were already on vacation, already far away on the ski slopes, all speed and sun. Paul's leg wasn't much of a problem: he had special equipment and took it easy. And Benjamin's plate was empty now, my demonstration in his stomach.

That was when I decided to act. I'd talk to them, I'd prove how smart he was, but later. I had a plan.

It was a handsome old building on a broad, chestnut-lined avenue. Children chased each other down the sidewalk, and their cries sounded different, heralding the arrival of spring. It was beginning to smell like spring, too, a timid dialogue between the trees, the soil, the sky.

We went into the lobby. There was a sign with a list of names. I showed Benjamin where to read *Nicolas Chalain.*

His name was followed by *Ph.D.* I had explained to him that we were going to see someone a little like his teacher but nicer. This man was interested in children and might show him some games. It would be fun.

Even so, he was starting to get very nervous. The elevator arrived just in time to distract him. I lifted him up so he could push the fourth button. I told myself, "When we take the elevator back down, it will be settled." And that gave me the courage to ring the bell.

A woman opened the door: around Mom's age. The age of all the women you see in the street, on the subway, the bus, everywhere — and sometimes you feel there's nothing but them. I asked to see Dr. Chalain, and she looked flabbergasted. He never saw people on Tuesdays. I must have written down the wrong day for my appointment.

I didn't have an appointment. I told her so. When I'd called, I'd been told there was a three-month wait, and I couldn't wait that long. I had to settle things before then.

I spoke very calmly so I wouldn't make Benjamin any more upset. He understood that we weren't wanted and pulled my hand toward the door.

"But the doctor won't be able to see you," she said. "He's in a meeting."

"I won't take long," I said. "I just need some information. We've come a very long way just to talk to him."

She looked at Benjamin, squeezing his eyes shut as he always does when he's afraid, then she looked at me, just the opposite, trying to sway her with my eyes. At La Marette, even on Sundays, people used to come to see my father without appointments. Mom tried to make him say no but he usually gave in because choosing to be a doctor meant choosing that your time would never quite be your own.

"I'll see," she said. "But I can't promise anything."

She took my name and left us in the waiting room. There

was another door to it, probably Nicolas Chalain's office.
We heard voices on the other side. Benjamin pressed against
me.

"Am I going to get a shot?" he asked for the hundredth
time.

I told him to take a good whiff: "Does it smell like shots
here?" He admitted that it didn't. It smelled like stories,
the same as his house, where there were lots of books,
too, and he'd be allowed to touch them if he studied hard
in school, coming home tired but happy.

"He's not a real doctor, he's a nice teacher," he said to
reassure himself. "He won't even check my heartbeat."

The door opened, the doctor appeared, and he didn't
look nice at all; instead he looked somewhat annoyed. He
took a look at Benjamin and me and motioned me to come
into his office without the child. I swore to Benjamin that
I wasn't abandoning him, I never would, and I followed
Nicolas Chalain. He closed the door. He was very tall,
massive, with a full head of white hair and a salt-and-pepper
beard. He asked me to have a seat.

"What do you want?" he asked. "I have office hours on
Monday and Wednesday, by appointment only. Why did
you come today?"

"About Benjamin," I explained. "The little boy who's
with me. I have to find out whether or not he's a gifted
child. Right away."

He raised his eyes, exasperated.

"Gifted! Listen here, Miss . . . Moreau. Every day we
get fifty phone calls from parents convinced they've hatched
a genius, who insist that they need to see me immediately.
Until now no one has just barged in. I should add that all
fifty prospective geniuses are really fifty darling and perfectly normal children, despite their parents' dreams. And
in the end, I'm sorry to say, those dreams do their children
a good deal of harm."

"Benjamin is different."

"That's what they all say."

There was a lump in my throat. Before long, I wouldn't be able to talk. I wasn't prepared for this kind of reception. I pulled his book out of my bag.

"Then why did you write this? Why did you say that if certain children aren't attended to early in life, their gifts may be wasted and that that's a crime? That they demand emergency care? I came because of that phrase you used: Benjamin needs emergency care."

My cheeks burned. Seeing his picture on the back of the book, I'd had such high hopes. He looked a little like a grandfather. He would understand. And I liked what he'd written. Could it be that like Pauline, like Paul, he was only interested in books? Not in the people in them?

A light knock, then the door opened, and without waiting for a reply Benjamin came in. He closed the door quietly behind him and stood still, his eyes glued to the rug.

"Why don't you go say hello to the fish, Benjamin?" Nicolas Chalain suggested.

Benjamin looked at the big aquarium behind the psychologist's desk, and I could tell he was tempted. In the soft light, all kinds of fish darted among the rocks and seaweed. His eyes came back to mine. I motioned him to go ahead, and he did, looking around from time to time to make sure we weren't about to pull any tricks on him.

With a heavy sigh, Nicolas Chalain sank into the chair behind his desk.

"Sit down."

I sat across from him. He took out a form. Benjamin's back was to us.

"The child's name, address, and age?"

I wasn't ready for that. It was stupid; I had simply thought he would see Benjamin, understand right away, be eager to help.

"Name?"

I gave him all the information. I didn't see how I could refuse, but it was only then that I realized what I was doing. "The first step is to tell his parents," Emmanuel had said.

"You're his sister?"

"His aunt."

"Why aren't his parents with him?"

That was the hard one.

"They're away on a ski trip," I explained. "And anyway, Ben doesn't interest them all that much."

A smile at the corner of his lips: "Are you sure they'd agree with that statement?"

I'd put it the wrong way. I'd given him more cause not to believe me. He pivoted in his chair and looked over at Benjamin, who was fascinated by the fish. Several of them seemed equally interested in him.

Dr. Chalain again turned to face me: "When did he first walk, talk? Do you know when he was toilet-trained?"

I wasn't sure about any of that, and I told him so.

"But you don't seem to be saying that he was particularly precocious."

No one had thought so. But what did it matter? Once he talked to Benjamin, he would see.

"What leads you to believe he's . . . gifted?"

He obviously didn't like the word. He said it crisply, ironically.

"He can read and add and subtract without ever having been taught to."

"How do you know that?"

I didn't use Gregory's name because of the big ears over by the fish tank, but I explained that he stayed up to play with his father's computer. Dr. Chalain didn't seem the least impressed.

"It's often surprising how fast children learn to use computers," he said. "They're much better at it than their parents."

"Benjamin wasn't using children's programs, though. He was playing games for adults and winning every time."

I could tell he didn't believe me, and I didn't know how to convince him. When I talked about Roughly Speaking, the mud castles in the garden, the calculator, the crosswords and kites, he raised an eyebrow as if I was only confirming the idea that I was a compulsive liar.

"All right. Let's have a look."

At last. He turned to Benjamin, who was still glued to the aquarium.

"I see you're interested in fish."

No reaction from Ben.

"You can see there are different kinds," Nicolas Chalain went on. "The Chinese fish are the black ones with the pretty black fins. And then there are those silvery ones there. Which kind do you think there are more of?"

Benjamin didn't answer. I got up. I had just realized that he wasn't looking at the fish at all, but at me, at my reflection in the glass. And he looked sullen, tight-lipped, as if he was angry with me, as if I'd fooled him. I got up to go to his side. With one hand Nicolas Chalain held me back.

"Let's leave the fish alone for a minute," he announced.

He scooped Benjamin up onto his lap, then turned his chair so they were both facing me. Benjamin was stiff as a board.

"I hear you like to read," the doctor told him.

Benjamin still showed no reaction. I didn't know what to do. I felt as though I was smothering. Nicolas Chalain pulled a book out of a pile on his desk and opened it.

"Do you know the story of Babar?"

Too easy; he knew it by heart.

"Could you read a little for me?"

Benjamin lowered his eyes and looked at the picture blankly, without a word. With his gaping mouth, he looked like the village idiot.

"Go on, Ben, read," I begged.

I wanted to slap him, and at the same time I wished I could take him in my arms and run out of the office.

The psychologist closed the book. He looked up at me.

"In the United States," he told me, "they're seeing what we call the superbaby syndrome. Parents want their offspring to excel, and from birth, sometimes even before, the children are programmed to learn. They do turn out to learn reading, writing, and arithmetic at a very early age, or how to play a musical instrument almost before they can walk. By the same token, when they're as young as three years old many of these children show signs of clinical depression, and whatever supposed advances they've made will probably be lost before they reach school age because people forget the most important thing: emotional development has to go hand in hand with intellectual development. When children are pushed too hard, sometimes they fall apart. Perhaps your nephew's parents are wise. Benjamin has plenty of time to develop his gifts. Why not give him the chance to be and to act the way he obviously wants to — like other children? Perhaps that's the kind of emergency care he requires at this point."

I felt tears welling up. He sounded like Roughly Speaking. But at least Roughly Speaking *knew* — and he didn't. Now he was being nice, and that was worse than anything. He thought he had shown me that I was mistaken, and, understanding my disappointment, he was trying to console me.

"But he really can . . ."

With a finger to his lips, he cut me short. He was watching Benjamin, and his expression had changed. Benjamin had just gotten his hands on a pad of paper on the desk: engraved notepaper. He seemed to have forgotten us, and softly, very softly, to himself, he was sounding out the letters. He read: "Nicolas Chalain, Ph.D., Consulting Psychologist, Associate Professor, University of Paris, Twelve rue de l'Arche, Paris Seventy-five.

"There are a lot of twelves," he said.

"I only see Twelve rue de l'Arche," Nicolas Chalain replied calmly, cautiously.

Benjamin turned to him and pointed to the paper. "Seven and five is twelve. And your phone number here is 4871–0004. Four and eight is twelve, and so is seven-one-zero-zero-zero and four. My Grandpa's number starts with six-three-three, that makes twelve, too. He had paper with his name on it like you, and he let me draw on it if I was quiet and stopped asking questions for a minute."

"Would you like to draw on my paper?" Nicolas Chalain asked, still in the same cautious voice.

Benjamin nodded. Without haste, like an animal tamer, the psychologist handed him a silver mug with a few crayons in it and waited. My heart was in my throat. Now was when I wanted to cry and shout, from relief. After a moment, Benjamin picked a red crayon. He bent over the paper, and his hand flew over it, skimming but not touching it; he was concentrating hard. Nicolas Chalain followed each gesture. After a minute or two, Benjamin put the crayon back and pushed the mug away.

"It's done," he said.

The psychologist's expression was even more attentive. He pointed to the blank sheet.

"What did you draw there, Benjamin?"

Benjamin eyed him gravely: "It's Grandpa," he explained. "He's dead, so of course you can't see anything. Want to know why I made him red?"

"You bet I do," said Nicolas Chalain.

~ 51 ~

Guilty as Charged

STILL TANNED from the sun on the ski slopes but
with a hard, unfamiliar expression on her face, looking
as though she hated me, here was Pauline. She came up
to me, grabbed my arm, dragged me into the living room,
slammed the door.

"Thanks for what you've done!" she said. "Thanks a
million! Nice work!"

I felt like going up to my room, locking the door: I
couldn't understand all this anger.

"You're always messing things up, ruining everything.
We all hoped you were growing up, but it never gets any
better."

"What never gets better? What have I done that's so
awful?"

"You take my son, you wait till I'm gone and drag him
to this so-called doctor. You tell him lies about us. The
two of you decide what to do about him. And now you
wonder what you've done wrong?"

I understood. Pauline felt guilty for not noticing that
her son was a genius; she was upset, and she'd felt embarrassed when Nicolas Chalain had called her, more so
when she'd met with him.

"A month ago I hadn't noticed, either," I said. "Ben covers it up pretty well, you know."

"Yes, I know," she growled. "He hides it because we frightened him . . . we don't pay attention to him . . . we're never around . . . we're not cut out to be parents."

"I never said that."

"So why didn't you tell us anything?"

"I tried," I said. "You didn't seem very interested. And I was afraid you wouldn't believe me."

"What made you think we wouldn't believe you?"

She stared me down. I didn't like her face: a stranger's.

"Why not admit that you just wanted to show off? 'My nephew here is a genius.' Am I right?"

"No!" Now I felt like shouting. I may have been wrong to do what I did without telling her, but that didn't mean she was entirely without blame, either.

"You told him not to play with Gregory; you threatened to sell him. He was beside himself. Gregory is his only friend."

Her eyes blazed.

"Yes, his only friend. And we were hoping he might make some more like himself, fresh and blood ones. We don't want him spending all his time talking to a machine. Did it ever occur to you that we might have our own ideas about Benjamin? You've always blamed us for anything that goes wrong. It isn't necessarily the parents' fault if a child isn't well adjusted, you know. The parents do the best they can, and then there are jerks like you who stab them in the back. Benjamin hasn't opened his mouth since we took him to that psychologist. He just keeps crying."

"You took him back? And Paul was with you?"

"Why not? Father, mother, child . . . that was the way your world-famous specialist wanted it."

I saw all three of them sitting across from Nicolas Chalain: father, mother, and between the two of them, like a prisoner, I saw Benjamin. He was the one I'd done the most harm to.

"I thought you'd go by yourself."

"You never do think straight. Well, Paul is furious! He's sick of your meddling. He wants to raise his son his own way. This time you've extended too far into *our* family."

How had my father put it? That people had private gardens and I should stop tromping through them with my heavy boots on? But he'd said it lovingly, not full of scorn. I wanted Pauline to disappear. And she shouldn't count on my feeling sorry. Because tonight she'd be in Paul's arms; she had Benjamin; she could say "home" and think of a place where she felt good. And I had nothing left, just a room that only served to remind me that sometimes a man used to knock at my door, I would pretend not to hear, and he'd say "Anyone home?" and sit down on the edge of my bed, looking slightly ill at ease. The day when a father thinks twice before tumbling onto his daughter's bed with her in his arms, he starts feeling shy. And she feels herself becoming a woman.

"If Daddy were here — " I said.

"Yes, let's talk about Daddy, while we're at it," she cut in. "You drag him to the mountains. You put him through that business with the guy in the basement. Thanks for that, too."

My heart skipped a beat: "What do you mean?"

"That you're always causing trouble. We talked it over with Mom, and she agrees."

"You talked about what?"

She didn't answer. I felt cold. Where *was* Mom, anyway? When I rode up, I'd seen the light in her room. That was the first thing I looked for when I got home: her light. An obsession. Afraid she wouldn't be there — or would. Afraid

Emmanuel would call me "my darling" — or wouldn't. It must have been Mom who'd lighted the fire in the fireplace. Why hadn't she come down?"

"What's Mom up to, anyway?"

"She's trying to calm Ben down. She's giving him a bath. She called Paul, too . . . to make excuses for you. That's how it's always gone around here. A little too easy, don't you think?"

I asked, "What you just said about Daddy, what did you mean?"

She looked at me, then glanced away: "Nothing."

"Yes you did. You were thinking of something. And Mom agreed."

"I meant that Bernadette warned you about that Tanguy, but that didn't keep you from bringing him here. You always do whatever crosses your mind without thinking how it could affect other people."

"Affect Daddy?"

She didn't answer. It was too much, too awful. It wouldn't come out. A bomb that could blow up in your face any minute, Bernadette had said. And it had gone off. Costing two lives. I collapsed on the couch. Mom knew. They'd talked it over. She agreed. I told myself, "It's all my fault," but I couldn't really believe it all was.

The door opened; Mom appeared. Her eyes swept the room, grew wide: "Isn't Benjamin down here? I thought he was with you."

At that moment the telephone rang. It was Tavernier. He'd just found a little boy on his doorstep in tears after crossing the road alone at night — a little boy in a bathrobe and slippers who didn't seem to want to go home and was crying too hard to explain why. What had happened? What should he do?

"We'll be right over," said Mom.

She hung up, turned to me.

"Happy?"

With Pauline in her wake, she went out. I followed them. They didn't want me, were erasing, eliminating me, but I went, I would go. Mrs. Tavernier answered the door and without a word led us into the living room. Roughly Speaking gestured to excuse himself from rising: Benjamin, shaking with sobs, was huddled in his arms. His eyes interrogated me. I looked away. He understood: I'd told, and this was the result. Even though he'd warned me. Like Bernadette warning me about Tanguy, and Daddy warning Pauline.

Pauline knelt by the chair and softly called to her son. Benjamin gripped his "Poppy's" neck, a skinny tadpole in his green pajamas. She called his name again: he looked away and saw me. His eyes told me that I'd betrayed him, that he'd heard his mother scream, seen her fight with his father, that she had cried and it was because of him, because he played at night when he wasn't supposed to with Gregory, his only friend.

Then he turned to Tavernier: "My daddy just wants some peace and quiet, if it isn't too much to ask, and my mommy says if he sells Gregory she'll go back to her own mom because it would be just like killing me. So can I just go to heaven wih Grandpa right now?"

"Poppy's" eyes brimmed with tears. I'd cut the kite loose from the string.

52

Relief Work

HOW COULD I look at her again, meet her gaze? "We talked it over. . . . She agrees." The string to *my* kite had also been cut. By Pauline.

It was still dark out when I left La Marette. It was raining. The sun was scattering the clouds by the time I got to Paris. Once, Emmanuel had told me about his street: "Not really like the city, with a convent school." It was time for school, and waves of children poured through an archway topped with a worn stone cross. In the schoolyard you could see a chestnut tree bristling with waxy buds.

The caretaker, in a flowered housecoat, was polishing the bronze doorknob of Emmanuel's building. She was very thorough, getting into the corners, contemplating her work with pleasure; they almost seemed like the motions of love. I asked her which floor Dr. Duplessis lived on. She hesitated. Rag in hand, she disapprovingly studied a girl far less presentable than her fine doorknob. But she decided to tell me anyway: Dr. Duplessis was on the top floor, I couldn't miss it, there was only one door.

I walked up. On each landing there was a mirror where I saw a sort of clown with wet, stringy hair, a tragic face, and big circles under the eyes. I'd come down with a cold during the night. With every cough it seemed to me I was coughing up myself: it was very painful. I rang the bell.

Emmanuel was in his bathrobe. He said my name but this time without "my darling." All of a sudden I froze. It was like the end of a race: you've given your all, and when you get to the finish line you realize that in one more stride you'll collapse.

He took my wrist and guided me into the entryway.

"Give me that jacket, you goose. It's soaking wet."

I followed orders. My only wish was to obey him. He took away my garment and came back with a towel.

"Now dry that head off for me."

I dried that head. When I was done, he said, "You're just in time for coffee!"

I hadn't said a word yet. He must have noticed, but he showed no reaction. I followed him into the big room he must use for everything, with a comfortable lived-in look, an unmade bed, books and magazines on the furniture, African hangings on the walls, a lot of life and also a smell of night mixed with the scent of tobacco and other, indefinable odors, the kind that wafted around Daddy and made me stop feeling like kissing him when I was twelve. My sisters and I would say, "It smells like a man in here," with an animal ring to it. . . .

"Come over here a minute!"

He led me over to the bay window that took up one whole side of the room. It looked out over the schoolyard. The children were lined up in front of the classroom doors. You could see the well-lighted rooms, the tables and desks, the blackboards: you were inside.

"You see, I don't have a big apartment, just one room. But I have a whole school, a schoolyard, a chestnut tree that's about to blossom, recess, vacations . . ."

I remembered his retarded brother. Because of him, Emmanuel's view of children must be different. For me, the kids down there were simply "normal"; to him they must be precious. And perhaps it was also because of his brother that he had gone all the way to Africa in the hope of saving a few other children.

He pointed to the couch, then went to get me a cup. In front of me, on the coffee table, there was a thermos bottle, some melba toast, and a yogurt — a real bachelor's meal. I gestured around the room, the bay window especially, and said, "It's a really neat place." I felt as if there were a plug in my throat, something like a champagne cork.

He took a look around, too, and said, "Yes, it is."

I remarked, "You must think this is a strange time of day to drop in on someone, especially without calling first."

He smiled at me. "I've been expecting you. I didn't know when you'd come, but I've been waiting." So I stared straight in front of me and told him I'd caused my father's death. The cork popped, and champagne splashed everywhere.

My head was buried in his bathrobe, his arm was around me, I let everything go. He didn't say anything. He didn't say, "What on earth are you talking about?" or "You're crazy" or "You're making things up." He let it come out. And in spurts, during the lulls, I told him everything: Tanguy, my father clutching at his heart, the will, his death . . . Until yesterday, I'd managed to keep going in spite of everything, at times I'd even forgotten, and then Pauline had said, "Thanks for Daddy."

Lifting my face slightly, I could touch his chin with my forehead. The nearest landscape was his neck and the gold chain with a medal hanging from it — not Saint Emmanuel; there isn't one.

I explained how Tanguy had died, too, that maybe it had been my fault but at least I could tell myself that he'd been a sad case and now he was out of his misery, while my father had been happy as a king, enjoying every minute, appreciating each breath of air, and I couldn't stop calculating all he was missing on account of me.

He remained silent. Sometimes he squeezed my shoulder a little tighter to show me he was still there. No, I couldn't accept his death. Impossible. All the time, with all my strength, I kept trying to swim against the current, to go back and say something to my father, and again and again I found myself with my face to the ground, smothering.

"Tell him."

I didn't understand. "Tell him," he repeated. "Tell him what's smothering you." I didn't dare. I was afraid, ashamed, and I felt ridiculous. What did he think? That he'd hear me? That he was in Heaven, wearing a halo? "Now!" he ordered. "Right now." I looked at the medal. I had another kind of ache in my chest, more ambiguous, like a wave, like hope. I murmured, "Sorry." Emmanuel held me so tight he hurt me. I repeated several times, "Sorry, sorry," and then I began to laugh because there was nothing else to do.

He filled my cup with coffee and added sugar until I cried, "Enough." I liked his hand on the slender spoon: a man's hand, strong. I could still feel it around me. I took a sip. Now it was his turn to talk, and I could guess what he was going to say: "You're imagining things, it's not your fault, the heart is a fragile and unpredictable organ" — all the words I'd said to myself a hundred times without managing to convince myself. But that wasn't what he said at all.

"Are you prepared to do something very difficult?" he asked.

I nodded. The most difficult thing there was! Any task, any new path, any mountains to move that he assigned me.

"I want you to go to your mother and tell her all that you've just told me."

My heart leapt. It was as if he'd hit me. He hadn't understood anything! Talking to my mother was the one thing
I could not do. Since my father's death I hadn't even been
able to say his name once in front of her. I couldn't. I had
no right. I told him that, and that I wouldn't go back there,
see her eyes, die. I'd even thought in the night about asking
him to take me to Africa. He could find work for me there.
I'd already learned a lot at the hospital.

He grasped my wrists.

"Remember, Cecile, how we talked about choices that
night in Malbuisson? Now you no longer have any choice.
You have to do as I say."

I cried, "But why?"

"To be able to live again. Because you could go to the
ends of Africa, or even farther, and you'd still be bringing
yourself with you, and the weight you're carrying: the weight
of your father's death, of not being able to forgive yourself.
You could move all the mountains in the world, and it
wouldn't make you feel any better."

He said that judging by the way Beatrice and Pauline
had described my mother, things should work out. And
maybe she didn't have quite the same theory about my
father's death that I did.

"Have you stopped to think how she'd feel tonight if
you didn't come home?"

I'd imagined her forgiving me, admiring me for my heroic work. I'd seen myself lying on the ground, dying for
a great cause, to everyone's admiration, and her on her
knees beside me, stroking my forehead the way she'd stroked
Pauline's the night before to convince her to go home with
Benjamin. I'd only thought of my own suffering, not hers,
as usual.

"I'd kill her, too, right?"

He didn't answer. He got up and went to open the big

window: "Listen — morning recess!" The air blossomed with the cries of children.

I leaned back against the couch, closed my eyes, and let myself rise with the sound of children playing. I floated. I may have dozed, I was so tired. When I opened my eyes, Emmanuel wasn't there. Recess was over, I had a blanket on my legs, and I heard a shower running. He had said, "If it's all right with you, I'll get dressed and take you home." It wasn't all right with me.

On a corner of the coffee table was a magazine about relief work, the whole cover taken up with a child's face. All eyes. I took the yogurt, opened it, and drank right from the carton. It was too sweet, it dribbled down my chin, but it was the best thing I'd ever tasted in my life.

53

The Pardon

THE MORNING was light and transparent. Rain, then sun right after, everything was flying: a landscape of wings and mirrors. We were already driving outside the city. I looked at the houses, some with gardens in front, and tried to guess how people lived. It was easier when there were sheets or bedspreads hung over balconies to air.

Emmanuel was talking. He was saying that when a wound is infected you have to go ahead and lance it, no matter how much it hurts, open it up to cleanse it, because if the smallest site of infection is left, the infection will always prevail.

It was ten o'clock. My mother's classes were held in the afternoon. In the morning she studied at home with cassettes. She had three courses on tape: shorthand, typing, medical terminology. That way the school saved money on teachers. I was going home because I was being made to, but I wouldn't talk. I wouldn't be able to.

He drove too fast. We were already going through the St. Germain forest. I rolled down the window to smell the trees. This was where the biggest local fair in the area was held each year. We used to go on scary rides for the thrill of feeling like we were dying. We'd bring home goldfish, balloons, cheap dolls. The fish would die, the balloons deflate, the dolls fall apart, but for a moment a feeling of newness would have blown through our lives, yes, out of nowhere. . . .

Emmanuel was still talking. He was saying that any operation leaves you feeling weak. You've used a lot of strength rallying your defenses, and it doesn't come back overnight. But one morning you wake up stronger and mysteriously happy because you understand the value of life so much better.

We were crossing the Oise. We passed Conflans, where the open-air market was at its height of mingled colors and sounds, like good paintings where life sometimes cries out so loud it's deafening. We turned toward the housing project. Among these tall gray buildings, like fireless chimneys, there was one where Tanguy had lived, crying in the wilderness of himself. When you've been close to suffering, Emmanuel was saying, and have been lucky enough to survive, you can sense it in others, and then you can help them, you are really "brothers," a word he used often, perhaps his favorite word. I could tell what my brother Emmanuel was doing with his words: administering anesthesia. He was keeping me from thinking, from being afraid, from opening the door and bolting out.

He turned onto the road to Mareuil, then found his way down along the river. Here was the gate to my house. He stopped in front of it. The shutters in the master bedroom were open, and smoke curled from the working chimney.

I asked, "How did you know the way here?" He looked embarrassed: "I came this way once when I was out on a Sunday drive. Just wanted to see what kind of barracks my little soldier has."

Then I told him that a soldier knew how to fight but I didn't. I was just the opposite, always afraid, I spent my life running away, and I'd never have the courage to talk to my mother. I begged him, "Please come in with me. I need you."

I saw his eyes soften. For a few seconds I thought he might take me in his arms, but he turned toward La Marette.

"Some things you have to do alone, or you can't take all the credit, and one day you might regret it."

I regretted only one thing: believing he'd help me. I told him so, and he didn't answer. I got out of the car he'd borrowed from a friend, with the word *Paramedic* painted on it and a blue light on the hood that, when it was flashing, helped you get places faster. I was just lucky he hadn't used it to bring me back to my misery.

In the living room there was a voice that wasn't my mother's. This strange voice was saying that thermometers, bandages, gauze, hypodermic syringes, stethoscopes needed to be ordered. It spoke of hemorrhage, fainting, nausea, contagion. My mother was sitting at the dining room table, across from the tape recorder, taking dictation from the tape. She stopped it when I walked in.

I went straight to the French doors overlooking the yard and opened them. I ripped out the page where Bernadette built a treehouse in the woods, and the one where my father put up a rose arbor; seasons full of flowers, nuts, and apples they say are gifts from the Lord. And then I let it all tumble out at once.

With a shudder through my whole body, I heard my mother get up. I felt her come close. She closed her arms around me as you do to love someone, but sometimes to smother them, too. She repeated several times, "So that was it . . . so that was it."

And as she spoke, she told me that she'd often see Daddy clutch at his heart, that he sometimes had pain in his chest from a pinched nerve, that the will he had written in December was simply to update one he'd had drawn up the year before, that yes, she most emphatically agreed with Pauline that I was always sticking my nose in other people's business, that I'd really made a mess of things with Benjamin, that half the time the way I acted was totally irresponsible, that I hadn't changed since the time when, for instance, I'd jumped fully clothed into the Armançon River near Grandmother's, trying to save someone from drowning, forgetting that I didn't know how to swim — and it was the drowning victim who'd pulled me out of the water, losing his snorkel in the bargain. I was still the little girl who brought tramps home, promising that my father would fix them up, she could cite me a million examples, but it was usually just because I got carried away by my big heart, the way I had with Tanguy, and if Daddy had planned to die of stress, he could have found all he needed in one day at the hospital. As she told me in a lower voice that since that night before Christmas I hadn't said more than ten words to her except for everyday conversation, I hadn't looked her in the eye, I'd avoided her, she'd been at her wit's end, she'd thought I was mad at her without knowing why, except the night I fixed her a nice dinner, a sort of party, but still clammed up, and now we would finally be able to breathe again, she had her Cecile back, her daughter . . . as she said all this, life surged back into me so violently that I felt like I was dying.

Or being born.

～ 54 ～

Easter

BERNADETTE DECIDED that for Easter she wanted the whole family in Normandy, at Mandreville, her in-laws' castle, in the Saint-Aimond family for three hundred years, if you please. We all arrived on Saturday with loads of Easter eggs and candy packed in each trunk. The Easter Bunny would hide them for Sunday morning: out on the grounds if the weather was nice, inside the house if it rained. There were huge baskets for the kids crammed with chocolate eggs and bunnies, not of the best quality, and dozens of colored eggs. The adults would get smaller baskets but with the finest quality chocolate.

At the end of a drive lined with apple trees in blossom, the castle looked pink, a checkerboard of brick and stone, with a multicolored roof, three towers with a view of the sea. The Saint-Aimonds were shopping in Deauville with Stephan, so Bernadette was the welcoming committee. First she introduced us to Bastien, the caretaker, who had a thatch of white hair beneath his beret and a ring of keys jangling on his belt, and Rose, his wife; we were advised to stay in her good graces because she was in charge of the kitchen. Rose wore three aprons, one on top of another, the same as Henriette, Grandmother's cook — that meant her cooking had to be good!

Proud as princesses, the twins dragged their cousins off to the room where there was supposedly a puppet theater, and Bernadette gave us the grand tour: reception rooms, billiard room, library, all full of paneling, tapestries, and hunting trophies. Then we went up the broad stone staircase that led to the bedrooms, beneath the severe glances of the various counts and countesses of Saint-Aimond, seated or standing, in their gilded frames. Four sisters in jeans and sneakers must be something of a change!

The rooms were princely, each with a fireplace, a canopy bed, and superantique furniture. Superantique as far as creature comforts went, too! The only heating was from big down quilts, and for freshening up there was a flowered pitcher and basin.

"They have too much to do, with an acre of roof to repair, to put in any more bathrooms," Bernadette explained.

There was one bathroom for thirty-five bedrooms! But it didn't matter: there was a wonderful sense of the past, plus the aroma of apples drying in the attic.

We found the kids in the kitchen, sitting down to mugs of hot chocolate and homemade sweet rolls. Rose wanted to serve us tea in the salon, but we wouldn't hear of it: we'd have a cup here, with her, and didn't she have enough to do with the seafood in puff pastry and the leg of lamb she was making for tonight?

"I have something to tell you all," Bernadette declared when our cups were filled.

She wore the expression she always had on important occasions, at once hardheaded and flustered. Well, she told us, with the money Daddy had left her, she'd begun to dream of buying a few ponies and opening a stable here at Mandreville.

"What about your husband?"

"He'd have to find a job around here."

"And what about his parents?" Mom worried. "What will they think of the idea?"

"I don't know," Bernadette said, "but I think it's high time to put some life back into this old joint!"

The Princess sighed. A joint like this would have suited her fine. For the moment, only Bastien and Rose were in on the deal. Bernadette was waiting for the right time to present her plan, but one thing was for sure: since she'd come up with the idea, her life had changed. It seemed as if the skies of Normandy filled her little apartment in Neuilly.

"You can count on my share of the will, too," I said. "I've been wondering how to invest it."

Everyone's eyes grew wide. Just because you're careful with a dollar, you get cast as a tightwad.

"Providing I share in the profits," I added, "and get to ride for free."

Bernadette kissed me, something that happens once in a blue moon. Pauline said she'd be in charge of PR, and the Princess volunteered as a weekend hostess. Without listening to Mom, who begged us to get our feet back on the ground, we were already set up in the castle and making a fortune when the rightful owners suddenly appeared in the kitchen: so this was where we'd been hiding ourselves! They'd looked all over for us.

"A kitchen is the best place for daydreams," I said, "with a cup of hot cocoa . . ."

Everyone shuddered. But that was all I said. Hervé de Saint-Aimond didn't say no.

And then it was already Easter! Everyone trooped over to Mass in the little church around the bend. Pauline and I stayed behind to hide the Easter eggs. The morning was blue and gold. We started on the lawn in front of the castle. Hedges, shrubs, a variety of trees, rabbit holes, and molehills made easy work of it. We left a few eggs sticking out as clues for our little treasure hunters.

"Remember," said Pauline, "how Daddy would never eat his Easter candy? How he'd hide it in his drawer and then when ours was all gone he'd pull it out and tease us?"

"It always annoyed Mom. . . ."

"She called him Father Pelican."

My sister came closer to me. She looked at me for a moment in silence. Every time I talked about Daddy, my throat . . .

"You know, I felt guilty about him, too. . . ."

"What?"

"That business with Paul, the trip to the mountains . . . I thought that couldn't have helped his heart either, that the thing with Tanguy wasn't the only . . ."

Our eyes met: case closed. We wouldn't mention it again.

Now we heard church bells pealing wildly. Noon! And all over the countryside other bells answered. The whole horizon vibrated, and children all over France were looking for eggs . . . and the screams we heard were from our little ones, running full steam, followed by the grown-ups, amused by their haste. Pauline gathered them around her and swore she'd just seen a bunny hopping by. They were bursting with impatience, but we had to wait until everyone was there before we let them start, including Rose and Bastien.

"One, two, three, go!" said Paul.

Gabriel was disorganized, darting all over the place, scattering his energy. Melanie and Sophie worked without letting go of each other's hands, busier giggling than finding eggs. Benjamin proceeded methodically, tiptoeing from spot to spot. So he could talk to a computer and still believe in the Easter Bunny! I loved it. Every time one of them found an egg and read the name on it there were happy cries and they'd put it into one of the baskets the parents were guarding.

Only one egg was missing now. The "two bunnies," Paul joked, had forgotten where they had put it, and catching the kids' enthusiasm, the grown-ups started hunting, too. Mom was the one who found it, with Bernadette's name on it. Applause! Now we were all accounted for.

Then I handed out the baskets, in order of age. The kids were relieved to see that the big baskets full of candy were for them. The men took theirs with slightly embarrassed looks, as if poking fun at the children inside them. Antoine started playing kickball with his egg. Rose and Bastien seemed thrilled with their baskets and happy to be included.

Afterward, following an old local tradition, we went to the castle farmhouse to taste the newly fermented cider. It was the time to drink it: the cuckoo had sung three times and the moon was right. On the wooden table were bottles, mugs, plates of pastries. The cider was rough on the palate. "It's sour," said Sophie, wincing. Gabriel asked for seconds just to show off.

As I admired a huge armoire carved with doves and roses, Bastien came up to me. His corduroy jacket smelled new, and he had on his best beret.

"Did you know, Miss Cecile, that in Normandy an armoire used to be a woman's dowry?

"When Rose was born," he explained, "her father cut down an oak tree. While the wood took its time aging and drying, the women worked on the trousseau. As soon as Rose was engaged, the cabinetmaker started work. The doves stand for love; the number of roses shows that the family was prosperous. A few days before the wedding, the armoire was brought to the bride's new house, filled with the trousseau, so the wedding guests could come and count the sheets, napkins, and tablecloths."

"It's all still in perfect condition," Rose remarked proudly, throwing open the twin doors to show neat stacks of lavender-scented linen.

"Back then, things were made to last," said Bastien, an arm circling his wife's waist.

Bernadette walked up. "I think Mandreville breeds happy marriages," she said in a booming voice.

Stephan whirled around in astonishment. Her cheeks were flushed: from drink or from excitement? Mom eyed her nervously.

"I have a dream," the horsewoman said to her husband. "We move to Mandreville . . ."

"But what would you do here?" Pauline asked innocently.

"Buy a few ponies," Bernadette answered. "Give children rides and lessons, just a small operation."

"Where would you get the money to start?" Claire said, looking perfectly astounded.

"With what Daddy left me," said Bernadette. "He loved nature, I know he'd approve. . . ."

Realizing now that she'd let the cat out of the bag, Bernadette looked at her attentive, silent in-laws. I seemed to read a sort of hidden smile on their faces. And I could see they'd expected this. So what was keeping them from saying yes? They knew that my sister was unhappy in the city.

"There's room," Bastien interjected after lengthily clearing his throat, "plenty of room here. And it would be good to have children around this old place."

"In your dream," asked Stephan, "what am I, the stableboy?"

"Of course not," Bernadette said indignantly. "The ponies would never make it. In my dream you're . . . a rising young lawyer in Normandy."

Mom held her breath. And it was to her that Hervé de Saint-Aimond turned. He was holding his Easter basket,

271

which didn't make him look serious at all. He didn't sound it, either.

"For a while now we've been wondering why Bernadette spent all her visits here out in the stable plotting something with Bastien. So this explains things."

Bernadette looked at her father-in-law's happy face. The blood had left her cheeks; she was white as a sheet.

"So it's not a definite no?" she said in a quavering voice.

"Or a definite yes," Stephan broke in. He pointed to the armoire: "Know what? I've had the same dream as you: living here. That must be what makes marriages last, right, Bastien? When you end up having the same dreams. But don't expect your rising young lawyer to turn Mandreville into a riding stable without studying every side of the question. . . ."

I didn't have time to enjoy my sister's reaction, because a car pulled up in front of the farmhouse. Because a man got out, and suddenly I no longer knew where I was. Nothing is more contagious than dreams.

"Oh, Lord," Pauline exclaimed, "the egg hunt got me completely rattled. I forgot to tell you, Pest . . . sorry, Cecile . . . Emmanuel called last night. He's spending Easter with friends near here, he wanted to see you, I told him to stop by this afternoon. Looks like you'll have to share your candy."

55

The Harbor

NARROW AND SLATE-CAPPED, the houses huddled along the waterfront to watch the spectacle of
many-colored boats rocking in the breeze in Honfleur's
old harbor. A fresh, easy light — sun gleaming on water —
enveloped the town. Everything floated.

"How do you like that one?" asked Emmanuel, pointing
to a tiny boat painted an unusual shade of blue, with a
spanking clean deck and a dollhouse cabin shuttered tight:
The Periwinkle.

"It's beautiful!"

"So what are you waiting for? All hands on deck!"

Amazed, I watched him head up the plank. He stretched
out a hand to me.

"But we can't! It's not ours!"

"Don't be so sure."

I took his hand and walked up on deck with him. He
removed the cover from a chest by the rudder, found some
cushions, sat down on one, and motioned me to the one
beside him. He smiled at my astonishment.

"See that hotel?" he asked, pointing toward the waterfront. "The owner's son is an old school friend of mine.
With Easter, every room was booked. So he let me have

his boat for the night. Just don't ask me to take you for a spin. I'm hopeless."

On the dock, people stopped and gawked at us enviously. We'd gone over to the other side, the right side, the sea. They were simply landlubbers. A fishing boat sailed slowly home through the harbor, the putt-putt of its engine like a heartbeat. Emmanuel sighed with contentment.

"I'm a mountain man, and now a kind of desert nomad, so the sea is magic for me. Exciting and restful at the same time."

"The sea can be an enemy."

"But never completely. A nurturing enemy, a love-hate relationship. You know how men talk about it. Like a woman."

I felt the sea breathing beneath my body. It carried and rocked me, gave its spray to the wind, wavelets to the sunshine. A woman . . . I liked the way he said the word; it moved me somewhere. I looked at him. He'd pushed up the sleeves of his sweater; his arms were strong, tanned. Was I really here with him? This morning I was hiding Easter eggs, making peace with Pauline. How was it possible that nothing inside me had signaled that I'd be seeing him in a few hours? There must have been some sign; I just hadn't noticed.

"Paul has a boat," I said. "And in the summer, with Pauline . . ."

"No," he said.

He touched a finger to my lips: "You've already told me all about Pauline, and Benjamin, and Claire, and Bernadette and her pony rides. Now it's your turn."

"Nothing to tell about me."

I blurted it out. He laughed and turned to look me full in the face, not let me get away.

"Listen to her! Nothing to tell . . . She shows up at your house one day at the crack of dawn, a complete wreck, but it was nothing! She comes into your life, turns everything upside down, messes with your head, disturbs your sleep, but don't take it seriously, everything's fine, nothing to tell."

His laugh got me started. He was right. My own private garden, my brush, my jungle was not a place I felt like exploring. That was probably why I was a squatter in other people's: so I wouldn't have to face my own. Sitting on the pier, barefoot, a boy played the guitar. The notes riffed in the sunlight, sought out my past, opened it like a fallen fruit. No! I was "now," not yesterday. I had to make the most of this moment consisting of Emmanuel and me, the sea, sunshine, and music. I didn't want to wait for tomorrow to tell myself it was good.

"Sometimes I have trouble living today. Or rather, enjoying the present. I always feel I'm 'before,' or 'after,' never 'now,' and it's not comfortable at all."

He smiled.

" 'Before' was you with your sisters; you were one of four, in a happy, unbroken family. 'During' was the hard times you've just been through; and 'ahead' is Cecile facing herself."

He took my wrists, held them tight, looked at me intensely.

"And 'now' is the two of us here. And you know that I came to Normandy just for you, don't you?"

My heart was thudding: sometimes you know things but don't really dare believe them.

"I'll be leaving for Africa at the end of the month."

"So soon!"

The words slipped out, and he smiled. But I liked knowing he was around, even if I didn't see him much; being able to tell myself that hearing his voice was as simple as dialing a number, even if I didn't call him. The idea that he was about to leave made me feel abandoned.

"I'm glad you said that," he told me. "Before I leave, I want to talk to you about Tanguy."

Something ground to a halt inside me. The end of feeling good, of the joy rising in me. It was awful. And yet those words were inevitable. I'd been expecting them.

"I know how much you loved him. You told me how much you shared."

Now, right away, I should tell him the truth; there had been nothing between us, as I had led him to believe. I wasn't sure I'd even loved Tanguy. He was handsome, and the first boy who looked at me differently. We had never had sex. The one time he'd tried, I'd run away. I had never made love. No man had even really kissed me. I wanted to tell him, but the words wouldn't come out.

"And you told me that you want to be faithful to his memory," Emmanuel said. "But it shouldn't be out of guilt."

I murmured, "I think Daddy got me over the guilt part."

He had come to my room every morning and explained that Tanguy had wanted to die, that he'd only used me, that he would have found a way sooner or later anyway. If I felt guilty about anything, it was about forgetting him so fast. The memory was fading. My eyes were dry when I thought about him, as if my father, in leaving, abandoning me, had taken all my pain, all my tears.

"The other thing," I said, "is that I feel so alone."

"You're not alone," said Emmanuel. "I love you."

He said it. This man told me he loved me, and the moment was suddenly suspended in time. I saw every detail of the waterfront: the couple strolling hand in hand, the tourist wearing an odd hat, the child licking an ice cream cone, the distant window cheerful with flowers that a woman was watering. Everything was very clear, almost raw, like an image I would lose. They say that in the few seconds before you die your whole life appears before you, flood-lighted. I must be having a foretaste.

"I love you because you're real," Emmanuel said. "Because you don't play games. One thing I've never compromised on is sincerity."

The lighting flashed off. Everything was gray. He never compromised. If he found out that I'd lied to him, he would reject me. I turned away. I didn't know if I loved him, but something was tearing me apart. He took my hands, joined them together, raised them to his mouth, grazed his lips over them.

"Don't be so scared, my darling, listen, I'm not asking you for anything. I realize it's too soon."

Then he got up, looking happy, light.

"And now, sailor girl, what would you say to some shrimp and white wine here on deck?"

We went back down among the earthlings. He slipped his arm around my shoulder, and we walked in the Honfleur springtime. On every streetcorner, the walls of a house, the wooden steeple of a church, the faded lettering above a door told us finished stories, suffering and joy long past. I longed to be able to start all over again, to meet Emmanuel for the first time, to be real and sincere, not play games. This huge weight in my chest, this regret, and at the same time, by his side, this sweetness, this feeling of being where I belonged — perhaps it was love. Not violent or wrenching, as it had been with Tanguy, but deep, engulfing. One certainty: him.

We bought a big sack of fresh shrimp, some dark bread, salted butter, and white wine. The sky was blood-streaked. I wished he would raise anchor and take me away by force, far away, beyond myself. We went down into the cabin to get the dishes. Everything was in miniature, clean, nice. We couldn't move without bumping into each other. I asked him, "Do you still wear your medal?" He turned toward me and pulled down the neck of his sweater to show me. It was a medal of Our Lady. I closed my eyes:

Mary, help me. And suddenly I was against him. He put his arms around me and held me tight, as I had wanted, as if to take me away; then he let go, he stroked back my hair, he took my face in his hands, pressed his lips to mine. He opened, penetrated them. My heart was beating so strong. I felt a kind of gigantic silence enfold us. The first, and you don't even know it. It was sweet, profound, imperious as well. I was drained.

His hands slid down my back to press me against him. I felt him. He stopped kissing me. He looked into my eyes and murmured something like "Want to?" His face wasn't the same; his eyes, his tense, almost harsh, expression were familiar: desire, Tanguy. I said no and pushed him away. I was afraid, ashamed, ashamed of my fear, afraid of my body that was becoming a river, afraid of his urgency against me, of what he'd discover, my lie, my lack of experience.

"Forgive me," he said. "I understand. I really do. And I swore to myself that I wouldn't rush you! But you felt so close to me all of a sudden."

We went up on the deck for our dinner. The day was fading, and along the waterfront, on the restaurant doors, on the masts of boats in the harbor, ribbons of light appeared. It was beautiful. A holiday. He told me about his work, the other world down there, which I imagined, I don't know why, as a prison with bars of sun and sand, with hands stretching out from them, hands he took as he had taken mine a while before. I answered, I asked questions, but I wasn't really there anymore. I was hopelessly "before." It had been so good when he had invited me up on deck, when the barefoot guitar player had unwittingly dedicated the notes of his song to us, when he hadn't said Tanguy's name or the word *sincerity*. Yes, so good.

Late that night he drove me back to Mandreville.

"Remember when I told you how you used to visit me at night when I was in Africa? I barely knew you, but that

didn't stop me from dreaming of you, without really understanding what was happening to me: a slip of a girl in
a strange nightshirt, making me show her her choices. . . ."

He wanted to know if he should keep expecting my
visits when he was back there, if I'd think about joining
him there for real someday, to learn with him how to live
in the present. I didn't need to answer right away. I should
think it over. The next afternoon, before he went back to
Paris, he'd stop by Mandreville to see me. All he asked
for was a word of hope. He didn't want to dream for
nothing.

56

Sand Castles

BENJAMIN LOOKED AT THE SEA. He squeezed our hands, Pauline's and mine, and craned his neck toward the moving mass exploding and spreading in the distance. His expression was eager and almost painful. Benjamin was discovering life, in all its violence and beauty.

Paul looked at Benjamin discovering the sea. He was no longer the writer or journalist in search of the right phrase, the right touch; he was the father of this tiny boy prey to his feelings. Paul watched this frail ship being launched into life, and his own face was also full of pain.

Pauline looked at Paul, the man she had wanted and who had given her this child. She looked at the father discovering the child, and her face shone with loving and giving, in spite of everything.

I looked at the liquid and roaring realm we are supposed to have come from, the water, salt, and power, each of which our bodies carry. I lost myself in the movement, I accepted the fact that, one by one, things and people disappear. I accepted it? For the time being.

"Can we bring some home?" Benjamin asked.

He let go of our hands and knelt on the sand, looking

at the sea's offerings without daring to touch them: shells, seaweed, debris.

"All you want," said Pauline. "It's all yours!"

Then he plunged his hands into the sand, took it by fistfuls, let it run through his fingers, laughed in happiness and amazement. Yes, it all belonged to us. Yesterday, on the waterfront at Honfleur, a boy had said the same thing with his guitar. We are lifetime owners of this beauty, these blues, ochers, greens, these smells, too. And we keep forgetting.

"Let's go wading," Paul proposed to his son.

Benjamin looked at his tiny feet, then at the sea, then at his mother.

"You have to listen to grown-ups," he said nervously. "They know best."

"They know that the sea won't eat you up," Pauline said with a laugh. "Go ahead, guys. We'll join you in a minute."

We watched them walk off, Benjamin holding Paul's hand. Without his cane or his shoes, Paul looked fragile. Benjamin was used to his father's limp and adjusted his stride. We sat down. Pauline put her arms around her raised knees, rested her chin on them.

"Dr. Chalain finished testing him," she said out of the blue. "Math is where he really stands out. I guess his scores are amazing for his age."

"What are you going to do about it?"

"The main thing is not to hold him back. The educational system doesn't have much to offer for kids like him. Chalain is trying to organize a group. Ben will be in it."

"What does Paul have to say about it?"

"He's proud, of course. But afraid of pushing him. He knows what it's like to be different."

She turned to me: "Apparently it was high time we did something about it. Will you help us?"

"I'd be glad to, but how?"

"You can love him. Love him a lot. The way he is."

In the distance, a small boy bent over to pick something up and show it to his father. Then they continued their walk. The beach was crowded, no surprise since it was Easter vacation and the weather was exceptionally fine. Everybody seemed to be playing ball. Our exceptional little boy would have to learn that playing is important; we'd have to help him find his place among other children. I stretched out on the sand, where winter still lurked. Pauline looked at me.

"And how are things with Emmanuel?"

"I think he likes me."

She laughed: "The way you say it! You almost sound annoyed."

Again his arms were around me, and at first he held me without moving. Then his mouth reached for mine, and he pressed it open. When I remembered, something stirred in my groin. Then his hands slid down my back, I felt him hard against me, I saw how he looked at me, and I was afraid. . . .

"I did something really stupid," I said.

"You don't say," sighed Pauline. "Tell me."

"I told him that I slept with Tanguy and it was heaven."

She laughed. "Only heaven would do. People usually try to hide their affairs, and you make one up. Why on earth did you tell him that?"

"I don't know. To make trouble for myself, I guess. The old Pest at work."

"So why don't you get the Pest to tell the truth?"

"I tried. I couldn't."

"Then just go ahead and do it with him, he'll figure things out!"

I straightened up and looked at her — her pretty face

that melts everyone's defenses, her slim body, her flat stomach, legs up to her neck. "Did it ever occur to you that it's possible to be afraid of sex, turned off by the whole idea?" I asked.

All you hear about is girls who start in the cradle, do it anywhere, with anyone, don't care. And what about the rest of us? The ones who don't dare, never try, but not always on principle, who'd like to but can't, one step forward and two back, who tell themselves they don't know how to love, are afraid they're waiting too long, they'll never find it, never "do it" — you never hear about them. It's not the kind of teenage sexuality they write about.

Pauline's eyes had drifted to the horizon. Her turn had come when she was just seventeen. His name was Pierre; he painted the sea.

"You won't be turned off by it when you're in love. You may be afraid, but that's something you give along with the rest, and in a way it's part of the pleasure."

So here was pleasure. Spread out on the front pages of newspapers, in close-up on the screen, in specialists' books, weighed and dissected like meat in a butcher's case, sexual pleasure, I won't say the word, everyone knows what it is, it rhymes with chasm. And there you are with your back to this wall of words, images, and cries, and you ask yourself: "Will my body know how? Will my brain love enough?" Would I ever bridge that chasm?

And you wish your father was there to push you, as he did when you were on the brink of learning to swim, ride a bike, go ahead, you can do it, all right, go on. But some fathers leave you high and dry without finishing their job, and now my father would never know the man who would bring me to the heights — if I did get there — he would never even say his name; and the thought of that killed me.

"Do you love him?" Pauline asked.

"I don't really know. When I imagine myself without him, everything's empty."

. . . But when I'm with him I panic. Now tears welled up. I got to my feet. All night long I'd asked myself that question. If I loved him, I had to tell him. If I didn't love him, it was over. It hurt. I ran into the seascape that never stopped being born, falling back on itself. The wind bit my face, spoke of the sea but also of a mountain meadow, the flowers and fruit to come, nature awakening, opening, dilating, bursting, reaching its own climax under the sun. All of that is a blessing, but its beauty is painful when you don't share it with anyone. Emmanuel . . . what had I done?

"Hey, stop!" Pauline yelled. "Are you crazy, or what? And you could at least help me. . . ."

I stopped. She didn't have enough hands to carry everything — Benjamin's shoes and sweater, Paul's cane — not enough heart to hold all her loves, her joys and pains. Lucky her.

They'd made a sand castle, fortified with seaweed, decorated with shells, and surrounded by moats.

"Next we'll make the church and maybe the ponies," said Benjamin, flushed with excitement and happiness.

"You'll never have time," said Pauline. "The sea's almost here."

Benjamin turned around, saw the waves breaking only a few yards away, went up to his father.

"Dad, how about if we move it into the trunk and head home?"

"You can't move sand," Paul explained. "Look."

A piece of tower crumbled in his fingers.

"The sea takes everything except boats," I said. "And even those have to be strong."

"All right, next time we'll build a big boat," Ben decided.

Meanwhile, we strengthened the castle's defenses. That's

why they're built in the first place, to defy the inevitable: time, and sometimes other kids who are jealous and kick the walls, throw things. We all went to work. People stopped to watch us. Sea foam was bubbling in the moats, the towers were slowly sinking, the shells drifting off in the waves, the walls eroding; the last piece of seaweed floated away. It was over, everything was smooth, things were as they should be again and people seemed happy; that's life.

Benjamin pursed his lips: "I don't like the sea," he said. "You can't stop it."

"Smart little boy," a woman remarked. "How old is he?"

"Four," Pauline answered.

Her tone was not friendly, and the spectators walked away, grumbling. We'd have to learn to accept Benjamin as he was, or else how would he ever accept himself?

The bells in Houlgate's church steeple chimed five. And suddenly waves were also unleashed inside me. I'd felt them coming closer for a while now, I'd felt my defenses crumble one by one, along with the words I'd repeated to myself all night long, the excuses I'd made, the dreams. Anguish swept over me. What had I done?

"I want to go now," I said.

"Something the matter?"

I nodded. Yes, something was the matter! Why had I come to the beach with them? Why had I asked them to take me? Emmanuel had said, "I'll stop by tomorrow afternoon." All he wanted was a word of hope.

His car wasn't in the drive. In the salon, Claire was playing chess with Bernadette. Bernadette looked somber: it was a safe bet she was losing. She's the world's worst player. She cheats, takes back her moves, makes you feel guilty. She always has to win, in everything.

I asked, "Any calls for me?"

"No, but your friend stopped by," Claire said. "He seemed disappointed that you weren't here."

I avoided Pauline's fierce stare. Yes, Pauline, I ran away. Hadn't she guessed? About all I ever did: run away or dream.

"No message?"

"Yes, he said to say goodbye for him. Is he going somewhere?"

He was leaving! Going away on the boat where he'd wanted to take me, where in his arms I might have learned to accept the movement of the sea, of time, the crumbling of childhood's castles, the death of a father. In the Africa he called "down there" with a light in his eyes, his door would be closed to me from now on. I'd lost him. And the silence that suddenly filled me, the loneliness, made me realize that I loved him.

"Nice going," said Pauline. "You win again."

57

Marie

BY THE MAIN ENTRANCE to the hospital, forehead on his knees, face hidden, a young man had been sitting for two days. He had traced a circle around himself in chalk and written: *I have nothing.* People quickened their pace when they saw him. Who could tell whether it was true that he had nothing, whether it was his own fault or others had traced a circle around his life? The only thing for certain was that he wasn't warm. *April is the cruelest month.* He had nothing to protect him from the rain, and perhaps he was hunched over to fight the chill as well as to hide his shame.

I asked Mom if I could have some of my father's old clothes, the untouchable ones in the back of the hall closet. I'd found a good use for them, and Daddy would have approved, I guaranteed it. Mom hesitated. She finally let me have them, as long as I promised to leave her out of it.

I understood why when I opened the bag. The smell rose to my nose, my throat, my heart. Here he was, Dr. Charles Moreau, much more vivid than in photographs or my memory. The smell of soil — he used his old clothes for gardening — the smell of pipe tobacco, the smell of wool mixed with his own odor. I took the best pair of pants, a sweater, his old suede jacket, and a shirt with the sleeves cut off. I put them in another bag, tied it to the back of my moped, and set it in the circle next to the young man. I wanted to tell him, "Please take them, wear them!" If he did, he'd be doing *me* a favor.

Marie, the accident victim, was still there, Room 306. Her parents had filled her room with the things she loved: a tattered bear, pictures, books, tapes. About the same stuff I had at home. There were snickers about my old teddy bear, tears over Marie's. She could have been me. A member of her family came every day to talk to her, read to her, put on some music. "You never know," her brother said, clenching his jaw. "Imagine that she can hear, just a little, but can't tell us." Around Marie's neck was a medal of the Blessed Virgin. Without her faith, her mother wouldn't have been able to stand it.

And what if God exists through our need of him? If He is the need, the straining toward something higher I have often felt inside, the clenched jaws of Marie's brother, her mother's flicker of hope? In that case He'd be called life.

That evening I went to see her. The dinner hour was over. The hospital begins to sleep then, even if the sun is still shining on everyone else. I sat down on her bed and told her it was springtime. A spring so long in coming, then exploding all of a sudden, working miracles everywhere from one day to the next. At home, the forsythia had already yielded to purple azaleas; people walked with their heads up in the tender green of the trees; and on the way back from Normandy I'd seen the golden lakes of flowering rapeseed waving against the blue of the sky, and it was so much a new beginning that my heart had ached.

And yet, I told her, there wasn't much happiness in the air — more like widespread depression. Specialists were studying the problem, had found all kinds of important reasons, when all they needed to do was to look a little deeper in people's eyes to understand. People didn't know how to believe, or what. They'd been told too many stories, had too much made-up happiness dangled in front of them, and at the same time they'd been deprived of what used to motivate them, those distant lights called values that made you want to move toward something better. They drew circles around themselves, like the man on the sidewalk. And yet as soon as you believe in something solid, even if it's only an idea, it changes everything. Just look at Bernadette!

A nurse came in. Was everything all right? Fine, thanks. Marie was breathing. Nothing was missing when I checked her: eyes, nose, ears, mouth. Except they weren't connected. The more you looked at her, the less you believed they'd ever start working again. There must be a word, a sound, a touch that would get the juices flowing. You wished you could be God and flick the switch. Him again!

I told Marie that a man loved me. I thought I loved him, too, but I'd spoiled everything. Since one afternoon on a boat, I'd felt as though I was wasting my life, wasting my time on the wrong path. It was certainly selfish of me to talk to her that way, since her own path was in almost total darkness, but with a sick person or a corpse you're bound to think of yourself, everyone agrees even if no one dares admit it; the only thing that counts is being ready to give if you're asked, and I was ready.

I was taking her as a friend! The ones she'd had before talked about her now in the past tense; now she would be my friend just as she was, and I would act as hers. I would come to see her regularly, I'd keep her informed, and on the outside I'd try to breathe for her, see for her, and, if I could, love for her, too.

On her cheeks, suddenly, I saw two tears roll down. It scared the living daylights out of me. I ran out into the hall and yelled: Marie was crying, Marie could hear, she was trying to tell me something. The nurse ran in. I showed her. She took a handkerchief out from under the pillow and wiped Marie's cheeks. I shouldn't get so excited. This wasn't the first time. All that week, almost every day, Marie's tears had flowed. It didn't mean she was suffering; in fact, it was probably a sign of healing.

It was seven o'clock when I left the hospital. The air was heavy with the smell of sunset, the mild night to come. The young man was no longer in his circle, and neither were my father's clothes. In place of them, some scribbling: the word *thanks*? I was probably imagining things. I have an unfortunate tendency to daydream; in my head, blocks of rapeseed bloom in every season. It would be nicer if they weren't complete with weeds and thorns and certain poisonous mushrooms I've cultivated since childhood.

Meanwhile, my father's old jacket was beginning a new career on someone's shoulders, and that was good. No one will ever dissuade me from the idea that in something you've worn, looked at, or loved a lot, you leave something of yourself, a sort of force that waits to be used again, and whether he wanted it or not, I had put some love on that young man's back.

I saw Marie's tears. A voice rose in me. It said I had no right to ruin my life. It screamed, "Go get him."

∽ 58 ∽

A Schoolyard, a Chestnut Tree

I TOOK THE TRAIN, the subway. Down there, no springtime, except dummied up on the walls. I ran down the avenue that led to "his" street. Don't think, just go up, say it all. My heart was beating hard. I let it calm down a minute in front of the school, "his" school, my eyes raised to the eighth floor, the bay window where a sheer curtain billowed: he was there, I could go ahead!

Something fluttered beneath my feet: the pink and white froth of chestnut blossoms. I looked around. The main door to the school was open, and you could see the huge tree invading the whole courtyard with its foliage. The children must have fun with it: chestnut fights, lacy leaf cutouts. I slipped into the schoolyard and laid a hand on the trunk.

It was cleaning time in the classrooms. The doors were open; there was a sound of vacuuming. He had told me, "I have a whole school, a schoolyard, recess." He'd shown me the desks, the tables, the blackboards. In a little while I would look at them with him again. A little while? It was really scary, but I did it: went into the nearest classroom, smelling of books, chalk, dust, and childhood, and on the board I wrote his name in huge letters: *Emmanuel*. He'd never believe it!

I took the elevator this time. I would talk the minute he opened the door: "I lied to you: Tanguy and me, nothing! Me and a man, never!" Then I would take him out on his balcony and show him his name, and he'd hear the words I couldn't say out loud. He'd take me in his arms. Since he would know, I'd let him do as he wanted: I'd like it, I hoped.

There was a step, a turn of the latch, the door opened, the words were ready on my lips. I stifled them. It wasn't Emmanuel. Facing me, in the small entryway, stood a man with glasses and a beard. Inside, a woman lay on the couch, reading.

I stammered, "I was looking for Dr. Duplessis."

"You've come to the right place," the man said with a smile. "Except he's gone away for a few months. He's lending us his apartment."

"Gone?"

It was impossible. I refused to believe it. If he was gone, what would I do? Where would I go? To whom?

"Would you like to come in for a minute?"

He stepped aside to let me by and closed the door behind me. He looked at me inquisitively. I murmured, "I didn't know he was leaving so soon. I saw him less than a week ago."

"He went to spend a few days with his family before he flies back to Africa," the man explained.

Hope returned, so violently that it hurt.

"With his family? In Pontarlier?"

"That's it, Pontarlier."

I went into the living room. I recognized each thing: the African textile on the wall, the coffee table, the shiny plant. I'd written everything inside me. On the couch, the woman sat up to look at me. She said hello in an astonished voice. I said the same. I went to the window and leaned out. You couldn't see the classrooms anymore. All you could see in the schoolyard was the green roof of a chestnut tree spiked with pink and white; it must be surprising, during recess, to hear children's screams and laughter rise from beneath it.

"Would you like something to drink?"

I walked back into the room: "No, thanks, I'm not thirsty."

The man was older than Emmanuel. He must be a doctor, too. I find that they have a different way of looking. He looked at me as if nothing surprised him. On the couch, the woman had closed her book. I spoke to him: "Do you know when he's leaving?"

"Next Monday."

"And will he be back here first?"

"I don't think so."

The woman got up, walked over to her partner, and took his arm.

"Could you give me his number in Pontarlier?" I asked.

"We don't have it."

She was the one who answered, and I knew she was lying. He looked away. They wouldn't give it to me. They didn't know me, and I could be trouble, someone Emmanuel didn't want to hear from. It had often happened to Daddy. People would call him at home, people he could do nothing for. Mom would say he wasn't there. She called it a white lie, I'm not sure why.

"I'm a friend," I prodded. "For Easter, he came up to Normandy to see me. I'm sure he wouldn't mind your giving me his number."

I'd blown it. I could see it in their faces. The more I said, the more alarmed they'd be. I understood now why people lash out when no one hears them. I wanted to shout that Emmanuel loved me: he'd held me in his arms right in this room, and he'd asked me to think about going to

Africa with him someday, me, yes, me! But they wouldn't believe me. They'd only have to look at me.

I headed for the door. Helplessness smothered me; I hated them, especially her. And anyway I could get his address from Beatrice, from Martin. I just had to ask Pauline to help me, it would be easy.

The man came up to me, laid a hand on my arm. "Don't just run away now! Emmanuel is supposed to call us tonight. Do you want us to say you were here? Can we give him a message?"

I turned around and looked at him standing there, so calm, apparently so much at ease.

"What's the matter, now?" he murmured.

What was the matter was that because of them, because of the way they looked at me, even I couldn't believe what Emmanuel had said to me. Once again I was certain that he'd made a mistake and couldn't love me, and I could hardly blame them.

I asked, "Are you sure he'll call?"

"Sure as can be. So what should I tell him?"

I closed my eyes tight, and in the burning tears I saw the dripping evergreens in the Jura forest. I stopped near the President, and I heard my father order Pauline to fight. A strange thing about fathers: the further away they are, the less you can touch them, the louder their words echo in you.

"Tell him I'll be in Malbuisson tomorrow night, at the hotel. My name is Cecile."

~ 59 ~

Winter's Funeral

TOWARD THE END of April, or in May, depending on the weather, my father used to bring my mother a big bunch of flowers, preferably yellow or red: "for winter's funeral," he would say. Mom would sweep the ashes out of the fireplace and fill it with the bouquet, arranged in the dented copper pot we got from Grandmother's.

Today, winter's funeral had been held at La Marette. The high flames of an armful of broomflower had replaced the logs in the fireplace.

"A present from Roughly Speaking," Mom told me. "I never would have thought he'd remember. By the way, he says he'd like to see you. He wants you to come over tomorrow."

"Tomorrow I'm leaving for the mountains again," I said. "Which train station would it be for Malbuisson?"

Mom's eyes widened; she gulped.

"Gare de Lyon, I guess. . . . Emmanuel?"

This time she got me.

"How did you know?"

"I know he's from Pontarlier: Pauline told me about him."

Try and keep a secret in a family like mine! I grabbed

295

Prince off her lap. I sat down on Pauline's stool in front of the fireplace, with winter newly buried, and explained that Emmanuel was about to leave for Africa again. I'd missed him that last day at Mandreville, I had important things to say to him, she should let me go and not worry about me because a mother's fears are contagious and stop daughters cold when they need encouragement.

"And where do you plan to meet him?" she asked, a good omen for what was to come.

"At the hotel where we stayed with Daddy, by the lake."

She lowered her eyes and twisted her husband's wedding band, which she'd had sized down to fit.

"I was just wondering what your father would have said. . . ."

When she mentioned him, it was always in this hoarse voice: hard to get the words out. I could talk about him in a normal voice now. And yet it had been barely four months, a little over a hundred days. I felt bad about getting over it so fast.

"I think he would have said, 'Go ahead.' "

"Maybe he would have gone with you."

"I wouldn't have let him. It's about time I did things on my own, don't you think? I'm almost nineteen."

She smiled to say yes. Warmed by her smile, the words seemed to float out of me.

"You know, I've been afraid of sex."

"And now?"

"I'm still afraid."

She reached out, supposedly to pet Prince; he shivered with pleasure. "But something has changed, right?"

"What's changed is that I've decided to do it. I'll have to sooner or later."

Her hand froze.

I went on: "According to statistics, more than two thirds

of all girls my age have already done it. And as you recall, your three elder daughters were no exception."

"So?" Mom asked. "You're you. They're them."

Just the problem. I was me. So, I froze up.

Outside, there was barking. Prince hurtled toward the window to let the passing dog know that it was encroaching on his territory. They had a brief exchange in their language, and then the intruder went away and His Highness calmed down and returned to the lap of the lady who brought the royal food and vitamins every day.

"What do you want me to do?" Mom asked. "Say 'go ahead' for that, too?"

My throat constricted: "I don't know. Maybe I want you to tell me that it can be good."

There was a silence. In the center of the yellow broom, Roughly Speaking had stuck a bunch of lilacs; it changed everything, you couldn't tell which to look at.

"Do you love him?" Mom asked.

. . . Every night before I went to sleep I laid my head on his shoulder and breathed in his smell, and a kind of certainty engulfed me: I was where I belonged. Earlier that day, when he wasn't at his apartment, I hadn't known where to go, or to whom.

"I'm pretty sure I do," I said.

"Then look at me."

Her serious face looked older. It was so different when she smiled. Was I cruel to talk to her about love when hers was lost?

"You see, what counts is giving," she said. "Not just your body, but giving yourself to each other, all of you. When that happens, it's better than all right — it's fantastic."

"But what if it's fantastic in your mind, in your heart, but not for the rest — the body, as you put it?"

She looked somewhat surprised but obviously understood. "You hear a lot these days about 'the rest,' as *you* put it. But making love is a skill you learn like anything else, and you shouldn't expect fireworks from the very first time."

I tried to reassure her: "As far as fireworks go, don't worry, I gave up on that idea ages ago. The same statistics say that more than sixty percent of women never get there, and they've obviously survived."

Then she began to laugh, and I loved it. She reached out and touched me the way she often had with Daddy, when it was her turn to protect him, stroking his cheek with one finger, as if to read him by heart.

"Don't give up quite so fast, honey. Just start with love, and the rest will follow."

My chest was heavy: with fear that it wouldn't follow, hope that it would.

"Do you really think so?"

"I really do."

I got up. I made her promise not to leave. Tomorrow she'd have plenty of time to rest, since I'd be in the mountains. Wouldn't I? I flew to the kitchen and inspected the refrigerator. I made myself a club sandwich with Swiss cheese, lettuce, sliced tomatoes, roast beef, on toast slathered with mayonnaise, a mile high, and took it back into the living room, where Prince came to favor me with a wealth of shamefully self-interested smiles: "But your figure, boy!" My sandwich leaked out all over; my mother pretended to see only my enjoyment, not the mess. After what we'd just said to each other, could she tell me not to lick my fingers? Tough luck!

"How long do you think you'll be there?"

"Just the weekend. Emmanuel leaves for Africa on Monday."

I looked at the clock: almost eleven. He knew now. The

man with the beard had given him my message. Maybe he'd described his visitor in the process. Suddenly I thought, what if he doesn't show up? I felt dizzy. Her eyes closed, leaning back on the throw pillows, Mom was recuperating.

"How do you get the Pill?" I asked. "I've heard about the day-after thing, but I'd rather die than ask for it at the drugstore. What do you suggest?"

She sighed a deep sigh and put her two hands on my shoulders.

"I suggest you wait," she prescribed. "Wait till you know and love him even better, till you have your whole life ahead of you, not just two days."

I tried to laugh. "Your whole life . . ." Mothers really jump to conclusions. I knew she would say that.

"Maybe the party of the third part wouldn't agree!"

"If he's the way Pauline describes him, I think he would," Mom said.

One morning, Emmanuel had said of my mother, "If she's the way she's been described to me, she'll understand." I smiled inside. If the whole thing didn't turn into a disaster, the two of them would get along fine.

~ 60 ~

Back to the Lake

SNOW WAS MELTING on the roadsides. Huge buttercups shared the meadows with patches of gentian. The color of the sky was dense, profound: different from the light, transparent sky of Normandy. Atop the rounded hills, evergreens kept watch.

And in the woodland meadows, here were the roan-and-white Montbeliard cattle whose milk makes comté cheese. I spotted the cheesemaker's squat farmhouse with its overhanging roof. The air was sharp. I breathed it in, as you drink from a spring, feeling it do me good. I laid in a stock for Marie, too: one breath for her, one for me. At this time yesterday I was at her bedside, and in a way she was the one who had sent me here, reminding me of the value of life.

The train dropped me off at Frasne. From there I took a taxi, asking the driver to leave me a mile or so from Malbuisson. I wanted to walk the rest of the way. The car roared off. I couldn't hear my footsteps in the hum of the countryside; time seemed to stop; Emmanuel was no more than a faintly sensitive spot. I had come here to find him, and instead I'd found Charles, my father. The smells, the blue-greens and green-blacks, the sweetness and the roughness of the landscape — we had first discovered these together. Together we'd stopped by this sawmill to admire the freshly barked logs, bright yellow, still alive. I had felt so sorry for the trees. But he had told me that it had to be done so other trees could have their share of light and their chance to grow.

A man passed and waved at me: "Good evening."

Evening was on its way. It gilded the motionless lake, with sparkles like suspended time. I went down to the shore and sat for a moment by a boat half hidden in reeds and water. I was the one who had decided to come here, no one but me, and that gave everything a particular importance, each step, gesture, look. It seemed to me that I'd broken my moorings, and probably because I saw how small a wake I left, behind all this beauty I sensed suffering. I felt, in the face of life, both very fragile and strong for having understood it.

"You came all alone?"

The owner-chef of the Hotel des Terrasses was amazed. I went directly into the kitchen by the side door, as I had in December when the hotel was closed to tourists. He recognized me right away and greeted me by name.

"I have friends here," I told him.

The name *Emmanuel* was on the tip of my tongue. But I didn't say it, so I wouldn't have to answer questions. Another cook was at work, wearing, like his boss, the tall white hat that symbolized pride in his work. The owner introduced me: his nephew, who'd come to help out for the summer.

"You'll see how different things are. It's our high season: we've been turning people away since Easter."

The French, of course, and Swiss and Germans who came for the scenery, the food, the local wine. I filched a morel mushroom from a heap on the counter, fragrant with the forest.

"Do you remember? My father loved these. He said other mushrooms slip down your throat too easily."

He laughed and sighed at the same time: "We felt really bad for you," he said. "What a shock! He was a wonderful man . . . and he loved his daughters."

He added that dinner was served between eight and nine-thirty: I was just in time.

A young woman led me up the stairway. I recognized the smell: wood and carpeting. Each place has its own smell. Mandreville: stone and marble. La Marette: wallpaper and wood fires. Here, they gave me their "emergency only" room, way at the top of the hotel. Tiny, with a dormer, it hadn't been redone, like the rest of the place. In its wooden hull, the bed was a hundred years old. Full of creaks! There was a pitcher of water on the dresser; the bathroom was down the hall. "Emergency only" — perfect for me. And with a view of the lake.

The girl closed the door. I threw my bag onto the down quilt. Now I was afraid. Emmanuel came back full force, and the reason I'd come here. And now it hurt. Would he show up? Loneliness swelled in me. Hotel rooms are deadly when you're in pain: no familiar object the eye can fasten on, no friendly voice to remind you of better times. "A wonderful man. . . ." He was.

I went to the window and opened it wide. I looked for the church that was supposed to be sunk at the bottom of the lake, and I think I prayed. With all my might, I addressed the uncertain gleam that for some is a blinding light. I addressed the force that can be an imperceptible twitch or a thunderbolt; I spoke to the special place where good and evil, death and life meet, and that men have always called God. I asked for a miracle: to find one certain person for me among the multitude, at once an ordinary person and perfectly unique, and to bring him here to me tonight, to give me the strength to talk to him; and to give him the heart to hear me, and to make it happen that in this world of strangers we would become, for as long as possible, indispensable to each other.

∽ 61 ∽

Reconciliation

I WAS IN THE LOUNGE, where, on a winter night of north wind and snow, I had met Emmanuel for the first time. The clock had struck eleven. He wouldn't come. I'd lost him.

One day, at a sidewalk café table, I had seen a young woman in front of an untouched drink. Crying. The tears rolled down her cheeks, and she didn't try to hide them, as if she no longer cared what other people thought. I guessed that someone had not shown up for her. Now I thought not of Marie but of that stranger, to whom a man's absence seemed to mean something like a death sentence.

One after another, the guests had gone up to their rooms. The owner was surprised to find me still up: was something wrong? I assured him that I was fine, just not tired, and I felt like reading for a while, that was all. I promised I'd shut off all the lights, that I wouldn't catch cold and would feel free to get myself something to drink if I was thirsty. Then he would feel all right about going up to bed. He had a hard weekend ahead of him: a first communion, a wedding.

I didn't read. I looked at the words without seeing them, and I heard what Emmanuel had said to me that first night:

"Life is a series of choices. . . . We have to find the strength to live up to them." Was it possible, for who knows what obscure reason, to choose your own loneliness? By lying to Emmanuel, standing him up at Mandreville, was that what I had done? I looked at my choice, and I rejected it. I wanted Emmanuel, wanted to hear his voice, for him to take me in his arms. I refused to have lost him.

I didn't hear him come in. I'd put my head in my hands and was struggling with the emptiness. When I lifted my head up, he was there. He had his jacket over his shoulder and was looking at me without smiling. I wanted to go to him, but he stopped me.

"Don't get up."

I didn't recognize his voice.

"I'd made up my mind not to come," he said. "And then it seemed wrong to let you travel all this way for nothing."

I tried to say "Thanks," but I couldn't. I hadn't imagined this coldness. Nothing worse could happen: a stranger. He sat down across the table from me.

"What do you want from me?"

I murmured, "I had to see you before you left."

He laughed, and in his laugh I saw the desert. Not love, not hate — indifference.

"Of course. This is just how you'd do it. The middle of the night, the crack of dawn, when you're not expected. Why did you have to see me?"

I knew what I wanted to say, knew it by heart; sometimes as I'd rehearsed my speech to myself it had even seemed moving, had brought tears to my eyes, because I'd pictured myself saying the words against his chest, in his warmth, with his help. But, like all the rest, those words had deserted me: they were for a man who loved me, not for this one.

"I wanted to apologize for the other day."

The laugh again: "Apologize? But why? It was just

another way of giving me your answer. Not very nice, or very brave, obviously, but at least very clear. I got the message. No need to come so far to apologize."

So it was really over. He moved slightly, and I thought he was going to get up and leave. He'd never know the truth.

"Nothing happened between Tanguy and me," I said. "That's why I stood you up at Mandreville. I was ashamed because I'd lied to you."

He leaned over: "Then why did you do it in the first place?"

I gathered all my courage. Talking like this, I felt I was losing myself, but if I didn't say it, I would lose him.

"I don't know. Maybe because I'm afraid — of you, of me, of life. . . ."

"Did you love him?" he asked.

It was like a blow, and I turned away.

"Look at me!"

His face had changed. No longer indifferent, he burned, demanded the truth.

"I don't think so. . . . I don't think I really loved him."

I felt empty. I'd just admitted defeat. I had wanted so much to believe that I loved Tanguy, probably because an illusion of love is better than nothing. And I was stripping Tanguy of everything: it meant that all I'd done was betray him.

"Why have you come to tell me all this tonight?" Emmanuel's voice seemed softer, his eyes, too. I didn't remember his eyes being this color, with these green highlights in the brown. I had come to tell him all this because I really did love *him.* I said, "Because when you're in Africa I want you to think about me all the time."

I said those words, words of surrender, and a barrier gave way; from deep inside, from hidden gardens, from the underbrush, from the old Pest tripping over her tongue, from unsaid words and stifled cries, a storm front mushroomed. The storm broke out of nowhere, with lightning flashes of pain, dull and distant rumbling. I choked. He stretched both hands across the table, palms open. I could hardly believe it. He said my name. Then I managed to move my hands, put them in his, and he closed his fingers around them; I knew I was saved, I put my face on our hands and let everything go.

"Finally!" he murmured.

Without letting go of my hands, he got up. He came to me, fell to his knees as he might have done for a child in Africa, and put his arms around me.

"You've taken your sweet time," he said.

I choked back my sobs, clung to him, and said, "That's not all, there's something else I have to tell you."

"Yes," he said, "yes . . ."

His hand pressed on the nape of my neck to bring me back where I belonged, and with my nose delighting in his neck, the smell of his hair, the warm scent rising from his chest, the indefinable and very different mixture that a household of girls could tell was the smell of a man, I continued.

"Not Tanguy, not any other man, ever."

The fear, the total lack of confidence in myself, inside and out, what he could see but also what I hid beneath the baggy sweaters my mother wrung her hands over . . .

A sort of tidal wave shook me: his laughter. Toward the end it sounded more like a sob, but that's common when you laugh with relief. Laughing and crying where extremes meet. He took my head in his hands. It wasn't easy to meet his eyes after what I'd just told him, even though I'd made a point of picking the longest, baggiest old sweater of my father's that I could find for this trip.

"What am I going to do?" he asked. "You know I only love you for the way you fill out a sweater. That's all I was after!"

The tragic face he put on made me laugh, too. He slipped his hands under my sweater around my waist. He lifted up my shirt to touch my skin, and it both felt good and frightened me. He wasn't laughing now. I remembered his face on the boat. Would he want to make love? Maybe my mother had been wrong.

I took his hands under my clothes and squeezed them.

"Is that all, now?" he asked. "Nothing else that needs airing out?"

"Yes," I said, "one more thing."

I tried to laugh to make him see that what I was going to tell him now wasn't very important, or at least much less so than the rest; anyway, I must have looked at too many adult magazines with Melodie, spied on Bernadette and Stephan through the keyhole once too often when I was twelve, but while everyone else couldn't wait to have sex and even enjoyed it, *I* was completely inhibited and just plain scared. Personally, I didn't really care; I'd talked it over with Mom, and she said things usually worked out in the long run. But he must have been with all kinds of girls who were great, experienced and everything, and he shouldn't expect miracles with me. Besides which, I wasn't protected against the risks involved. Now he knew everything.

I expected to hear him laugh again, but not at all, not for a second. He held me even tighter, brought his lips close to mine without touching them, and waited for me. I felt his breath and then the immense relief of having things cleared up between us, and this time I came to him. I felt the sweetness and the summons; I was the one who opened him. And just as on the boat in Honfleur, the wave rose, but this time I didn't resist, and he was the one who finally pulled away.

"We won't try anything you don't agree to," he promised.

I agreed to another kiss. I felt so empty when I wasn't holding him, but he stood up.

"I have something important to tell you, too, and it can't wait another minute: I'm starving!"

We went down to the the kitchen, tiptoeing like burglars. The owner had done a lot of prep work for the next day, and we found all the layers of the wedding cake in the refrigerator: meringue, filling, cream-puff decorations. It looked delicious, but we resisted the temptation and found some leftover asparagus and cold cuts instead. As we ate, Emmanuel told me that he'd figured it all out a long time ago: Tanguy, how afraid I was, and my sweaters and all that. The harder I tried to act like a liberated, experienced woman, the more clearly I showed I was a frightened little girl.

I was indignant: "And you didn't say a word! You let me make a fool of myself!"

"I tried to give you a way out. But you didn't bite. You had to discover the truth yourself, and accept it."

"But what about when you talked about my sincerity?"

"Sincere people make bad liars."

"And you really would have just left?"

"It would have given you time to think."

"What if I never came after you?"

"I knew you would," he said.

62

The Family Tree

LATER, HE WALKED ME to the door of my room and took me in his arms again. I didn't want to leave him. I pressed my hands hard to his back to tell him so and to feel him even closer, but he undid my hands.

He told me he wanted me very much but didn't want us to settle for a few hours, a night or two. He wanted plenty of time for us. There was no hurry: we had a lifetime ahead of us.

I was trembling with fatigue, emotion, and happiness. He picked me up and set me on the bed, which, naturally, groaned in protest. He would sleep on the couch in the TV room — it wouldn't be the first time — and bring up my breakfast tray in the morning.

I kneeled on the bed, lifted my arms, and asked him if he'd mind helping me off with my sweater before he went. At least we could get that step over with! What rose in me when he complied, slowly, making the pleasure last, made me think that I might turn out not to be frigid after all. He laughed and said, "I'm going to have a rough night on account of you. . . ."

I loved it; then he left.

I settled into the pillows, pulled the quilt up to my chin,

and looked out the open window at the night and, on the other side of the lake, a village called Saint Point, also supposed to be a proud and friendly place. It was night, but dawn inside me. Something was being born. I felt a kind of tingling run through me. I couldn't wait. I said to Marie, "We're on."

I was taking off! What fueled me was the love I carried inside me like a new, demanding child. Everything has a life span: men, plants, animals, but also feelings. Everything has its dawn, its full sun at noon, its twilight, and its night. I was at the dawn of my love. It was already leading me forward, and I was letting go of hands. Without rejecting any of it, I was leaving my old life behind. To my father and mother; to Claire, Bernadette, and Pauline; to Benjamin, Gabriel, Melanie, and Sophie; to all the friends of my childhood, I said goodbye for now. I was starting down my own path.

I imagine family feeling as a tree, as the sap running inside it. No two branches are the same, with the same number of smaller branches, leaves, or fruit, but all take their nourishment from the same source. Some branches may break, others fail to develop; it's often a question of light, you could say love. But there is also the weight of snow, the lashing of storms, there is sickness, and lightning that can take a chunk out of the tree in a few seconds. You think it's lost, but if the roots are deep the whole keeps living in spite of it.

Family feeling, to me, is not an isolated tree. It will give shade, shelter, and oxygen to those who desire them and stop to take them. And the tree needs others around it, thrives on them.

Yet it happens that certain people, rootless, feel uneasy, are even hurt when they come across such trees. I've known some. Faced with the tree's flourishing, they feel their

311

solitude more acutely, and the wealth of leaves or fruit reminds them of their own poverty. They say the fruit is sour, they try to cut down the tree, and if they can they carve their name in painful letters, leaving scars thát never completely heal over. Yes, I've known people like that.

On the Moreau family tree, grown on the grounds of La Marette, I see myself as one of the four main branches, with my parents forming the trunk together. They loved each other so much! My branch is a bit shorter than the others and turned more toward the mossy side than toward the sunlight.

But now everything was changing. A man had come, and there rose in me irresistible desires for light, for fruit. On the tree a new shoot was forming; others would join it, and still more would come to surround it. My hunger was for forests.

And already, somehow, I breathe with you, my love. Together we will climb high. We'll reach for the sky, and sometimes touch it, I hope.